# THE
# COVE

# THE
# COVE

## ALICE CLARK-PLATTS

R A V E N  🐦  B O O K S
LONDON · OXFORD · NEW YORK · NEW DELHI · SYDNEY

RAVEN BOOKS
Bloomsbury Publishing Plc
50 Bedford Square, London, WC1B 3DP, UK
29 Earlsfort Terrace, Dublin 2, Ireland

BLOOMSBURY, RAVEN BOOKS and the Raven Books logo are
trademarks of Bloomsbury Publishing Plc

First published in Great Britain 2022

A catalogue record for this book is available from the British Library

ISBN: HB: 978-1-5266-0427-9; TPB: 978-1-5266-0428-6;
eBook: 978-1-5266-0429-3; ePDF: 978-1-5266-5231-7

2 4 6 8 10 9 7 5 3 1

Typeset by Integra Software Services Pvt. Ltd.
Printed and bound in Great Britain by CPI Group (UK) Ltd, Croydon CR0 4YY

To find out more about our authors and books visit www.bloomsbury.com
and sign up for our newsletters

To my daughters

If there's fire on the mountain
Or lightning and storm
And a god speaks from the sky
That means someone is hearing
The outcry

*The Cure at Troy*, Seamus Heaney, 1990

# 1

## ADAM

*Sunday*

The kayak sped over the water: an arrow spun over glass. The prow forged ahead. A weak sun glanced off his shoulders as it edged above the horizon. The sea was flat. Salt caked along the ridges of the inflatable kayak. Adam's tanned toes gripped the pale grey rubber of the boat.

The taste of rum lingered in his mouth. His eyes were bloodshot and his cheekbone throbbed. As the sun inched higher, he lowered his head, urging the kayak on towards the curve of the headland. His breath was sea-curdled, mixed with the booze from last night, heavy with brine. He paddled hard, left then right, his body arched, his knees bent rigid.

Above him, a bird. Wings spread wide, it followed the boat, gliding in the blue, its eyes forward like Adam's.

He rounded the cape, catching a last look at the beach behind him, receding behind the bluff. Around the promontory, the sea was muddled. Waves splashed against jagged outcrops, mussing the sheen of the previously still water.

He edged closer to the coastline and the seabed shallowed, exposing rippled sand; the spiky black of urchins; delicate fronds of plants that flattened and recovered as he wound the paddle through the water. The kayak buffered and swayed with the swell. He pulled hard right, steering the prow from the rocks.

Ahead of him, just under a kilometre's kayak from where he'd started, was the neighbouring resort of Timba, its perimeter marked by the hazy shadow-line of a cluster of huts, their shutters still closed in the early-morning light.

His shoulders felt tight. His hangover was hampering his progress. Thirst scorched his throat. The water he moved through shimmered around him, taunting him. Cool, deep and undrinkable. He forced himself to carry on. He wasn't ready to go back. Not yet. They wouldn't be awake. And there was no way he wanted to be the only adult on breakfast duty with the children.

He bobbed for a minute before turning the boat and heading back into open water, butting the nose of the kayak over waves that, out past the reef, sparred with each other like boxers. Now he was tired. He stopped and rested the paddle on his knees. The kayak drifted, bouncing rhythmically along with the swell. He lay back and closed his eyes.

He awoke and the sun was higher. His skin itched with salt and sunburn. He lurched, checking with panicked fingers that the paddle hadn't fallen overboard. It hadn't. It lay propped against his shins. But where his hangover had been flayed clean by his sunburnt sleep, his thirst now raged.

Thankfully, the current had brought him further round the coast and a little closer, inland. A glimpse of white sand flashed ahead of him. Above it, he could just make out a fissure in the rocks where he might find shade and water and muster the energy he'd need to scull back to the resort. He picked up the paddle and cleaved the blade through the water, turning the boat towards the shore.

A single squawk and a bird landed on the jut of the cliff high above him. He watched it for a moment. It was the creature he'd seen earlier. Its wings shook as if it were laughing.

Everything was quiet, with only the far-off splash of water against the shoreline rocks, the wash of the current lapping against the boat. He looked at his fingers resting on the paddle bar, regarded his wedding ring.

He coiled round, straining to see the brow of the headland in the sun-dissolved distance. Behind the curve of that shoreline lay the beach where he was staying with his wife and children.

The bird took flight, and the movement caught his attention, made him glance up into the bright of the clear and empty sky. Someone was there. A figure, over by the split in the rocks above the white sand of the cove. They shouted something. It sounded like hello. They raised a hand in greeting.

Adam adjusted his cap, ran his tongue across his lips. His booze-soaked temper, carved solid through the waves like the kayak, dissipated now like foam on to coral.

He lifted a hand in reply.

He focused only on the rhythm of his paddle, on the water, flat ahead of him. He kept an even line, straight and sure.

Over to that slice of sand with its cool, dark cave. Heading towards the figure on the rocks.

To the person that was waiting for him.

# 2

## ELIZA

*Friday: two days earlier*

The colours of the mainland blur and fade as the boat picks up speed, swerves on a pinhead, and heads into open water.

Eliza grips the holdall on her lap as sea spray dashes her face. Next to her, inside a huge yellow life jacket, Chloe's eyes are stuck on the path the boat cuts through the waves, as if her life depends on it.

Eliza releases her daughter's damp little palm from her fingers, giving a wan smile as she tries to control the whipping of her hair by the wind. Her eyes are drawn to Adam, who's standing at the back, somehow managing to sway in time with the arrhythmic jolts. One of his bare feet rests on an ice box as he keeps balance with light fingers curled above him around the rolled-up awning of the boat. He catches her stare and grins before bending to say something to Lou who sits, muscles tensed, holding the baby tight. She passes the message on to Raffy who immediately leaps up and runs to his dad, ignoring the frustrated wave of the elderly Malay boatman, his wrinkled hands batting the air for the child to take a seat.

Eliza turns away, twisting her hair at the nape of her neck, veering horizontally as the boat curves round again. This weekend is a gamble. She and Noah don't know the Carters well. Yes, they've shared a lot of long lunches and a raft of drunken evenings – one of which spawned this very trip – but the friendship has grown very intense, very rapidly. They only met Lou and Adam just over eight months ago.

It doesn't look as though Noah will be much help at smoothing things along either. Opposite, her husband frowns as the boat slams violently down over the crest of a wave. In his lap, Sam yells with excitement at the roller-coaster ride, but Noah doesn't even smile. He's in such a foul mood, Eliza can feel tension radiating heat from him as potent as nuclear fallout.

Surely, they must be nearly there? The proximity of the resort to the mainland was one of its many advantages, so Adam had enthused over the vat of double gin and tonics when the plan had been hatched for a long weekend on Pulau Kalah. Paradise lay only half an hour's drive from their house in Singapore, up to the immigration border at Malaysia, where they'd crossed before heading through the city chaos of Johor Bahru. Then a couple of hours up the east coast, passing forests slashed and burned to make way for rows and rows of palm plantations, until they reached the little port of Mersing.

There, they'd parked their Hyundai in the dust of the gravel car park, handed their bags and passports to the Turtle Cove staff and set sail on the resort boat. Only a twenty-minute journey and they would be on the island, pushing their toes into sand.

'Look!' Chloe shouts.

A smudge of white has appeared on the horizon.

'It's the beach!'

Eliza lifts her head, and her heart slams into her throat.

The island is on fire.

Flames blaze violently behind the peak of the mountain that overlooks the beach. They curl over the top, licking greedily down its slopes. She can almost feel the heat of it, burning at her chest. She grasps at the side of the boat, her pulse racing.

'Amazing colours.' Adam's voice shatters the illusion. 'Must be nearly time for a sunset beer, eh mate?'

'You're not wrong. Gagging for one,' Noah calls back.

The beach is empty of fire. It is filled only with the early hues of the most beautiful sunset.

They draw closer to the island and the engine begins to slow and stutter. Eliza rubs clammy hands over her face, breathing slowly inside her palms. She's on edge and in desperate need of a drink, but her stomach tightens at the thought of Noah and Adam getting stuck in this early – before the kids are even settled.

They sail nearer still. Tiny shapes and shadows gradually become huts and palm trees, and then the whole vista resolves into the wide sweep of a cove. The boat's engine is cut, and they idle to shore. She scans the coastline. As is usual when they travel, Eliza has done her research.

Turtle Cove Resort is on the north-easterly tip of Pulau Kalah. It's a small island in the shape of a skewed bow tie, six kilometres long and one kilometre wide with only four beaches accessible by boat. Rising up in the distance is the cloud-covered summit of Gunung Api – Fire Mountain – a baby dormant volcano. Jungle tangles its way down its slopes, humidity steaming from a forest of lush fern, the thick trunks of vines winding haphazardly amidst shady, rustling patches of leaves.

From the boat, it looks impenetrable.

As the seabed grazes the bottom of the tender, the crew jump out and wade through shallow water, shouting in Malay to the staff on the beach, tossing mooring lines to secure the vessel. Everyone is grinning, the still-present sun casting deep shadows from palm trees on to the sand.

Eliza waits at the prow, holding her sandals as the elderly boatman makes a surprisingly sprightly exit over the side. The children have already gone. Sam, Chloe and Raffy hurtled away as soon as they beached and are now busy high-fiving friendly-faced resort members.

'I'll go,' Noah says, pre-empting a childcare request from Eliza.

'It's fine,' she says. 'I can see them.'

Noah rolls his eyes and jumps out anyway, shaking hands with the staff who greet him.

'I know it's only twenty minutes from the mainland,' Lou says quietly from behind, the baby in her arms. 'But I hope there's a doctor here. Even twenty minutes feels a long way from civilisation, somehow.'

'We're not going to need a doctor, Lou,' Adam says, hopping into the water himself. 'No one's going to get sick. We're going to have a great weekend.'

Lou lifts an eyebrow as he leaves them, striding through the shallows, helping the staff carry the bags to the shore.

'He's right, though.' Eliza moves over to stroke the baby's head. 'It's going to be lovely. We're going to be really looked after. A chance to completely relax. The kids will love it. We all will. No one will need a doctor for anything.'

'Oh yes.' A tall Malay man has come up to the boat as they've been talking. 'We treat all our guests at Turtle Cove like family. Here, please let me assist.' He holds a hand out to Eliza to help her climb down from the boat. 'Even now, we still have the greetings cards from guests who stayed many years ago. We have a saying in Malay: *air dicencang takkan putus.*'

As Eliza's feet sink into the warm, clear water, she looks up at him curiously.

'*Parted water is never severed.* It is the same with us, madam. It is the same with family.'

Something in this man's face is so peaceful and welcoming that, just for a moment, Eliza forgets she has only just met him. 'Blood is thicker than water, isn't that what they say? That's what my mum used to tell me anyway.'

The man gives a little laugh and a shake of his shoulders. 'Oh, yes, madam. And I am Zikri.' He curls his palm, beckoning her to follow him up the beach. 'Welcome, madam, today you are finally here. Welcome to Turtle Cove.'

# 3

## LOU

The baby is asleep at last.

She looks down at her daughter's jet-black cowlick that spikes from the collar of her life jacket. They'd called her Laila – *night* – because she'd been born at midnight and her hair was the colour of it.

She doesn't seem to understand the concept, though. At four months old, Laila sleeps for an hour at a time, on and off, a non-stop flickering light throughout the twenty-four hours of every single day.

Lou can't work it out. She's performed the same routine that she had with Raffy. She's done nothing different. But where her son had every night sunk into slumber with the relish that her husband has for the first gulp of a gin and tonic, Laila fights sleep; scrunching her face red and angry, fists tight, railing at the idea that she could lose her grip on the world, even for a few hours.

Now, though, the rhythm of the boat must have lulled her, plucked her rabid hold on consciousness away with the sleep fairies for a while. Lou looks down at her, nestled in the papoose on her chest. Her heart pours with love for her.

When she is asleep.

Lou can feel the weight of the shadows under her eyes. She needs this weekend. She needs sunburn on her skin, salt on her lips. She actively wants the grit of sand in the bedsheets.

Four months. That's all it's been. Four months since Laila arrived. But in those few months, Lou has become a different person. She's tetchy, she snaps at Raffy all the time. She can't bear to be touched, and especially not by Adam. All she craves is sleep. Not even sleep. Just quiet. Some place where no one asks her any question, asks her anything at all. Where no one tugs on her sleeve. No one even looks at her. They just let her be. Let her breathe.

She knows how ungrateful she sounds. She has girlfriends who have longed for children. Her friend, Marie, has been through three rounds of IVF with no success. And before Laila, ever since they'd had Raffy, she had been desperate for another baby. She had been an only child herself. She didn't want it for her son. She wanted him to have a playmate, a partner in crime. And so, even though there were hundreds of reasons why she shouldn't have done it, she'd persuaded herself, and she'd persuaded Adam.

At first, they hadn't worried. They were tired... always, they were tired. Then Adam hadn't got a new book contract. So they'd worried about that. And then Lou's business partners, in the asset finance company she'd founded the decade before, had voted to sell the company to a larger one and they'd worried about that for a while. But then the business had sold, and suddenly they didn't need to worry about money any more.

And then she'd been offered Singapore.

Everything about it made sense. The package was good. Adam could write. And the main draw... they'd have childcare. Now they knew her as Marisol. But back then, she'd been a visionary creature. Someone who could willingly play with Raffy, build his Lego, spend an hour spooning pureed bananas into him without stressing that work emails were building up unread. The offer was a no-brainer.

Adam's next book was snapped up and before they could really take stock, they were living in a beautiful colonial-style house next to eighty-two hectares of heritage botanical garden and everything was paradise.

It was just that they couldn't conceive.

She wonders if it was that period of time – when she was desperate, tracking her cycle; when sex became a chore rather than a spontaneous pleasure – that has led to her anxiety now. She had longed so much to be pregnant again, and had convinced

9

herself so effectively that it would never happen, that when it finally did, she was so frightened it wouldn't last that she couldn't really be happy about it.

Her entire pregnancy felt like trying to catch a butterfly: it could sit on your palm for a second but as soon as your fingers started to close to keep it safe, it might flutter away, off into the wind, its bright colours fading with the light.

So when Laila had appeared – first as a blue dot on a litmus paper, then a thumping beat on a black and white screen, and finally as a purplish bundle of screaming mouth and dark, dark hair – at each moment, Lou had been too terrified to believe in her. Even now, when she looks at Laila sometimes, she is shocked to find her actually there, warm and alive, lying in her arms.

She passes the baby to Adam who has returned to the boat and stands ankle-deep in the turquoise water. She climbs carefully over the side, enjoying the tepid caress of the sea against her skin.

It's just motherhood, not rocket science, she reminds herself. Adam has said it enough times. The constant demands, the lack of sleep, the need for a well of patience deeper than the ocean itself. Every last bit of it is entirely normal.

Lou straightens as Adam hands her the baby. She slips her back into the papoose, her heart rate quickening as Laila's eyelids flicker. It's all perfectly normal.

So why does she feel so strange? As if she's looking down at her body from up there, in that blue sky above them. Watching them all disembark. She and Adam, and Raffy and the baby. Noah and Eliza, with their eight-year-old twins.

Lou takes in a gulp of the salt on the air and splashes her way to the shore.

On the beach, just beyond a small grove of palm trees, is the resort accommodation. She had chosen Turtle Cove for this long weekend. Its rustic nature had been the appeal, a deliberate choice on her behalf. It was somewhere entirely different from the luxury hotels where they usually stayed. A place where she could get Adam off his iPhone and Raffy off his PS4. She wanted to see the ocean, show their daughter the stars without the light pollution of the city.

A tiny island idyll with only ten huts, and no Wi-Fi. Half-empty at this time of year, the usual crowds put off by the imminent monsoon that wouldn't actually be here for another month, the resort manager had explained over the scratchy telephone line. The rains were late this year due to El Niño. They'd have the pristine beach to themselves.

She'd felt a thrill at that. She was beating the paradise-chasing tourists from Europe and Australia. She had the inside knowledge as a resident of Singapore. She was almost a local.

But more than that. They would be alone on their desert island. Away from the constant socialising in Singapore, the partying, the drinking. They would be calm, peaceful. Here, she would finally have the space to tell Adam that their relationship was over.

Of course, her fantasy of a small, intimate family holiday hasn't worked out quite like that.

Lou reaches the beach, taking in the semicircle of thatched cabins with their verandas and rattan chairs facing the sea. Striped beach towels and swimming costumes hang over the rails to dry. To the left of this accommodation is a larger building with an atap roof and walls open to the elements. On the sand, in front of this restaurant and bar area, Cove staff members line up with glasses of a welcome juice the colour of sunset. Lou watches as Eliza accepts one with a smile before going into the bar, fanning her face from the blast of afternoon heat.

Adam had invited the Fishers to come along this weekend, at the club after an especially raucous Saturday-afternoon drinking session that had spilled on into the evening. He'd painted such a beautiful picture of Pulau Kalah it had been impossible for Eliza and Noah to refuse. Sure enough, the following week, they had booked their ferry crossing and accommodation, and suddenly it was a done deal.

What could Lou say? If she objected to them coming, she looked unfriendly and, truthfully, she *does* like Eliza. And it's great that Raffy has some buddies to kick around with, she thinks, caressing Laila's head. But they don't know the Fishers particularly well and having an attractive woman around Adam brings its own usual, and unwelcome, complications.

The upshot being that the Fishers' presence has changed the dynamic. Rather than a quiet family weekend where some important decisions would be made, now it's going to be something different, something less… contained.

And Lou doesn't know if she can cope with it.

'Ma'am?'

She turns and accepts a drink from a young girl in a Malay dress, tasting the flavours of coconut and rum on her tongue. She glances up the beach to find Adam, who is standing facing the sea, the frown lines smooth on his forehead for once. She smiles at him and he raises his glass to her.

Maybe she's overthinking things. Maybe she just needs to treat this weekend as the last chance for them to all be together as a family. And then, when they return to Singapore, it will be a new beginning for them all.

Raffy appears and tugs at Lou's T-shirt just as she feels her daughter wriggle on her chest. Lou holds her breath as tiny shoulders butt against her ribcage. The baby's blue eyes snap open, round with fury at being woken by hunger, her mouth a crumpled peony as she prepares her onslaught.

Panic clutches Lou in a fever-sweat as Laila flings her head back, sucking in the air she needs to scream a cry that rattles through the palm trees like a freight train.

'Mama. Where's Monkey?' Raffy skips in front of her, his hands on his hips. 'Mama!'

She can't make out what he's saying over the noise of the baby. People are looking at her, frowning at the racket. She can see them muttering. Judging her failure to stop her baby's cries ruining the serenity of the beach. The glass drops from her hand, and she buries her head in shame, into Laila's ear, her cheeks dank with tears.

'Please, baby,' she whispers. 'Please stop crying. Please.'

She rolls on her heels, searching for Adam, needing him to help. Why does Raffy always come to her first? For once, could he not ask his father?

But Adam is already halfway towards the bar, clapping Noah on the back as they walk. As Lou looks at his retreating form, wearing the French rugby shirt he loves, the collar crooked against the nape of his neck, she feels a rush of hatred for her husband so hot and vicious that, for a moment, she cannot breathe.

After a beat, it passes.

She forces herself to concentrate on her son. She puts a hand on Laila's back, pressing it firmly as if that will quell her own panic.

'Monkey's in the bag with Daddy, Raffy,' she says and he dashes off after Adam.

She squares her shoulders and follows them, bouncing and jiggling the outraged Laila in her papoose, apologising to the young Malay girl who has bent to retrieve the glass from where it has toppled.

# 4

## Eliza

Eliza sits in a low-slung rattan chair, looking out on to the ocean. Palm fronds frame her vision and the ice in her gin and tonic causes condensation to run along her fingers. She breathes in softly, allows her eyes to close for a moment, enjoying the sound of water lapping, the quiet hum of guitar music playing through speakers behind the bar.

When she opens them, she can see Noah further up the beach, striding back and forth between two rocky outcrops. He's staring angrily at his phone, shoving it into the air, waving it around as if he's presenting it to the sea. He can't get any signal. He has told her this several times in an outraged tone of voice. As if he didn't know this would be the case, as if it is somehow her fault.

She sips at her drink and smiles at a couple on a table nearby who had arrived on Pulau Kalah only an hour after them. Newlyweds, they are holidaying with the girl's parents and, along with a young family of four from Lancashire and an older couple from the Netherlands, are the only other guests on the island.

She curls round to look behind her. Children are not allowed in the bar. She can see Sam and Chloe on their knees on the seat of their chairs in the adjacent restaurant. They are being entertained by the resort manager, Lars, and one of the university-age backpackers who drop into Turtle Cove for months at a time – to work as pseudo-babysitters, to scuba-dive and make some money before heading on to Bali or Thailand, or home.

The free childcare was yet another benefit of the weekend. The kids' club had a seemingly endless timetable of activities to keep the twins occupied. The staff even fed them in the evenings before taking them up to the purpose-built treehouse where they could play games, watch movies and hopefully fall asleep until their cocktail-soaked parents came to carry them back to their huts.

She smiles, watching Lars prance around in front of the children, telling them an embellished version of the *Billy Goats Gruff*. Lars is tall with white-blond hair, a tell of his South African heritage, although he speaks with a near-perfect English accent. He grew up on the island, and his chest is taut with muscles hewn from diving every day, from lugging oxygen tanks from boats to the dive centre, from all the chasing around of the kids that he does from morning until night.

Sam and Chloe are bewitched by him. Their faces track his every move, as he acts out the trip-trapping of the goats over the ugly troll hiding beneath the bridge. There are two backpackers on duty: a stocky mouse-haired British girl called Julie, who is soon to enter Sandhurst; and Zoe, a more glamorous-looking American, who wears indecently short Daisy Dukes and seems far more interested in Lars than doling out plates of chicken and rice and chopped-up veggies for the children. Nevertheless, the kids cram the food into their mouths without even noticing, so entranced are they by the story.

'He's quite the entertainer, isn't he? Everyone loves a clown.'

Adam rolls his eyes at Lars, then lowers himself into the chair next to Eliza and gives a self-satisfied sigh. One of the Malaysian staff, wearing the Turtle Cove uniform of a traditionally patterned shirt, immediately appears to place a gin and tonic in front of him. 'Thanks, that's great. Cheers.'

He clinks glasses with Eliza.

'This is the life.'

'Where's Lou?' she asks.

'Showering the kids. They're covered in sand from the beach. She'll be along in a minute.'

Eliza smiles at him, idly wondering why he isn't helping Lou, and also why Raffy is missing the storytelling by Lars. She says nothing, though, just sips at her drink.

'Noah having problems with the Wi-Fi?'

She raises her eyebrows. 'Not a good weekend to be offline, apparently. He's in the middle of some big closing. I think he can get Internet over on the other side of the island, though. Timba, I think it's called? There's another little resort there. I read it's where the turtles actually lay their eggs? It's a bit more rustic and low-key than here.'

'It may have internet, but it probably won't have air con,' Adam agrees, turning to look out at the sea. 'This location is incredible, isn't it? You can't beat that view.'

They sit in silence for a few minutes. Adam shifts in his chair and Eliza is conscious of his knee close to her thigh. She can feel the heat of him, the warmth of the sunburn on his leg. She leans forward to put her glass on the table, moving her own leg to the right, away from him.

'Here's Lou,' she says, nodding her head to beyond the fringe of the atap thatch of the bar. Adam turns and waves.

Lou looks dreadful, Eliza thinks. Her eyes are ringed charcoal with tiredness and her navy T-shirt is stained with what looks like dried milk. She's got Laila hoisted on her hip and Raffy is scowling, clearly furious about something as he marches along next to her. Lou seems close to tears.

Adam gets up and goes to them. Eliza watches as he kisses Lou on the cheek before taking Raffy's hand and leading him across to the kids' table and Lars.

Eliza stands and beckons Lou over.

'I don't think I can,' Lou says, giving a worried glance at the barman. 'Children aren't allowed in the bar.'

'They don't mean babies,' Eliza says. 'They just don't want screaming kids running around, spoiling everyone's peace and quiet.'

'Ha,' Lou answers, sitting in Adam's seat and reaching for the rest of his drink. 'Have they met my daughter?'

The baby stares at Eliza from Lou's lap. She is perfect, Eliza thinks. She's at that plump, peaches and cream stage, her dark hair framing deep blue eyes.

'Oh, she's gorgeous,' she says, reaching over to squeeze a chubby arm. 'She can't be that much trouble, can she?'

Lou gives a laugh as she downs Adam's drink. 'God, I need that. Raffy was apoplectic about missing the story. You know how he can get so fixated on things. But I couldn't cope with both of them in the shower, so he had to wait while I did Laila first and then we were late.' She looks at the table, at their empty glasses. 'Shall we get another? I think I'm officially giving up breastfeeding this weekend.'

'Really?' Eliza is surprised then notices Lou's expression. 'Not that I'm judging. Not at all. I had twins. Breastfeeding them wasn't just hard. It was a military operation. No, I mean...' She gestures over at the barman to ask for another round. 'I just thought you seemed pretty determined to see it through when you were pregnant. I thought you said you'd do it for a year.'

'Things change,' Lou says, looking down at Laila. 'We don't always know what the future holds, do we?'

Eliza considers her for a beat. When they met in the playground of the primary school where the twins had joined Raffy's class when they moved to Singapore, there were many reasons she hadn't wanted to like Lou. Looking at her immaculate appearance and demure smile, her beautifully turned-out little boy, she'd assumed that Lou was a career mother. Someone who'd hitched her wagon to a successful husband and spent her days menu-planning and online shopping.

So she had been pleased to discover that Lou was actually one of those women that Eliza could really talk to. Not just the endless conversations about weaning, and toilet training, and sleep patterns that she had with most mothers of children the same age.

Eliza and Lou talk about books and films. About their jobs. About their lives before they became mothers and when – somehow – that became what defined them. How their children behaved; their decisions about screen-time, about snacks, about swimming teachers, and schools – when did all of that become what defined them?

Had her mother been the same with her? she thinks back. She can't remember ever being bundled from ballet class to swimming gala, or her mother standing in the playground wearing Lycra and

17

gossiping with the other mothers. But maybe she's forgotten it all, like so much of that time when she was little. Most of it has been pushed into shadowy corners of her brain where the light can't reach.

She looks over at Lou's exhausted expression, the absence of her normally pristine clothes and hair, and wonders if she is coping with the addition of Laila. She hasn't seen much of her since the baby arrived. Lou was already pregnant when they met, and she hadn't thought it right to intrude on that newborn period when a family has to change its shape to include the new member. But maybe that was a mistake? Maybe Lou has really been needing a friend.

'No. We don't know what the future holds, at all. Not at all,' Eliza says now. 'So you should definitely drink and be merry this weekend. Adam can look after the baby for a change. And we'll all help. Many hands...'

Lou adjusts Laila's dress, pulling it down over a wodge of nappy-stuffed bloomers and patting her bottom. 'Adam's writing a new book,' she says. 'Unfortunately, he's brought his notebook here.' She gives Eliza a wry look. 'Usually a hugely important thought will come to him just as the baby needs changing, or feeding, or putting to bed. And, you know, you have to work fast when inspiration strikes.'

Their drinks arrive and Eliza raises her glass to Lou. Just behind her, she can see Adam helping Raffy with his food and then Noah jogging up the sandy steps to the restaurant to join them, ruffling Sam's hair as his son drinks his juice.

'Well, I'm here. The other kids are older, they can run around with the staff. Let me take Laila for a bit so you can have a break.'

Lou smiles gratefully at Eliza, bouncing Laila gently on her lap.

The sun hits the edge of the horizon and its last rays bleed into the ocean. While they'd seen the beginnings of the sun's descent from the boat, Pulau Kalah is directly on the equator – the actual denouement of the setting sun is quick. There are only a few brief minutes of purples and oranges before the beach becomes dusted with shadow and then night.

'Isn't sunset sad?' Lou murmurs, her eyes on the ocean as she sips at her drink. 'It's beautiful but I always find it sad. The end of another day we'll never get again.'

Eliza turns to Lou with an anxious expression, but the sound of laughter flips the moment and they both circle round to see the small group of children leave the restaurant in a Pied Piper crocodile with Lars at its head.

Hurricane lamps flicker as Adam and Noah join the women in the bar, cold pints of beer in their hands. Eliza watches them chat, confident and easy, their legs spread wide. Noah remains a little subdued with work anxiety, but even he begins to relax as the beer hits his bloodstream, and she does her best to ignore the speed with which the drinks disappear, to allow him to take this break without her hectoring him for once.

It's only as they make their way into the restaurant as a four-some, when Lou turns to hand the baby to Adam, that Eliza realises she has woefully underestimated what's happening. It must have been hidden under the deft lighting in the bar, the hues of the sunset as it streaked through the rafters, but now Lou's face is painfully visible.

And the look of desperation that Eliza witnesses before Lou turns to go to the ladies before dinner is so visceral that, for a moment, Eliza physically feels it too. She almost follows her in, goes into the ladies behind her and tells Lou to go. Tells her to leave this place right away and find a doctor, find some help right now.

Because, looking at Lou, it hits her that this is a woman at breaking point.

And Adam, her husband, doesn't appear to have noticed it at all.

# 5

## ADAM

He can't stop thinking about her.

He's tried. He's pushed it to the back of his brain. Something to avoid like his tax return. He's played sport. So much sport. Squash and football. Out with the boys. He's run every night. Hard runs through the humid heat, pushing his lungs until he can barely scrape in enough oxygen to walk the last kilometre home.

He's turned to Lou. He's begged her to sleep with him. To take away the images in his head. But she won't. He barely has to touch her before she looks at him as if he's insane. She covers it quickly enough, but he sees it flash across her face as he rolls over to her in bed. The slight dip of her mouth. The deliberately blank expression.

Lou sinks into unconsciousness when the baby sleeps, as if she's been knocked over the head. Then he slides out from under the duvet and pads through the cold of their air-conditioned bedroom into the bathroom, where he watches himself in the mirror and he comes.

Thinking of her.

This isn't like him. It's never happened to him in this way. And the weird thing is, they'd known the Fishers for weeks before it did. When they met, he hadn't given Eliza a second look. When they became friends, they'd had dinners and gone to the club. Sat for seemingly endless Sunday afternoons around their swimming pool, pretending to lovingly watch the children while keeping a more interested eye on the stock in the wine cooler.

He'd never thought anything more about her, other than she was bright and funny. And obviously beautiful. She'd probably been a total stunner when she was younger. Now, she was hitting middle age. She clearly highlighted her blonde hair and her skin was a bit blotchy from too much sun. She was fit; he knew she ran regularly. But her body wasn't amazing. Nothing like some of the twenty-year-olds he'd seen in bars and clubs – when he was ever allowed to go to them.

So what had happened to him?

He's thinking this as he strolls back from the kids' club just beyond the restaurant. He's regretting leaving his flip-flops outside their hut. The ground is littered with tiny pine cones from the trees that shade the periphery of the beach and they stab into his soles, making him hobble.

It must be the book, he thinks. This happens sometimes when he's deep in the writing process. He'd started this one around the time that Eliza had begun intruding into his thoughts. It's not coming as easy as the ones he's written before. He writes airport thrillers. His character – Roman McFee – is a private detective for insurance conglomerates. He investigates corporate fraud that leads him into perilous situations involving guns and hand-to-hand fighting. Sales have been bad for the last couple, though, and he's had to change things up a bit. Give Roman a female sidekick. And he's struggling with it. He can't get into her head and the chapters are progressing slowly.

He looks ahead to where the lights of the restaurant seep on to the sand. A bird is bleating an incessant night-time call and it knocks into his head, making him irritable. He can see the table where he left them all to go and check on the kids. Noah's got his arm around Eliza and it provokes a stab of envy in him that almost makes him laugh, it's such a rare feeling.

He likes Noah, but he grates at him too. It's the air of vague amusement the man has, as if nothing's really worth his time. And why should it be, with his million-dollar law practice, his Jamie Foxx chiselled cheekbones, his box-fresh T-shirts?

He shouldn't have invited them along on this weekend. But he hadn't been able to help himself. Too much booze, and she'd given him a look at the club, he was sure of it. A little flirty look, a hand on his shoulder as she left the table to go to the ladies. The idea of being with her for three days solid. Her, in a bikini, on a beach in the moonlight.

Before he knew it, he was telling them all about it. Waxing lyrical about the benefits of eco-resorts, giving something back to the local community, reducing carbon footprints, blah fucking blah.

Adam grimaces as another pine cone cuts into his skin. It was all bullshit, of course. He'd actually voted for the Oberoi hotel in Ubud. But Lou had read about this place on some mums' blog. She'd pleaded for the kids' club, the au naturel vibes. She'd clearly had some kind of surfer-chic fantasy: of Raffy swimming all day long, bleached curly hair, salt on his skin, running barefoot. Except doing that was impossible with these bloody things on the ground.

And now they're actually here, and he's having to watch Noah fawn all over Eliza while she and Lou make big eyes at the South African man-child who claims to be running this place. Lars something or other... The bloke couldn't run a piss-up in a brewery – not legally, anyway, given he's clearly as dodgy as fuck. And why does he never put a shirt on?

'How are they?' Eliza asks with a smile as he walks back into the restaurant. Is it him or do her eyes linger on his as she takes a sip of wine?

'All good. Watching *Finding Nemo* while that army girl looks at her phone.'

'Has she got signal, then?' Noah sits forward, pushing his rimless glasses further up the bridge of his nose.

Adam shrugs. 'That guy Lars was saying earlier that they block the Internet throughout the resort. They've got some weird notion about enforcing relaxation on the guests.' He looks at Noah frowning fiercely at his iPhone and gives a laugh. 'It's working well, clearly. It might be better over there, I suppose. The kids' club is nearer the resort office, and they must have some kind of Wi-Fi to run the business.'

Noah gets to his feet. 'Sorry,' he directs this to Eliza. 'But I do really need to check if anything's come in from Germany. I can look in on the kids as well,' he offers to mollify her.

'Adam's just done that,' Eliza points out before waving a hand at him. 'It doesn't matter. Go ahead.'

'We'll be heading off in a bit anyway.' Lou looks down at her feet where Laila is asleep in a baby seat. 'I'll have to feed her soon and I'm knackered. Don't want to be too late tonight.'

'I thought we could put the kids to bed and sit outside the huts on the beach?' Adam suggests, looking round at them all.

'Sure,' Noah says. 'I'll bring the kids over after the film and see you there.'

'We'll order another bottle,' Adam calls after him.

'Not for me,' Lou says. 'I've had enough.'

Adam feels his shoulders tense. Even if you forget the Eliza thing – and anyway, Lou hasn't got a clue about that – why is Lou always such a drag these days? She never used to be like this. When they'd first got together, he couldn't believe his luck that someone as fit as Lou was also such a laugh.

She'd always been one of the boys. Impossible to offend, able to drink anyone under the table. He knows things are different now, he does get it. They're older. They're parents. Even he doesn't have the stamina he had before. Or the liver capacity, frankly.

But at least he's willing. They're on holiday, for God's sake. Why does Lou have to make parenting such a bloody drama? Raffy is knackered. He's tired enough, he'd probably sleep on the beach if they asked him to. And Laila is fine in that seat thing.

'Why don't you feed her a bit later?' he asks Lou. 'If you wake her up now, she'll only take an hour to go back down again. Then you'll get all stressed. Just leave her until she wakes up on her own and have another glass of wine.'

'I don't get *all* stressed, Adam.' Lou shoots a *this is what I have to put up with* look at Eliza. 'I don't want to disrupt her routine just because we're away. Also,' she says, reaching down into a bag by her feet and retrieving an inhaler, 'my asthma's playing up, for some reason. I'm just not feeling up to it, that's all.' She takes in a puff, giving Adam a tight smile as she does so.

Adam sighs, swallowing down the snap of anger that's surfaced at Lou talking to him like this in front of Eliza. 'Of course.

23

And you're tired, I know. But look,' he turns to where the moon is streaming on to the ocean, slicking its top with light, 'it's beautiful out there. Let's just have fifteen minutes to enjoy it without disturbing Sleeping Beauty.' He smiles at them both, hoping that Eliza will see how patient he's being with Lou.

For a moment, they sit without saying anything.

Adam's mind races with aggrieved thoughts. He's not selfish, he's a good dad. Lou has levelled the criticism of selfishness at him a couple of times recently. But, Jesus. They've got Marisol. Raffy's at school most of the time. And Lou will be back to work in a couple of months.

He goes out with Raffy for most of the bloody day on Saturday. Takes him to tennis and football so Lou can have some rest. Actually, he likes it. His son is becoming a real character. He likes their little chats. The kid's so passionate about the weirdest of things.

The baby – at this stage – isn't really his thing. He loves her, of course. Loves her fiercely. Would do anything for her. But the point is that she's *fine*. He keeps saying this to Lou. The kid could be growing up in a crack den. As it is, she's got two decent, hard-working parents, a beautiful house, everything she could ever want.

'I just think it would be nice to have a nightcap by the sea,' he says eventually, breaking the silence.

'For God's sake, Adam!' Lou gets to her feet wearily, hoisting the baby seat up from the ground and crooking it over her elbow. 'You have a bloody nightcap if it means that much to you.' She turns to Eliza. 'Sorry... I'm just knackered. I'll be on better form tomorrow.'

Laila starts to squirm in her seat. She makes a small sound, like an animal stirring from slumber.

'There she goes,' Lou says, shooting daggers at Adam. 'Right on schedule.'

A schedule you've created, he thinks, but doesn't say.

'I'll see you in the morning,' Lou says to Eliza. 'Maybe you could bring Raffy to bed once you've had your nightcap,' she directs to Adam.

He nods. He knows she wants him to get up and follow her. She wants him to go and get Raffy now and bring him to their hut. To put him to bed while Lou feeds the baby. For them all to turn the light off and go to sleep at the same time, together.

But he doesn't.

He watches the seat bang against her hip as she makes her way down the beach alone and then he turns to Eliza.

'Another drink?'

# 6

## NOAH

He watches a moth dive repeatedly on to the curve of a hurricane lamp. Its wings stutter against the smoky glass, its tiny eyes fixated on the flame.

He remembers learning about them at school. How moths evolved to navigate by the light of the moon. But then came science and invention, and suddenly the world was made up of a billion artificial – electric – moons. With eyes like telescopes, moths can't see for looking.

Fatal attraction, Noah thinks, as he watches the moth tip over the lip of the lamp, watches as its wings shrivel and burn. He lays a hand across the top of his glass as Adam goes to pour more wine.

'Not for me, thanks mate.'

He turns a cork round and round in a circle on the table in front of him, only half-listening to Adam and Eliza talking. Adam is beginning to slur his words. He's chain-smoking Malaysian cigarettes from a packet he must have bought behind the bar.

The nicotine haze is making Noah's eyes water. He wants to get out of here. He has to email the documents over to the office by tomorrow. What kind of place doesn't have a working Internet connection in the twenty-first century? Yes, he gets that this is a family holiday. But, unfortunately, corporate law isn't something linear.

It's like a virus. It doesn't recognise public holidays or family gatherings. It sweeps into every aspect of your life. And, if you're lucky, you can manage to steer it into a direction that works for you – if only for a few years. Suck the financial marrow out of it before it moves on to decimate another man's life, leaving nothing behind but a mortgage-free house, a decent pension and, hopefully – still – a marriage.

He looks up, trying to catch Eliza's attention, but she's as fixated on Adam as the moth was with the light.

He clears his throat. 'Guys, I'm thinking it might be time to call it a night. We should check on the kids...'

'They'll be fine. Lou's right next door. They'll totally be asleep,' Adam says, flicking a tower of cigarette ash into an empty water glass.

'Yeah, sure. But even so. We've got the dive tomorrow and it's only the first night. There's lots of time to—'

'Noah, come on,' Eliza says, reaching over the table and taking one of Adam's cigarettes. 'We *are* on holiday. Can't you chill out for once?'

He watches disbelievingly as she lights the cigarette and exhales a stream of smoke above his head. Her eyes are glassy, her mouth a mulish line.

'It sounds awful,' she's saying to Adam before taking a big gulp of wine. 'I mean, I never knew my father. But I'd like to think, if he'd been around, he would have been a stand-up guy, you know?'

Noah cringes at the girlish stupidity he can hear in her laugh. What is she doing? Is she flirting with Adam? That isn't like her. Eliza doesn't flirt. He's never had to worry about that sort of thing with her before.

'Pipe smoking, slippers by the fireplace, teaching me how to ride a bike...'

'Yeah, well. My old man was around, but he was nothing like that,' Adam replies.

Neither of them are bothering to include Noah in the conversation, and their disrespect claws at him like a moon-ghoul, made up of shadows from the beach beyond the restaurant lights. His mother always told him that thunder might be impressive, but lightning does the work.

Often, he forgets this.

He stares at the bottle in front of him, still more than half-full. His saliva buds buzz with desire for the taste of it. He could have one more glass. Just to be able to sleep.

27

His fingers inch across the table, then withdraw.

No, not tonight.

He has to keep it together, keep control.

He rubs a thumb along his jawline. He can feel his nostrils flare as he stares hard at Eliza, but he breathes. Manages to bank it down.

'He was a legendary lech,' Adam goes on, irritatingly oblivious to any tension. 'Proper randy old sod. You have to hand it to him, though. Even when he was doddery, he still managed to charm them. I'd lost count of the women he'd messed around with by the time he entered the pearly gates.'

'Really?' Eliza asks. 'Jeez... And what did your mum make of that? Must have been really hard for her.'

Adam shrugs, considering the restaurant rafters and rubbing at his hair until it sticks upwards with the effect of a haphazard halo. 'She ignored it mainly. Dunno why, really. Suppose that's what they did in that generation. Even ignored the kids, unbelievably.'

'El...' Noah says quietly.

'What kids? What do you mean?'

Adam sniffs and crumples his cigarette into the ashtray. 'Oh, Dad had a few brats with his tarts.' He laughs and his cheeks flush a little. 'Sorry. That sounds rough. But those times did cause some hardship at home. Mum was understandably... a tad peeved.'

'How many?'

'Did we get any more fags? I thought we'd bought some,' Adam says, checking his pockets. 'Ah. Here they are.' He throws a packet on to the table with a flourish.

'How many kids did he have?'

Noah sucks at his teeth, his bare feet arched and rigid underneath the table. 'El?' he says again, his head bent. 'It's late, babe. Like I said, we booked that dive earlier – for tomorrow. Remember?' He looks up. 'Shit, El. What are you doing?' He leans over and lifts her palm, flicks what's inside it away onto the ground. He stares at her. 'You had a hot rock in your hand, babe. From the cigarette. You didn't even notice.'

Eliza's gaze has been bolted on to Adam, but now she turns to Noah as if waking from a fever-dream.

'Can't be sure. But Mum never—' Adam stops mid-flow as he sees what's happened. 'Oh fuck, are you all right? Did you burn yourself?'

Eliza shakes her head as she pushes back her chair.

'Come on,' Noah repeats, his voice strained. 'Let's go.'

'Oh, are you guys leaving? Won't you stay and help me finish this?' Adam darts a look from one to the other as Eliza gets to her feet. He sloshes the wine bottle at them to demonstrate his point.

The restaurant is empty, the music off. The sound of a car engine drifts in from outside and a sweep of headlights crosses the ceiling. A door slams and a group of shadows melds and hovers behind the bar. Must be Lars, Noah thinks. 'Nah, mate. I'm beat. And this one's shattered too.' He stands and puts an arm around Eliza's waist, a slight pressure in his fingertips.

Ears pricking at the low voices that filter in from outside, Adam seems to rouse himself. 'Yeah, OK. Well, you two go. Have a wander back under the stars,' he winks at Noah. He sounds genial, but there's something hard beneath his smile.

Eliza lifts a hand to him as they say goodnight. She seems in a daze, Noah thinks. Has she drunk that much?

The sand is cool and damp from the outgoing tide. The moon's fingers reach over the water as they stroll up the beach to the huts. Bats circle the dark outlines of the palm fronds above them.

'What was that about?' Noah asks.

'What was what?'

Noah clicks his tongue. 'With Adam.'

She starts to say something, but he can tell she doesn't get it.

'He wants you, you know that, right? You should be careful with him. Could give out the wrong idea.' He walks on a little before he realises Eliza has stopped. 'Shit, what? What's the matter? It's a compliment, isn't it?'

'You don't understand.' Her voice is hollow.

'What's to understand, babe? It's Adam Carter, pissed-up and rambling, flirting with my wife while she smokes his fags.'

His point made, he moves on again, making slow and deliberate footprints in the cold sand all the way to their hut. At its steps, he glances back, but she hasn't followed. She's standing at the shoreline, looking out to sea.

He grips the rail. Why does it have to be this hard? When they first met, coming home to Eliza after work or a night out with his mates had felt like a single malt whisky after a boring and average meal. When he sees her like this now, it feels like indigestion.

Far away, against the horizon, a silent fork of lightning spears the sky.

He watches her in the moonlight for a few more minutes, then jogs up the stairs. He slips into the hut and tugs off his clothes. In the room adjacent to theirs, he can hear the heavy breath of their sleeping twins. He climbs into bed and lies there, waiting in the dark with his eyes wide open.

Waiting for Eliza to come in from the sea.

# 7

## LOU

*Saturday*

'Mama?'

Raffy's voice digs into Lou's consciousness. She opens her eyelids a crack but it's still dark. Above her, she can feel the thin waft of the fan that rotates above the tented mosquito net covering the bed. Next to her, she can smell stale booze leaching from Adam. Out of the corner of her eye, she can see he's naked, lying on his side, turned away from her. She squeezes her eyes back shut, praying that Raffy didn't notice she opened them a little.

It's too early. The sun isn't up. It feels as though Laila only went back to sleep five minutes ago from her last feed.

'Mama? I'm hungry.'

Outside, a thumping noise starts up. A regular *boof-boof* noise that Lou realises must be other children playing with the basketball and net in the small playground that's right outside their hut. Predicting this possibility, she'd thought about removing the ball last night but had forgotten in her tiredness, her eagerness to fall with Laila into bed, into a sweaty, dreamless sleep.

*Boof-boof.*

'Mama. The other kids are up.'

'It's not seven yet, Raff. It's not light,' Lou murmurs, putting an arm over her eyes. 'The baby's sleeping. You need to go back to bed.'

'I'm hungry.'

Lou swivels her head to Adam with the vague notion of getting him to deal with Raffy. But he is out cold. She prods his back with her fingers, but he doesn't respond.

She groans quietly. 'I don't want to wake up Laila. Daddy's sleeping. I can't leave her here, not with him like this. Can't you wait, Raff? Just until it's light outside?'

*Boof-boof.*

'The other kids are awake. Why can't I go and play with them?'

His whine is increasing in volume. Lou opens her eyes fully. He's standing next to the bed, a small ghostly figure behind the mosquito net. He's already got his shorts and bright orange T-shirt on, holding the ever-present Monkey. She peers at him. The clothes are the ones he was wearing yesterday and are covered in dollops of ketchup and chocolate ice cream.

'I can go by myself,' Raffy says. 'Mama. I can go to breakfast. I know where it is. It's just over there.' His shape turns to the slatted window in the direction of the restaurant.

It's not even a three-minute walk through the pine trees that stand parallel to the beach.

'Where's Sam?' Lou whispers. She puts a hand into the travel cot lying next to her on the bed. Laila is still breathing softly, the deep slow breaths of sleep.

'Outside. With the ball. We can go together. I'm nearly nine, Mama. It's not fair. *Please.*'

Raffy's tone is determined. Knowing him as she does, he'd happily stand there debating the pros and cons of the rights of children for another hour at least. And Lou is hit with a wave of exhaustion that physically prevents her lifting her head from the pillow. Her eyes are weighed down with stones.

'OK,' she mumbles. 'You can go with Sam to breakfast. But do *not* go down to the water. You hear me? Straight to the restaurant to eat and then stay there. Play a game and I'll be over in ten minutes.'

'OK, Mama.'

He's gone in a flash. The wooden door of their hut opens for a brief moment, letting in a chink of a blue sunrise, and he's out.

She can hear chattering outside then one last *boof* and then bliss-ful silence.

Lou leaves her hand in the bassinet and falls immediately back into a heavy sleep.

When she wakes, her hand automatically reaches into the cot to feel for Laila. She touches the flannelette sheet, a little damp from where Laila's full nappy must have been. Her fingers move around the tiny space and then they stop. Her palm lies still and flat in the bassinet.

Lou sits up and stares down at it.

The cot is empty.

Adam is also missing. His side of the bed is rumpled, his clothes scrunched up into a ball. Lou pulls back the mosquito net and swings her legs out of bed. She pulls on the shorts that lie on the floor. Grabbing her bag, she shoves her feet into flip-flops and leaves the hut with her nightshirt still on.

Then, ahead of her, she sees Adam. She calls out and he stops and turns. He is holding Laila to his chest. She runs over.

'I didn't know where you were... I woke up and you'd gone, and she'd gone... and...' She knows she sounds close to tears as she reaches for Laila. Adam gives her the baby and runs a hand over the dark stubble on his chin. When he speaks, his voice is gravelly and hoarse.

'I thought I'd let you sleep. Thought it would be obvious I'd taken her,' he says, clearing his throat. 'More to the point, where's Raffy?'

'He came over to breakfast with Sam about half an hour ago. What's the time?' she asks.

'Eleven.'

'What?' Lou blinks up at him before turning to the restaurant. She starts walking towards it. 'He went hours ago. I can't believe I've slept so long...'

'He'll be fine,' Adam says, following her. 'He'll be with Noah and Eliza. Playing with the other kids.'

Lou reaches the steps to the restaurant, taking them two at a time. Laila's head nods along with the rhythm, enjoying the gallop in her mother's arms.

Chloe is reading while Raffy is playing Uno with Sam, glasses of chocolate milkshake at their elbows. Lou bends to give him a kiss.

'Hi Mama.' Raffy points to a collection of shells and sticks of white coral on the table. 'We went beachcombing. Clearing the beach of rubbish too. Look. I got these shells, and also this.' He holds up a yellow plastic comb with several teeth missing.

'Wow,' she says with a laugh, looking in relief at them sitting happily side by side. Both boys have turned browner and blonder with the effects of the sun. Raffy's already wild and curly hair has gone out of control with salt and humidity. They look like twins themselves. 'Sorry I'm late, Raff. Mummy fell asleep. Have you been OK?'

'He's totally fine,' Eliza says, looking up from her coffee and paperback at the adjoining table. She's wearing a duck-egg-blue kaftan, her hair pulled away from her face. She looks incredibly pretty, Lou thinks, suddenly conscious of her nightshirt and bed-hair. She can't remember the last time she read a book.

'I'll get you a coffee,' Adam says.

'Sit down. Are you hungry?' Eliza asks. 'They've stopped breakfast but I'm sure they could do you some toast or yoghurt or something.'

Lou sits next to her with Laila on her lap. Her heart is pounding, and she feels utterly ridiculous. As if she's made a huge fuss over nothing. Why can't she behave like a normal person? Nobody else seems to get so upset over little things like oversleeping or going to breakfast. She shakes her head, not trusting herself to speak as Adam puts a mug of black coffee and a glass of water in front of her.

He stands, planting himself between Lou and Eliza. Behind him, Lou can see Noah in the small alcove off the restaurant, staring down at his phone. She goes to take her coffee but it's too hot to drink. She pushes it out of the reach of Laila whose chubby hands bat the air precariously. Reaching into her bag, she palms one of the pills the doctor gave her and slips it into her mouth at the same time as she sips her water.

Sam is shouting *Uno* as Lars walks up the stairs. His hair looks darker than normal, damp from the sea. He is shirtless, the top half of his wetsuit hanging down from his waist.

'Ah, guys. Just the people. I've been out this morning. It's absolutely beautiful.'

'Out to the wreck?' Adam asks.

'Yeah.' Lars gestures behind him where the newlyweds are coming up the beach, lugging their oxygen tanks and fins. 'Got back ten minutes ago. It was stunning. Hey kids,' he ruffles Chloe's hair, 'guess what we saw this morning under the sea? Two manta rays. As big as this...' He holds out his arms. 'Swam right next to me. And a lionfish. Did you see that on the wall chart?'

The children are wide-eyed.

'Did you see a shark?' Raffy asks. 'Did you know that – here in the archipelago – there are black- *and* white-tip reef sharks?'

'Yah, I did. But we didn't see any this morning, Shipmate Raff,' Lars replies. 'Maybe this afternoon with your dad, though, hey?'

Lou looks over at Adam. 'Are you going diving? You hadn't mentioned doing one.'

'Yeah. We thought we might. We booked it last night. Spur-of-the-moment thing, as the resort's practically empty at this time of year and Lars said there was tons of space. You don't mind, do you? It's the only day we can, really. I mean... you could come?'

Lou cocks her head. 'And the children... ?'

Lars looks over. 'I'm sure Zoe or Julie wouldn't mind taking the kids if you wanted to come, Lou?'

'They can't take the baby.'

'I'll stay.' Eliza gives an eager nod. 'I can look after Laila. You can leave a bottle and I'll walk up and down the beach with her in the sling.'

'It's fine,' Lou says. 'Don't worry.' She feels her cheeks turning hot. Why is she the one being singled out again? As if she's causing a huge hassle for them all? 'I can't dive anyway.' She gives Eliza an apologetic smile. 'The asthma, you know?'

'You have done it before,' Adam points out. 'In Thailand, remember?'

'About a hundred years ago. Really, Adam.' Lou gives a brittle laugh. 'Thanks so much for the offer, Eliza, but I'm very happy to hang on the beach. I've had a good sleep. I just can't believe it's so late...' She strokes Laila's hair, feeling horribly self-conscious.

Lars claps his hands together. 'Great. Well, the boat will leave at two, right after lunch. It will go on the dot which means you need to get over to the dive hut twenty minutes before to get your kit organised. I need your PADI cards before lunch too, please. Don't forget sunscreen, water, and a hat or cap for the ride out to the wreck. It'll take us about half an hour, and we should be back for sundowners around six. OK?' He grins at them, his teeth white against his deep tan. 'Conditions are awesome. It's going to be a sick dive.'

Noah comes over as Lars leaves and slumps in a chair next to Eliza. 'Fucking Germany,' he says.

'Babe...' Eliza says, glancing over at the kids who have started another card game.

'Sorry.'

'Dive's all arranged,' Adam says, then hacks a loud cough.

'You sound awful,' Lou says, looking up at him. 'Did you smoke last night?'

'Only one or two,' he answers without meeting her gaze. 'Yeah, I know. Stupid.'

Lou sees him dart a look sideways, down at the top of Eliza's head. Jealousy flashes in Lou, a spasm of heat across her face. Then it cools. This is why it's over, she reminds herself.

'Right before a dive, too,' she says.

Adam's eyes flit momentarily to the ceiling. 'Anyway,' he says, tapping Noah's shoulder, 'swim before lunch?'

'Yeah, I'm not getting anything out of this,' Noah says, shoving his phone into the pocket of his shorts. 'We can take the kids if you like. Leave you two ladies to your coffee?'

Adam leans down to kiss Lou. She can smell the alcohol from last night, the whiff of tobacco. 'Love you,' he says lightly. 'Come on, Raffster. Let's hit the beach.'

She watches them all go, Raffy chasing along behind Adam, his short legs struggling to keep up. They look like an advertisement, she thinks. For holidays in paradise. The two good-looking men, taking their beautiful children through the palm trees for a swim in the clear blue water.

So why does she feel so removed from it all? Why is her pulse racing as if something truly horrific is lurking behind one of the picturesque huts on the beach?

'Are you OK, Lou?' Eliza's voice breaks into her thoughts.

'Yes, yeah. I'm fine.' She forces herself to smile, knowing that the pill will kick in soon and then she'll feel better. 'It's so beautiful here.'

She pulls her coffee towards her at the same time as Laila reaches out. The baby gets there first and the cup is jettisoned, out over the edge of the table, toppling in the air until it bounces on the ground, brown liquid sinking into the sand without trace.

# 8

## ELIZA

The island has disappeared rapidly: it's shrunk from the sight of the length of the beach, to a line of yellow and green on the horizon, and now there is just blue as far as the eye can see.

Sunlight flickers through gaps in the awning as the boat progresses, the smell of diesel fading as its speed increases. Opposite Eliza are Noah and Adam, elbows bent on the side, their gaze fixed steadily on the prow. Lars is standing next to Zikri, the Turtle Cove staff member at the tiller. Lars's hips rest easily against the back of the pilot seat. He looks completely at home, a long, tanned arm propping him up as the boat bounces over the waves.

The couple from the Netherlands are with them on board. They nodded a brief hello as they stepped on to the boat but have since spoken only in Dutch as they've fixated on synchronising their dive watches.

Eliza breathes in the brine on the air, the conversation from last night rattling inside her skull like coins in a tin can which, on top of her hangover, is making her feel sick as a dog.

Why had she started talking about parents? The topic always upset her, and particularly so with Adam. He was so insensitive. She knew this about him. So why did she think she could have a proper, decent heart-to-heart about something so emotive? She'd been a complete idiot and she'd only got herself to blame. Now she feels vulnerable, that she's been exposed and opened up, raw to the bone.

She takes a quick look at Noah, his handsome face shrouded by his cap. If only she could talk to him about it. If only he wasn't so controlling. So jealous. So liable to drown his insecurities with any type of booze that came to hand, rather than taking the time to actually listen to her.

But it's become too ingrained with them, this pattern. She isn't going to change it now.

She licks salt from her lips and tries to trick herself that everything is fine by focusing on the afternoon ahead.

She loves boat trips: the emptiness of the world around them, the absence of noise other than the sound of the engine. She loves journeys full stop. The opportunity to be still, to sit in that moment of time, to consider nothing except where you are right now.

She thinks back to the trip in her twenties that she took with Noah through Chile and Argentina. Endless dusty miles weaving up and down precarious mountain roads. They had an iPod but no Internet. No such thing as podcasts then and the rickety bus journeys were too bumpy to be able to read. Nothing to do except stare from the window and watch the vertiginous drop alongside grow steeper as they went higher and higher into the clouds.

All she did on those journeys was dream about where they were travelling, go over old memories, and listen to songs that, when she heard them, years later, would take her back to the rhythm of that bus ride, the feel of Noah's thigh next to hers, the stickiness of their sweat-sheened arms, the whole possibility of what lay ahead of them at the end of the journey.

Of course, their arrival would never match the fantasy she'd imagined. It would be a confused melee of hawkers and people offering them rooms to stay, flies clinging to the perspiration on their lips and eyelids, a need for a cold beer and a shower. But sitting there, on the bus, all that was yet to come. Until you got there, you could pretend that paradise awaited. Nurture that exhilaration that no one else in the world knew where they were right then. The freedom of it. Even their parents, if they were wondering about them, imagining their travels in South America, had no idea what they were experiencing right at that moment, no idea what they were seeing or thinking. It was a secret only they had.

That's what independence is, Eliza thinks now, looking down at the waves smashing against the side of the boat. That reckless moment of self-belief that you can handle everything yourself. Right before you realise it's all a sun-drenched illusion; just a marketing campaign devised in an office suite that's paying for some executive's kids' private education.

She'd learned that lesson like a slap in the face, a few weeks later, when they'd arrived in Santiago and she'd received that terrible call about her mother, down a scratchy telephone line all the way from London.

That was what travel gave you, the knowledge that you – that everyone in the world – was ultimately alone.

She looks again at Noah and this time she smiles at him from behind her sunglasses. He nods back but he's distracted, she knows. He's not thinking of where they are right now, where they're going. He's thinking of Germany, and all the work he's supposed to be doing. About how he can generate enough data on his iPhone to be able to coordinate his associates and trainees who are all working in the Singapore office over the weekend while he's out here, stuck on a dive boat with her.

Zikri cuts the engine, and the boat begins to idle as Lars comes to the back to release the anchor.

Eliza shivers a little as a breeze grazes her bare arms.

They take anchor close to the wreck.

The reef is called Terumbu Sinar.

'Reef of the rays,' Lars says during the dive briefing. 'And we should see many.'

'What was the wreck?' Adam asks.

'Just a fishing boat. It sank around eight years ago.' Lars shrugs.

'I thought this was a marine conservation area,' Eliza asks. 'People aren't allowed to fish here, are they?'

'People have to eat,' Lars says. She can't see his eyes behind his mirrored sunglasses, but he smiles at her. 'It is forbidden, and they should be restricted. We monitor them. Report activity to the government. It's a losing battle, though. Look around.'

There is nothing other than the deep blue of the ocean. A puff of white cloud above and a splash where the waves foam over a prong of the reef sticking out of the water.

'There aren't exactly police stations or government offices knocking around here. But look, let's not worry about that today. You're going to see some awesome stuff this afternoon.' He claps his hands and looks around the boat. Everyone seems ready.

'OK. Let's go. We'll stick together and loose buddy. Adam, you come with me, and then Noah and Eliza, and Karin and John. You can see the top of the reef there. That's our orientation point. The wreck isn't deep, it's only twelve metres down from there. Zikri, are we all on the same time?'

'I make it 3:05 boss.'

'Everyone on that? Good. OK. We'll be down for forty-five minutes. We'll snorkel over to the reef and descend. When you're down, do try and avoid touching anything. The wreck isn't particularly stable. And we're not going inside. It's a small boat. The main lure is its attraction for the marine life. But please respect the ecosystem and stick together. As always, keep eyes on me in case of any need to surface early. It'll be warm and light. We're going to see some wonderful sights. Have a great dive, guys.'

Eliza swims out with Noah. They've dived together a lot, whenever they can, since their South American travels. It's one of those things they will always have in common. A familiarity between them that brings back memories of holidays, their youth, those days when they would look at each other and have to leave the bar or restaurant, wherever they were, and just jump into bed. That feeling of when their bodies linked as if they were pieces designed only to slot in with the other. Diving with Noah brings all of that back. As they descend, for the first time in months, Eliza forgets all the anger and resentment. She feels in synch with him for once. She feels happy.

The water is cool despite the rays of sunlight that pierce the surface. As they go deeper, and they can see the outline of the wreck, the coral is bright and vibrant with colour. They swim down, past a starfish spread out on a purple rock, a school of butterfly fish, and darting orange clown fish. Down further, the water is hollow with cold, it undulates with sun-warmed patches, then back to the darker blue of the deep.

Eliza kicks her legs, following the neon yellow of Noah's watch strap. Then they are above the splintered cabin of the boat. She can see the others on the far side of it, silhouetted against the streaming light. The cabin roof is crusted with limpets and molluscs. She feels Noah touch her arm and looks up to see a figure paddling next to them. She thinks it's Lars. He's pointing behind them and there are two giant manta rays, skimming a sandbank, scooping up and then down, lapping the water under their majestic fins.

Noah gives Eliza the OK sign and she returns it. She treads water vertically, looking down at the rays, watching her own fins tap-dance in the water right above them. If she could somersault and bring her head lower, she could touch them, feel their skin that gleams like porcelain.

The explosion comes out of nowhere.

At first Eliza thinks that the O-ring seal on her regulator has blown. Everywhere, there is swirling silt from the seabed. She can't see. Her fingers scrabble at her neck, trying to feel over her shoulder, down her back.

Her ears pound with pressure. She can feel the water being sucked away, dragging beyond them as if in the pull of a vacuum. She can just make out the shape of Noah next to her. She feels him touch her hand, move it down from the top of her oxygen tank at her shoulder blades.

The blast wasn't from her regulator.

The paintbox of coloured fish that had swum around them a second ago have pulled in as one, and now they flee in neat packs, zipping away through the water until they disappear from sight.

Eliza covers her ears with her hands. There is a high-pitched scream; a buzzing, ringing sound. Beside her, then in front of her, Noah lurches this way and that, searching through the murky water for Lars.

She taps his arm. *Should they ascend?*

He shakes his head. No. They have to find Lars. He is the dive leader. Noah looks at his watch. They have twenty-three minutes left of the dive. Whatever the explosion was, Zikri must have heard it. He and Lars will have a protocol for this. They need to stay safe and regulated until they are told otherwise.

Noah doesn't say this, but Eliza knows this is what he's thinking. She looks around, peering in the dim light drowned in
floating, spinning sand, trying to find where the others are.

She tugs Noah's arm, again. She thinks she sees Adam. Over
by the wreck. He's holding on to a hanging piece of rotting wood
that once must have been the boat deck. She hooks her index
finger at him, the sign of a question.

*What do we do?*

Adam makes the *stop and hold* sign.

She can't see Karin and John. Then Lars appears, emerging
from the gloom. He hovers next to Adam and makes his hands
into fists, points both his index fingers downwards.

*Buddy up. Stay together.*

Another bang rips through the water.

The noise is magnificent, Eliza thinks, even as she is knocked
horizontal on to her front by the vibration, her head forced to
curl down to her knees, her oxygen tank bulky against her back.
She can almost see the sound. It rears up as a shape in the water,
taking form in clear valleys, troughs of light. It pushes through
the dive group, circling them, the force of it turning them upside
down and round and round.

She loses Noah. His hand slips from hers.

Silt from the seabed has wheeled and spun into tornadoes
that block the light. She can't see which way is up. She squeezes
her eyes shut for a brief second, forces herself to remember her
training.

Watch for the bubbles in the sediment, water droplets in her
mask. Bubbles always go up. The pain in her ears is twisted into a
knot that gouges through her head, as if into her brain.

She opens her eyes.

*Watch for the bubbles.*

She's had vertigo once before on a dive. She hadn't gone
underneath the water for a year after that. That feeling of bliss,
of freedom, of weightlessness had vanished. It had turned into
pure, hard fear. No breath, no air, no light. Dying under the
pressure of your own lungs, getting ever tighter until it all goes
dark.

She feels that same dread now. Her fingers curl reflexively, reaching for air. Inside her flippers, her feet start to point. She wants to kick. To push down and propel herself up to where there is light, where there is air.

Someone grabs at her elbow. She whips round, clawing at them to steady herself.

Adam's eyes stare at her hard from behind his mask.

*No.*

His fingers jab through her wetsuit on to her arm.

He's too close to her. He lifts a hand.

Panic rises. She back-pedals. The muscles in her jaw unclench as if she is preparing to scream. Then he reaches for her and, as he does, he knocks the tube connected to her regulator and it tumbles from her mouth.

She stares, horrified.

He is going to hurt her.

He keeps hold of her in a tight grip as he rapidly scans the water, his hair curling like waving strands of kelp. She tugs herself free, sculling back, trying to get away. Her vision pops, her lungs feel vacant and light, blown free of oxygen.

He rears up, his expression wild behind his mask. He jerks his head, and she looks down.

He's holding her regulator. Offering it to her.

She can't tear her gaze away from his as he puts it gently back into her mouth. He presses the purge button and seawater expels in a tiny gush.

She drinks in breath, her legs and arms in spasm, shaking with relief. He nods at her, satisfied she's all right. Keeps a loose hand on her arm as he hunts the murky water for the rest of the group.

She treads water, feeling the steady flow of oxygen calm her heart rate. She disassociates. A silver reef fish moves in slow motion beneath her.

They wait.

The violence of the explosion disappears as quickly as it came. The sand settles and drifts. Their visibility clears. Lars emerges from the other side of the damaged wreck, Noah at his elbow. Behind him, Eliza can just make out the Dutch couple.

They gather together, all present.

Lars gives the thumbs-up sign. They will abort the dive and ascend. They all return the sign and Noah swims over to Eliza.

*OK.*

Slowly they head up. At only twelve metres down, it's not long before they reach the surface. Immediately, Lars takes off his mask and yells to Zikri.

'*Awak OK tak?*'

'Yes, yes. OK. Over there.'

They turn in the direction that Zikri is pointing. Eliza squints. There is a tiny shape in the distance on the water.

'*Nelayan,*' Zikri shouts. '*Dinamit.*'

They gape at him, all of them understanding, despite the Malay.

'That was a dynamite explosion?' Adam asks, moving quickly through the water over to Lars. He pushes his mask up on to his head and his face is white beneath his tan. 'In the water, here?'

Lars frowns, continuing to stare intently at the distant shape. 'Everyone back in the boat,' he says. 'Everyone out of the water, now.'

They front-crawl fast to the ladder, climbing up, handing their kit to Zikri. Lars is the last one in. He heads straight to pull up the anchor and shouts something in Malay. Zikri starts the engine and then the boat is moving, cutting through the water, making a wide circle around where Zikri had indicated the source of the blast.

'For fuck's sake. We could have been killed,' Adam says, ripping off his mask and dropping it on the deck. 'You said that fishing was banned. They're using dynamite to fish, yes?'

'It is. What they did is illegal.'

Lars has moved to the front of the boat, arms folded, looking back towards the reef.

'You have to tell the police,' Eliza says. She rubs her ears with her hands.

'Are you OK?' Noah asks.

'I can't hear much. That was terrifying. I thought... I couldn't tell which way up I was...' She hears the sob in her voice and swallows. 'Yeah, I'm OK,' she says.

'Lars,' Adam barks. 'Mate, this isn't on. If that had gone off anywhere nearer us, we'd be pieces of flesh floating round in the water. You can't bring people out here if there's any chance that could happen.' He gets to his feet. 'Lars, man. Look at me.'

'Sit down. Adam, please. Put on your life jacket. We'll get back to shore and talk about it. Not now. We are safe now. Please be calm and we can talk at the resort.'

Eliza can see Adam weighing up whether to do as he's told. After a beat, he sits, leaving his life jacket on the seat unused. Then he turns to her. 'You OK, Eliza? Had a bit of a moment back there.'

'What kind of moment?' Noah puts an arm around her shoulder, concerned.

Adam smooths back his hair and cuts his eyes at Lars over by the tiller. 'She had a sort of panic attack. Thought I was trying to hurt you or something, didn't you? She tried to push me away and ended up losing her regulator. Seriously, I am fucking *livid* about this.' He takes a breath. 'It was all right in the end, though, wasn't it? We got through it.' He nods at Eliza, as if they've shared something. Been through an experience together.

'Was it? Are you sure you're OK?' Noah pulls her into him, his hand on her hair.

She feels dizzy. It's not right, the way he's putting it. Making out as if she'd been pathetic when he'd been the one to come up on her in the water with no warning. She wants to tell him off in front of everyone. Tell them it was his fault she'd been afraid. He'd been too rough with her under the water. He'd frightened her.

'Eliza?' Noah says.

'I'm fine,' she says, putting on her shades. She wraps her arms around herself. 'It's fine.'

Silence and exhaustion envelop the boat as it speeds back to the island. Eliza looks at the blue of the horizon, watching as the line of the beach comes gradually into view. The explosion has rattled them.

There's a rumble in the sky and she shivers. This sound is different from the explosion, though – a familiar echo. As the boat cuts the engine and glides into the shallows, a bank of black and purple clouds gathers angrily up above the resort, nestling on the top of Fire Mountain.

Lars sees her watching and gives a grim nod.

'Storm is coming in,' he says.

# 9

## ADAM

He feels the rage course through him as if it were actual liquid burning acid through his veins. He can't stay still. Watching Lars lounging at the bar entirely at ease, half-naked as usual, that ridiculous earring in his ear, he wants to grab a rattan chair and shove it into his disgustingly oiled chest.

They could have been killed. He would have left Lou a widow and his children fatherless. One stupid decision to go out with a man – basically a *child* – and his life would have been over.

He should have trusted his instincts because he hasn't liked Lars from the moment he met him. Last night he'd deliberately stayed behind to talk to him after Eliza and Noah had gone to bed. Not only to erase the mental torture of the image of the pair of them in bed together, but also to probe Lars. Find out a little more about him.

A thriller writer knows a plotline when he spies one. And Lars has got 'cheap action movie' written all over him. He's too confident, the way he moves around the resort. Sort of catlike. He's got that irritating quality where everyone drops everything just to hear him speak, as if he's some kind of god and not just a drop-out surfer who runs a bar in the middle of nowhere.

Dodgy, illiterate, egomaniac. That's what Adam's pinned him as, and from what Lars had told him last night, he isn't too far off. Over some unbelievably strong local whisky, Lars had boasted that he basically ran Pulau Kalah – that nothing happens on the island without his say-so.

But dynamite? That's too fucking much.

He thinks about Eliza – how terrified she'd been – and it makes him shake with anger. As soon as they'd reached the shore, he'd jumped out of the boat, leaving his dive kit behind. He'd stood on the sand, waiting for Lars and Zikri to bring everything in.

He'd appreciated the presence of six-foot-tall Noah coming to stand at his side, arms folded, although he suspected Noah was more concerned with protecting Lars from Adam's fists than the other way round. But Lars had stayed calm, passing all the gear to the resort staff to take up to the dive hut. Above them, the sky had darkened, and the air felt thick and humid. Lars had considered the clouds before coming over to Adam.

'Mate...' Adam had begun.

Lars held out his hands. 'Come. Please. Come inside and we'll have a drink. We've had a shock. Let me get you a drink.' He hadn't waited for an answer, leaving Adam and jogging over to the restaurant.

Adam had followed and now stands, almost trembling, watching Lars hand round bottles of beer, his fingers itching to make contact with something, anything.

Noah and the Dutch couple stand in silence. Eliza stays standing, her wetsuit unzipped to her waist revealing her bikini top, her hair wet and spiked from the sea.

The beer is ice-cold in his palm as Lars places it there. He takes a long drink, his eyes never leaving Lars's face. He brings the bottle down and lets it swing from his fingers. He sucks at his teeth.

'How many times has this happened?'

'On our trips? Never.' Lars's stance is relaxed. He pushes his blond hair back from his forehead, drinks from his own beer. 'There was an incident. A fish bomb about eighteen months ago. Two tourists were killed. Two Chinese guys.'

Adam takes a step forward.

'But it was fifty kilometres from here. On the edge of the conservation area. We knew about it, of course. The whole archipelago crawled with investigators, police. Insurance agents.' Lars shrugs. 'I think they found the guys. They were dealt with. But here on the island... we don't have a problem. The locals are educated. Look. Sit down. Let me explain.'

'Let's hear what he has to say, Adam. Come on.'

Adam turns to respond to Noah and, instead, his eyes find Eliza. She seems so vulnerable, her eyes pleading, before she takes the chair closest to where he stands.

'Noah's right,' she says. 'What's the point of fighting? And we should hear what Lars says before we see Lou. We need to be able to explain.'

He can't help it. He's immediately mollified by the concern she has on her face.

'I don't want Lou worrying,' he concedes, sitting down. 'She'll never let me dive again otherwise.'

Thunder growls angrily above them as Noah props himself on the arm of Eliza's chair. Adam can't help the flare of jealousy this sparks. But then, she chose to sit there, next to him. She took that seat before anyone else could.

Opposite him, Lars puts his beer on the table and leans forward, his elbows on his knees.

'The Orang Laut are sea people, right? They were the first immigrants to this part of the world, before the colonials came. They live off the sea. They work it, travel it. They're nomads. Some of them are pirates, sure. They need to eat. They need to provide for their families. Life has changed for them. They've had to settle. Get jobs. It doesn't sit right with many of them.

'And the monsoon season is hard. The waters rise, they're dangerous to sail and to fish. Climate change has altered the seascape. Holms and spits where, in the past, they'd land for shelter have gone. With all the industrial backhanders, overfishing in general... supplies have dramatically decreased.'

He sighs. 'Dynamite trading is a business. Just like drugs, or guns, or humans. People trade dynamite like they trade everything else. The fishermen think it will help get them an easy catch. It doesn't, of course. What it does is the blast actually rips open the bladders of the fish, so they sink to the bottom still alive. It's a very painful death because they can't move, fresh water can't pass through their gills, they can't breathe.'

Adam looks over as Karin, the Dutch woman, tuts and shakes her head. He can see Lars has his audience in the palm of his hand.

'And the worst thing is that, typically, it's the kids who are made to free-dive down to collect the dying fish after the explosion. So you can only dynamite in shallow waters so they can get to the haul. It means the explosion happens right on top of the reef. Most of the reefs are destroyed beyond recovery after a few explosions. The coral is obliterated, it turns to dust and rubble.

'But, look. That isn't what happens here. You've seen our eco-tourism initiatives. If we turned a blind eye to this kind of thing, we'd be committing economic suicide. It wouldn't make any sense. We'd be destroying the very thing that people come here and visit to see – the reef, the turtles. And what would happen if one of our guests was injured or killed? Our business would die.'

Lars takes a breath and sits back in his chair.

'I will report this. Zikri and I have got the coordinates of the explosion. Normally OK, we have no witnesses. We only see the aftermath days later if we dive over the bomb site. So, you know, maybe in a funny way, this will be a good thing. Because we *can* report it. And hopefully the government will find the perpetrators.'

As Lars finishes this speech, Adam glances at Eliza, who seems transfixed by Lars, nodding as if she entirely agrees with everything he's said.

'Are you serious?' he laughs. 'You don't honestly believe this bullshit?'

Eliza looks at him, confused. 'What do you mean?' she frowns. 'Adam, I don't think we can blame the resort. How were they to know? The local communities here,' she turns to Lars, 'what do you do to stop them endorsing this?'

'We educate them. We try to. The staff all come from the islands. Many of them live in the kampong here with their families. They know this type of fishing doesn't make any sense, economically or ethically. It kills the environment that actually provides for them. We explain this. Persuade them to go back to the traditional methods they've been using for hundreds of years.'

'Oh, come on!' Adam slams down his empty beer bottle and the Dutch woman gasps at the impact. He gives her a withering look. 'This is utter bollocks, Lars. You said it yourself last night.

You explained how things worked here. That the locals had to be kept in line and a few backhanders meant business could run smoothly. Is that not what you said? Tell me I'm wrong. Tell *them* you didn't say that.'

There is a lull in the music in the bar.

'I think you misunderstood me, Adam,' Lars says, standing up. He stretches his arms above his head, linking his hands in what looks like an idiotic yoga pose, Adam thinks.

'What I said was that *of course* we have to work with the local communities. We are guests in their country. But we can guide them. Help them with adopting new technology.' Lars sighs again. 'Look. I know it was scary. I totally understand. But please believe me. The resort isn't at fault. We would never put you in danger. I'm really very sorry.'

'Hi there.'

Adam turns to see Lou standing at the entrance to the bar. The baby is asleep in the sling wrapped round her. The children are behind her, bringing up the rear.

A whispering breeze has picked up, gently buffeting them as it meanders in from the sea. Outside, palm leaves rustle and the usually fluffy white sand has taken on a damp sheen as if it has been mopped flat. The Dutch couple mutter goodbye and take their leave.

'When did you get back? How was the dive?' Lou assesses them. 'You all seem very glum. Wasn't the visibility any good?'

They look at her in silence.

'What is it? Has something happened?'

Adam gets to his feet as Raffy runs over to him.

'Hey, Raffy mate. No need to worry, darling. Everyone's fine.'

Lou cradles Laila's head. 'What do you mean? What happened?'

'There was an explosion.' Eliza goes over and brings Sam in for a hug. 'When we were under the water. We got... a bit turned around.'

'Turned around? What do you mean, an explosion? Like a bomb?'

'It was dynamite,' Noah says, picking up Chloe so her legs straddle his waist. 'A fish bomb.'

'A fish bomb?' Raffy exclaims. 'A bomb that kills fish?' He stares up at Adam in outrage, pulling at his sleeve. 'Daddy, that's so wrong. I saw a film about it on YouTube. All the fish were murdered, and the coral was all smashed up under the sea.'

'It's OK, Raff,' Lou says. 'Don't you worry, buddy. We can do some research, OK? Find out about it and see if we can help. I'm sure it wasn't as bad as it sounds.'

'Did you see one today, Daddy? Are you going to stop it?' Raffy's voice trembles and his eyes glisten with tears.

Adam looks pointedly at Noah before crouching down. 'No, Raff. It's all good. We were just talking about what a bad thing they are and how everyone should be told to fish properly so that the reefs are protected, that's all.'

'Absolutely,' Lars says. 'And we're going to do an activity on the reefs and the coral tomorrow after you've been snorkelling, yah?' He claps his hands and spreads his arms wide. 'But look. Now it's time to make pizzas! Guys, come over here. Look what Julie has got for you.'

Adam stands up and shakes his head in disgust as the kids trundle off behind Lars towards the big dining tables in the restaurant where staff have laid out pizza dough and toppings. He turns to Noah and Eliza, disbelief etched on his face.

*The guy is a knob.*

Noah shrugs in response. 'Yeah well... it's probably not our fight, you know? I'm going to go back to the hut while the kids eat,' he says. 'Have a shower and check my phone.' He squeezes Eliza's shoulder. 'OK?'

She doesn't look up at him, Adam notices.

'Adam?' Lou says. 'Can someone please tell me what's going on?'

'Come here,' he says, pulling her close and hugging her. 'It's fine. Like Noah said, there was a *tiny* little dynamite explosion. But it was miles away...' He shoots Eliza a quick glance and, for the merest second, she meets his eyes. 'So we barely even knew about it. We were down by the wreck and the swell got big, that's all. We got bumped around a little. Then we surfaced and came back. It's all good.'

'Lars has been explaining,' Eliza says, as Zikri the barman arrives with more drinks. 'There are some fishermen that use dynamite as a way of fishing. It's dangerous and illegal and it destroys the reef. But they're doing everything they can to stop it.'

Adam snorts loudly as he takes another beer.

'So, no one was hurt?' Lou clarifies, looking round as if to check. 'But you heard the noise of the explosion? And just got caught in a big swell?'

'Yeah, we heard it all right,' Noah says.

Adam frowns. Seriously, why doesn't the guy just take out a bloody advertisement?

'But it was fine. No damage done.' Noah grabs himself a beer. 'Right. I'll see you in a bit.'

'God...' Lou says, unwrapping Laila from the sling and taking a seat. 'That all sounds very scary. I hope Raffy isn't going to be too upset. He gets fixated on these things.'

'How's your afternoon been?' Eliza asks. 'How were the kids?'

Lou gives a smile and jerks her chin upwards as another sign of the coming storm cracks the air. Above them, one of the pendant lights begins to sway.

'It rained,' she says. 'And then it stopped.'

'Lars says there's a storm coming,' Eliza says.

'Yes,' Lou says, rocking Laila from side to side.

Adam watches Noah go, wondering, yet again, what it is that Eliza sees in him, when he feels Lou staring and forces himself to come back and focus on the conversation. But then Eliza leans forward and he can't help but notice as her breasts swing low in her bikini. It's like electricity firing down to his groin, making him catch his breath.

He looks up and sees something pass through Lou. A thought. A wave of discomfort. Like the breeze brushing their skin, turning uncomfortably cool. Then she smiles brightly, straightening her shoulders.

'Yes, a storm's definitely on the way,' she says. 'I can feel it in the air.'

# 10

## LOU

'Ma'am, can I have a word?'

The others have just left for their dive. Watching from a rattan chair in the bar, until the shape of the boat disappears from sight, Lou tries to get a bellowing Laila to take her milk from a bottle. On the sand, right by the steps into the bar, she can see the three blond heads of Raffy and the twins bent in concentration, making sandcastles, but it won't be long until they're bored. Raffy has thrown sand twice at Chloe, and Lou knows the next time will result in a fight.

She just has to get Laila to sleep in the sling. Then they can go further up the beach and she can sit in one of the chairs under the palm trees and the kids can paddle in the surf. If she walks up there now, the heat of the sun will surely goad Laila into a greater rage. So she's staying here in the relative cool, trying to persuade this crying banshee that sleep is what she needs.

But the effects of her earlier pill have worn off and Laila won't take the bottle and Lou is getting the panicky feeling that seems to come all the time at the moment. It starts with pins and needles creeping up from her toes and then her ankles. And then her breathing shallows and it feels as if malevolence swims around her, cloaking her vision, until all she can see is darkness, and all the badness in the world.

She shuts her eyes, trying to calm down. She knows she could just put Laila on her breast. But if Laila gets fussy about the bottle, she can't be left in the hut tonight with the babysitter, and Lou won't be able to join them all on the beach. And she wants to be like that for just one night. Wants to feel like her old self. Be that fun, relaxed and *normal* person she once used to be.

Now, the friendly-faced waitress, Sara, bends over her. 'Ma'am?' the waitress repeats. 'I'm so sorry. But can I ask…?'

She's just a girl, Lou thinks. Barely in her twenties. She's pretty, with her midnight-dark hair tied up in a ponytail, a slim physique dressed in the Malay staff uniform. She's looking anxiously over her shoulder at a group of four guests, lounging nearby in the bar, games of Rummy and Scrabble on the tables between them, creamy umbrellaed glasses of piña coladas in easy reach.

'We've had some people… they say that the noise…' Sara gestures kindly at the crying Laila. 'Would you mind taking her away? Maybe to your hut?'

Lou gazes down at Laila in despair as her cries lift to a level that make it sound as if she is actually being flayed. Her own chest feels tight.

'I'm so sorry,' she says. 'I'm trying to get her to sleep. It won't take long… It's just these chairs are much more comfortable than the ones in the restaurant. To feed her in, you know.'

She looks over to see who's complaining. It's the newlyweds and their parents. They stare at her with a slight shake of their heads, a lift of their eyebrows. So sure of their position. So certain that the solution to their problem is to remove it. To erase the harried mother and her nightmare baby and pretend she doesn't exist. That this paradise is theirs to delineate and manufacture for their own enjoyment and nobody else's.

'I mean, there are only four of them. It's not like the bar is packed full. Couldn't they just wait a little?'

Sara shakes her head nervously, wringing her hands. She darts another look back at the table of annoyed guests. 'I know, ma'am. But they… they say that children aren't allowed in the bar…' Her eyes fill with compassion that these guests have used the one strategy impossible to argue against.

Beyond Sara's shoulder, Lou can see the sign carved from a piece of driftwood: NO CHILDREN IN THE BAR.

Lou feels her limbs grow hot, as if anger and self-pity have leaked into the very blood in her veins and are propelling her upwards, causing her to grip on to Laila with such intensity that, for a moment, the baby stops in surprise. She looks up at her mother, sensing that this normally cosy cushion of either smiles or tears has transformed into something different.

Laila doesn't know rage. Only her own, borne of the frustration of immediately unmet needs. But she has never witnessed rage in others. And it halts her. Her little brow furrows with interest.

In the brief respite of quiet, Lou takes a breath. The waitress cows, her head bent as if in awe at what she senses is about to come.

And she is right.

Lou gets to her feet and moves closer to the table where the family sit. She stands, magnificent under the rafters, her greasy hair hanging in rivers around her face, her baby clutched to her bosom, her stance wide.

'Yeah, I'll fuck off, don't worry,' she calls to the group. They freeze and stare at her. The father – a grey-haired man in a white shirt – gives her a placating smile.

'Your language…' he says, waving a hand to indicate Lou's audience. Down on the beach, Raffy and the twins have stopped playing, much more interested in this adult altercation.

'Please don't patronise me,' Lou says, her voice calm although her heart beats wildly. 'You just carry on, sitting there, enjoying yourselves. Don't worry that you're excluding me, just because I've got the audacity to have children. Living, breathing human beings, who *are* allowed to be here, you know? Children *are* allowed to have holidays and play and open their mouths and not be bloody silent as the grave because it might disturb your precious drinking.'

She pauses, breathing hard, looking back at the children where Raffy is eyeballing her with undisguised admiration. He will never have seen her like this. She gives him a quick wink then turns back.

'Yeah, I'll take them away, down this incredibly hot beach, so that you won't be bothered by us. I mean, you've obviously had children. Clearly you've forgotten.' She glares at the daughter. 'And someday *you* might have them. So I hope you remember this day. But don't worry about it, seriously.

'And don't...' Lou lifts a finger to them '...don't ever consider that it might have been nice to have come over and said hello. And – maybe – say, I don't know, do you need a hand? Or, what's your name? Or... something. Anything. Anything to make me feel like a human being and not just an irritation that you have to get rid of like a bloody mosquito. That you don't even have the balls to come over and ask me to leave yourself. You have to get this poor girl to do your dirty work for you. You make me *sick*.'

The grey-haired man gets to his feet. 'Now, hang on—'

'Oh fuck off, grandpa,' Lou spits. 'Go back to your game of bridge or whatever boring shit it is that you're doing. Soon you'll be dead and these kids will be running the world. And they'll be a lot fucking nicer than you.'

She turns on her heel, beckoning the kids to come with her. They scamper along, following her as she stalks up the beach. Chloe turns back and sticks out her tongue at the man in the bar. Laila's head bounces on her mother's shoulder, staring at him with her big blue eyes as they go.

They hear the rumble of thunder as they move between the tiger stripes of shade on the sand from the palm fronds. Above them, the clouds begin to bush and grow, soaking up the water from the air, transforming them into scudding shapes of black and purple.

By the time they've reached Lou and Adam's hut, heavy pellets of rain tap rhythmically on to their heads and the ground, the weight of the drops making tiny dents in the sand. They climb the stairs to the little wooden veranda and Lou sinks into a chair.

The kids scatter inside, instinctively knowing that Lou must be left alone.

She sits and breathes and waits for her heart rate to slow. And as the deluge comes, she looks down to see that Laila has finally fallen asleep.

# 11

## Eliza

The air is soupy and thick with rain and she looks out from their veranda on to an underwhelming sunset. The beach is empty but for a couple of late swimmers cutting through the water, making the most of the remaining light.

In front of her, an orange ball sits abandoned on the patch of concrete used as a makeshift basketball court. Next to it lies the inflatable kayak they brought to the island with them from Singapore. It's quiet. Any noise from the bar seems muffled by cloud and the insistent incoming shuffling of the tide.

The children are eating supper over at the restaurant and Noah has showered and gone on yet another hunt for some Wi-Fi. With time before dinner, Eliza has brought her reading-club book outside. She's changed into a long-sleeved maxi dress as a defence against the hum of hovering mosquitoes. Occasionally she has to duck her head as moths begin to claim the night, flying and thwacking the little electric light above the door to their hut.

The book is set in the Deep South but Eliza can't concentrate on it. It's full of descriptions of food: iced tea and something called hominy grits. She shuts her eyes and opens them again to look down at the page. But there's a high-pitched tone in her head. It rattles through her, making it impossible for her to see the printed words.

From nearby, Eliza hears the beeping call of a bird.

'Did you see that lightning?'

Her eyes snap open.

Adam is right in front of her, leaning on the balcony rail, smiling at her from behind his sunglasses. The V of his T-shirt cuts down his chest and she can see a clump of his dark chest hair.

'What?'

He jerks his chin upwards. 'Big fork of lightning right above us. The sky's always busy in the tropics,' he grins. Black clouds scuttle above and he stands back with his usual confident stance, assessing the beach, hands in his shorts pockets. 'I'm going on a beer run if you want something from the bar? Or come over as well, maybe? Have an aperitif before dinner?'

'Oh thanks.' Eliza hears a tremble in her voice and is immediately furious with herself. Why is she being like this with him?

Adam is inscrutable behind his shades, but his lips are amused as he waits for her to answer.

'Um, gin and tonic?' she says. 'Sorry. I think my brain's been fried since the dive trip.'

'Yeah, it was pretty scary. I don't know,' Adam exhales, shaking his head, 'I'm not sure about Lars. Seems a bit too good to be true. Know what I mean?'

'I think he's OK. You have to have a certain amount of charm to run a place like this. I couldn't work in customer service. Too many people.'

Thank God, she's loosening up as she talks.

'Yeah. Lou had a run-in with some of them. While we were gone. They told her she had to leave the bar. Because of the baby.'

'What?' Eliza uncrosses her legs and straightens in her chair, her book dangling from her fingers. 'That's awful. This isn't the Ritz, is it? Where's she going to put Laila? Out on the beach on her own?'

Adam laughs and drops his hands over the rail in front of her. 'Well, in fairness, my darling daughter isn't known for her subtle conversation.'

'Where is Lou?'

'She's taken Laila for a walk up the beach. Trying to get her down before we eat.' He turns towards the restaurant. 'Right. I'll go and get the orders in. Reckon we could all do with a few sharpeners before dinner.'

'Thanks. I'll come on over in a minute. Noah should be on his way there already,' Eliza says. She re-crosses her legs and, as she does, her toes brush against his fingers hanging over the rail. The contact makes her stiffen. Her cheeks burn.

Adam smiles and takes his hands away, rubs one across the nape of his neck.

'Cool,' he says. 'See you in a bit.'

He seems to wait, hover for just a millisecond, before he moves. Then he turns and strolls down on to the beach.

Eliza sets her mouth and picks up the book, smooths out the pages, brings it to her face and stares at the typed words. Someone in the book is making cornbread and pitted peach jam from a recipe that's been in their family for generations.

Somewhere nearby, a chair creaks and a wind chime clatters in the breeze. She thinks about Lou walking further up the beach with Laila, trying to get her to sleep. How her own mother would have done the same thing with her, in the absence of her father. How lonely she must have felt, pacing the carpet in their tiny flat, praying for Eliza to stop crying. How grateful her mother always was to the Indian family who would regularly visit and sometimes bring her plates of food on Eid: vegetarian samosas and Indian sweets. Not only for the sustenance, but for the warmth and the care, for the time they took to include them into their family.

Even after all these years, Eliza knows she hasn't properly dealt with her mother's death. Hasn't coped with the grief. When it happened, she and Noah had flown back to London from South America, into a firestorm of coroner's certificates, autopsy reports, dealing with the funeral, and she'd walked through it all in a daze. She'd nodded and smiled and hugged and cried. But all of it had been meaningless.

The day after the funeral, she'd gone back to the flat. Walked down the steps to the basement – steps she'd taken a million times before in her life. Always, she would open the door with her key – that brass key – and the door would swing open on to the tiny hallway.

She could see straight through into the kitchen where invari- ably her mother would be standing, either at the stove or, more likely, on the other side of the kitchen bench on the phone, fag in hand, brandishing it like a wand as she gossiped with one of her friends. She'd look up and see Eliza and a delighted smile would light up her face. She'd wave at her, telling her to come in, to put the kettle on. Its steam would fog the little window above the sink, and they'd sit at the kitchen table with its green plastic tablecloth, chatting and drinking endless cups of tea.

That day, though, the kitchen was empty and cold. The garden – only a patch of patio tiles, really, but with an overhead trellis where the wisteria grew – had been decimated by the winter. She'd gone to the back door and stared out, remembering hot summer days, dragging out the television to watch the tennis at Wimbledon with a long extension lead, balancing a piece of cardboard on the top so they could shield the screen from the glare.

The night before she left for South America, they'd sat outside, sharing a bottle of wine.

'This is the best bit, darling,' her mother had said, breathing in the scent of the summer flowers. 'The night *before* the adventure. It's always so much more exciting than the real thing.' She'd taken her hand and Eliza had looked down at it, traced the veins on top. Hands as familiar to her as her own.

'I love you very much, Eliza,' her mother had said.

'Don't get sad, Mum. Have some more wine, come on. I'll be back before you know it. And there's the email now. Don't forget what I've told you about it. You need to get to grips with it. That's how we can stay in touch.'

'Ah yes, of course.' Her mother had cocked her head, amused. 'The email.'

Fourteen weeks later, and her mother was dead. Hanging from the very trellis they'd sat under.

Time moved on and sometimes it felt like the part of her life with her mother had been only a dream. That this was the reality – her family with Noah and the twins. Her beautiful children whom she would never abandon no matter how hard things became.

She'd learned to put her mother in a kind of box. A box of pain that was better never to be opened. It could sing with longing and radiate its heartbreak, but it couldn't touch her. And if it couldn't touch her, it couldn't hurt her.

At least, it hadn't been able to touch her. Not until very recently.

Music is turned on in the bar and, nearby, someone shouts a laugh.

Adam.

The image of him buzzes through her brain.

She frowns and puts the book down, her thumbs like vices on its cover. She stares out at the view, at the changing hues of the sand.

The sun must be high above Fire Mountain, but its light is meeting the shadows of the approaching storm. She watches as its rays are swallowed, as the gloom spreads in patches. She looks on as the line of darkness lengthens steadily, growing deeper with every passing moment, moving closer and closer to the sea, covering anyone still left on the beach.

She continues watching, forces herself to watch, to keep her eyes wide open, until finally the beach is wrapped in shadow and lying under the colour of night.

# 12

## Noah

He walks quickly across the clearing where, to his right, the dusky range of hills that rise from the middle of the island are caught in a halo of sunlight. He heads in that direction, through the spindly fir trees that are dotted around the resort, and wanders towards the administrative offices.

He needs to find Lars and ask about getting on to the Turtle Cove Wi-Fi. He'd tried to do it this morning, but ridiculously the staff wouldn't give him the password until Lars got back from the morning dive. And with all the drama of the fish bomb, he'd forgotten to ask him about it on the boat.

He hadn't admitted it to anyone – least of all Eliza – but it had been a bit hairy, he'd thought: under the water when the explosion had happened. When he'd got separated from Eliza, there'd been a moment when he'd thought that was it and he'd never see her again. When they'd surfaced and he'd gone to her, she'd looked so fragile. Her skin washed of colour, as pale as bleached coral. The image stops him for a minute, underneath a palm tree, and he stands there thinking, running his hand along the hatching of its trunk.

Eliza isn't delicate, though. She isn't weak. She's one of the toughest people he knows, with everything she's had to deal with. Coral is a good analogy for her, actually. It looks like it could snap into a million tiny pieces but actually it's strong as steel. Except recently... Since when? Since they've been in Singapore, he thinks. She's seemed more vulnerable, maybe?

Her reaction on the boat was out of character. And then, last night. What was that about – the smoking and the drinking with Adam? That isn't who she is.

He shakes his head. Adam's way too cocky, he thinks as he starts to walk again, crunching tiny pine cones flat under the soles of his Vans. Yes, fish bombs are bad, fair enough. But it's not the first time he's seen one and it won't be the last probably. The bomb didn't detonate on their heads, did it? No one was actually hurt. So why is Adam making all this fuss with Lars? He just wants to bring attention to himself, that's what it is.

Noah hadn't *totally* minded coming on this weekend with the Carters (until he found out it clashed with the closing of the Bonaparte deal). But he hadn't been that keen either. Adam and Lou are an all-right couple. Better value than a lot of the Singapore crowd. But it's different, isn't it – going on holiday with someone? Hanging out for a couple of beers on a Friday night is not the same as being with them twenty-four seven. Having to watch how a man talks to his wife. Watch how he flirts with another man's woman.

'*Fuck!*'

Noah halts at the sound of the shout. He's outside one of the staff accommodation huts. The main administrative office is a little further on. As the sky has darkened, they've turned on the lights in the restaurant ahead of him. He can hear the steady beat of a Bob Marley song. Where he's standing, someone has hung their boxer shorts and T-shirts on a wire strewn between two posts of the atap. They flap a little in the warm wind that's begun to pick up and dance through the air. A few metres away, he notices an older Malay woman rocking in a chair in front of the door of her hut.

'*No!*'

The yell is accompanied by more shouting. It's coming from the office and Noah moves towards it. Whoever is speaking, does so in rapid Malay. The person is agitated, upset. Noah carries on in the direction of the voice. It's barely ten metres away.

Like the other huts, the admin office is a single-level build-ing with an atap roof. Unlike the others, it has a wide, shaded veranda at its front with an open window and ledge looking out on to it which acts as a small reception area. When they'd arrived, Noah and Adam had waited there for Lars to painstakingly fill out their passport details in the resort logbook and give them a receipt for the fee they'd paid to the Malaysian government for the privilege of staying within a marine conservation area.

Noah stops and waits to hear more.

'*Saya memberitahu anda pada hari Isnin. Kita ada tetamu. Fuck!*'

It sounds like Lars's voice, and he is furious.

The hairs on Noah's arms prickle. Who is he shouting at?

'*Anda tidak boleh menyerang tetamu dengan fish bom...*'

Bomb... Fish bomb.

He peers round the edge of the window. Inside, a figure is silhouetted against the bare light bulb that begins to violently swing from the ceiling as the tempo of the wind increases.

It's definitely Lars but he can't see much more inside, it's too dark. Maybe he's reporting the explosion to the authorities just as he said he would.

'*Fuck, buat apa nak bazir dinamit macam ni!*'

Noah ducks back with a frown. He wouldn't curse at a government official. So who is he talking to?

*Bazir dinamit.*

Dynamite...

'*He's a little shit is what he is.*' There's a loud slam as if Lars has thrown something down. Maybe the phone? Noah hears what must be the flick of a lighter. The aroma of cigarette smoke.

Who is he talking about?

It sounds as if Lars knows something about the bomb, knows who might have been involved – the '*little shit*'.

Noah looks over his shoulder at the restaurant. No one will be able to hear this argument over the noise of the music in the bar. He can imagine Adam sitting there, beer in hand, still banging on about today and how he's going to single-handedly sort out the dynamite fishing cartels of South East Asia.

If Noah mentions he's overheard Lars talking like this, Adam will ratchet the news up to a full-blown conspiracy. He'll become intolerable.

Noah bites his lip, considering the square of light from the window that hits the concrete floor by his feet. Above him, the sky grumbles insistently. It's going to piss it down very soon. Clouds fly through the air, cutting through the last shards of sunlight as they merge.

At the same time as a gigantic crack splits the sky, the door to the office is flung open and bangs against the wall in the wind. Without thinking, Noah backs off, edging round the building so that he can't be seen. Cold drops of rain trickle into his collar as he kicks himself for leaving. Now he looks guilty, as if he were spying on Lars, when it was actually all quite innocent.

And he still hasn't got the damn password.

For a moment, he wants to laugh, even as his heart thumps in his chest.

Then, as the torrent comes down, he turns and begins to run.

# 13

## LOU

She reaches the bottom of the stairs of the hut as hard splashes of rain pucker into the sand. She turns back half-heartedly, debating whether to get an umbrella, then decides to forget it.

She races down the beach in the rain, then pulls up, feeling something biting at the soles of her feet. She stops and faces the ocean, and it's as if the ground is rippling. Tiny waves move across the beach as if the very earth is liquid.

*Crabs.*

A thousand or more translucent spindly crabs are running sideways across the sand in lines. A minuscule, endless battalion of bony legs, kicking and writhing as they scatter.

'It was disgusting,' Lou says to the others, sitting heavily in a chair in the bar. Rain drums the roof and the rattan blinds bang against the atap walls with the rhythm of the gale outside. 'There were zillions of the buggers. All of them see-through, like jellyfish. But crabs.'

The waitress from earlier – Sara – leans over the table to clear glasses. 'Spider crabs,' she laughs. 'They like to come out and dance in the rain.'

'Right,' Lou shudders. 'Of course they do.' She sighs and takes a sip of white wine. Adam is quiet, she thinks. He's studying his beer as if he's watching an Ashes test. Eliza is muted too. She's wearing another beautiful dress. A shimmery concoction of coral and white, her face tanned from the sun.

'And what's with the weather?' Lou downs the wine in her glass. 'It can't make up its mind, can it? Sunshine one minute, hurricane the next.'

'It's the monsoon.' Noah's glasses are speckled with water while his T-shirt is soaking wet and stuck to his chest. 'We're about a month off the real thing, but the weather's changeable at this time of year.'

'Great,' Lou says. 'Brilliant idea of mine to come here now, then.'

'At least the kids are happy,' Eliza says, smiling at Sara as she brings them another bottle of Sauvignon in an ice bucket. 'When I came over just now, I saw Lars fielding them over to the playhouse to go and learn how to tie knots and craft bows and arrows.'

Adam rouses himself at last. 'Course he is,' he says with a weary tone. 'Bloke can't just get them to play Connect 4, can he? Who does he think he is, Bear effing Grylls?'

'I think he's great,' Eliza says. 'The kids love him. And if they're happy, they're not bothering us. Plus,' she smiles over at Lou, 'he's pretty easy on the eye too.'

'Ha!' Lou says, reaching for the bottle and pouring herself another glass. 'You're not wrong there. Even if he is about twelve.'

Adam presses his lips together. 'He may be *easy on the eye*, darling, but I'm not sure you'd want to be mixed up with someone who's clearly taking advantage of the locals here for his own benefit.'

'What do you mean?' Eliza asks.

Adam shrugs. 'Like I said earlier. I had an interesting chat with him last night. His opinion of the Malays is pretty low. He clearly thinks he's above them in terms of intelligence and business acumen.' He leans forward and grabs a handful of peanuts from a bowl on the table. 'I got the sense that he was playing a few games here, that's all. Not very pleasant ones.'

'Oh, come on, Adam,' Lou scoffs, her eyes bright from the wine, amused by the childish look on his face. 'You just hate him because he's good-looking, spends his life diving and is a hundred years younger than you.'

'I don't hate him.'

Lou waves her glass in the air. 'Dislike. Envy. Are irritated by...' She stops. It's too much.

'Right. Whatever.' Adam inhales through his nose and fiddles with his watch strap for a second or two. 'Anyway,' he says at last. 'At least Laila's sleeping well here, isn't she?'

'Oh, she's only doing it to make a point when you lot are around. Trying to prove me wrong. That actually she's a model baby and every complaint I've made about her is just a downright lie.'

Adam's brow furrows again. The joke didn't land and Lou feels as if she's made yet another faux pas.

Next to him, Eliza clears her throat and crosses her legs. Her impossibly long legs, her toes painted a striking red colour that she'd told Lou was called Lobster Roll. Lou is suddenly aware that she hasn't changed out of her swimsuit after her walk with the baby. Once the babysitter had arrived, she'd been so desperate for a drink that she'd left immediately and then had to make that mad dash up the beach to escape the crabs. She's damp underneath her kaftan. Her hair is thick with sea salt and she can feel mosquitoes nibbling at her shins.

Adam shifts in his seat and she sees his eyes linger on Eliza. Feels the familiar knot of anxiety that comes from years of being married to Adam and wondering when his next infatuation will begin.

*Fuck it.*

The pill she took back in the hut has started to kick in and any care she has about her appearance is fading into something mushy and distant, tamped down by the low lighting in the bar, the thrum of the bass of the music that's being played.

A good-looking man wearing a khaki shirt and shorts comes into the bar, his hair wet from the rain. He leans across the bar and talks to Zikri, then glances over at their table, catching Lou's eye. He gives her a brief smile before rotating back round to his drink.

At the contact, Lou feels herself blush, so to cover it, she turns cheerily to Noah.

'What happened to you anyway? You look as drowned as me.'

Noah picks up a corner of his sodden T-shirt with a finger and thumb and nods. 'That I am,' he says. 'Got caught in the rain coming back from the admin office.'

'Did you manage to get any Wi-Fi?' Adam asks.

'Still no,' Noah shrugs, throwing him a quick glance. 'Must have just missed Bear Grylls after he went along to the kids' club.'

He drinks from his bottle of beer. 'Anyway. How's your latest book coming along, Adam? What's Roman up to in this one?'

Lou sips her wine and watches as Adam changes position, his expression taking on the usual mixture of conceit and craving for approval that talking about his writing normally brings.

'Ah, you know. Slowly. This one's tricky. Trickier than the last. Complicated plot,' he arches his back in overstated weariness. 'A new character I haven't really got to grips with yet.'

Whatever issues they may have, Lou has to admire Adam for being so honest about the difficulties he faces when writing his books. He could pretend they came easily to him. But then, maybe the admiration of others wouldn't be worth as much? Success is only really success when it's been hard-fought. If overcoming the monster wasn't a struggle, where's the valour of battle?

'It is amazing. Being able to write like that,' Eliza says, shaking her head at the peanuts Noah is offering. She leans forward. 'I know you mentioned him last night. But your father was a writer too, wasn't he?'

Lou looks at Adam in surprise. He rarely discusses his father. Before he died just over two years ago, their relationship had always been fraught, particularly after Adam got his first publishing contract and Roman McFee became a bestselling series. Why had he been talking about him last night? she wonders.

Adam nods. 'He was a professor of English literature. He wrote a lot of academic books.'

'No fiction?'

Adam looks down at his beer bottle and peels a corner of the label away from the green glass. 'He wrote one novel, yes. I thought you knew, actually. He wrote *The Kingfisher*?'

'Oh, God, yes. Of course he did. Benjamin Carter. I must have forgotten.' Eliza curls her legs up on to the chair, wrapping the material of her maxi dress elegantly around her calves. 'That was a fabulous book.'

'Yeah. Well, it became a sort of albatross for Dad. He never finished another novel. He wrote a lot of books but... I think, well...' Adam sits forward, putting his bottle on the table. He looks over in earnest. 'I don't think he could ever accept that *The*

*Kingfisher* was the only book he had. That saying, that everyone's got a book in them? I don't buy it. If it were true, why don't people actually write them? But I think it *is* true that sometimes an author can only have *one book* in them.

'That was my dad, I think. He had all this acclaim and was so well regarded. Especially academically. But for him...' Adam's face clouds over as he picks up his bottle and takes a drink '... it was never enough. The fact of *The Kingfisher* was never enough. It had to be bested to be valid. He had to prove that he was – I don't know – *consistently* a genius? Not just a one-off.' He looks up and smiles. 'Sad, really. I think he died very dissatisfied with his life.'

'Even though he'd actually been hugely successful,' Eliza says.

Lou reaches for her wine glass and happens to see Eliza's expression as she turns away from Adam. It takes her aback. Eliza's face is cold, just for an instant. Hard and unforgiving.

The beating of the rain on the roof has gradually slowed and Zikri comes out from behind the bar to begin rolling up the blinds. Outside, the sky is purple, the last pale strip of daylight struggling to stay visible beyond the horizon. Out of the corner of her eye, Lou notices as the man at the bar who'd smiled at her gets up and goes.

'Well, I love your books, mate,' Noah says, slapping a hand on Adam's shoulder. 'I'd read them even before we met you. Love all those car chases and set plays in casinos. Just like Bond. Brilliant.'

'Where did your dad teach?' Eliza asks, uncurling her legs and lifting her hair from the back of her neck. Her face has softened again, her eyes are warm and interested.

'King's,' Lou answers. Through the mist in her brain, she can sense Adam getting agitated and changes the subject. 'So, what time are we eating? You guys have all showered and changed. I should really do the same.'

'Not for a while,' Adam answers, putting a hand on her leg and giving it a grateful squeeze. 'But you don't need to change. You've only just got here.'

'I'm feeling quite merry already,' Lou says, considering her once again empty wine glass. 'Oops. But I feel disgusting. Covered in sea and salt. And I can give Laila a last feed before dinner. It's not far. I'll be half an hour tops.'

'If you're going back, I'll come with you,' Eliza says. 'I want to get some mozzie repellent.'

Lou stumbles a little as she gets to her feet. She'd better take it easy. The doctor had told her not to mix the tablets with alcohol. And she's barely drunk anything in the last year because of the pregnancy so her tolerance is low.

'The crabs have gone,' Eliza observes as they walk up the beach.

'So they have.' Lou shivers. 'Still horrible, though. To think of them all, burrowed under the sand, sitting there, waiting in the dark under our feet.'

'Ha, maybe you should be a writer,' Eliza laughs. 'That's a decent imagination.'

Lou lets out a sigh as they approach their huts.

'Are you OK?' Eliza asks. 'Since we got here you've seemed on edge. A bit...' She doesn't finish her thought, stopping at the foot of the steps leading up to the Carters' veranda.

Lou sits down on the bottom step, her face shadowed by the moon split by clouds. She lifts a finger as if to trace round its circumference then gives an embarrassed laugh. Her hand drops. 'A bit, what? Overwrought?'

'Well, yes. Maybe. More... I don't know, sad? Is everything all right with you and Adam? I don't want to... well, we haven't known each other that long...' Eliza twists her wedding ring around her finger. 'But I do think he could help you a bit more. You've got a lot to deal with, bringing such a small baby to the beach. All the sand, and mosquitoes. It's hard, with Raffy too.'

Lou looks up and, for a moment, Eliza's expression makes her want to cry. It's so filled with empathy and concern, as if she really understands what Lou is feeling.

'My mum was on her own,' Eliza explains. 'With me, when I was a baby. She told me how... *remorseless* it was.'

'Oh,' Lou says. 'But I'm not on my own.'

They look at each other for a minute.

Lou swallows. Eliza's right that they don't know each other well. And Lou likes her. But does she want to open up to her like this? Tell her how Adam's repeated philandering has withered their relationship into something so brittle it feels like it has claws? That she doesn't believe anything he says any more? That everything's getting so confused in her head she doesn't know what's true and what isn't? That sometimes she can let her mind wander into dark places where anything might be possible?

Even with Eliza.

On occasion Lou's noticed her looking at Adam. It's not a blatant attraction. Sometimes, Eliza seems more curious than entranced, whereas Adam is clearly infatuated. She's seen it a million times before. The zoning-in, the spotlight he shines on the woman of the moment, that raffish laugh, the way he musses his hair oh so casually, flexes his biceps as he lifts a pint glass to his mouth for Christ's sake.

And then Lou wants to smack herself around the head at the pointlessness of this particular debate. Because, even if Eliza thinks Adam is the sexiest man alive, does Lou really care about it any more, anyway?

'We're OK,' she says eventually. 'It was my stupid idea to come to the island. I was desperate for a break, from the monotony at home. The endless feeding, changing, sleeping,' she laughs. 'Because of course, all of that would disappear once we arrived here.' She shakes her head, looking down at her lap. 'It's just stressful, the first few months with a newborn.'

'Hardest thing in the world, motherhood,' Eliza says.

'Well, you sound a bit down yourself, if you don't mind me saying.' Lou puts her head on one side, considering her. 'You're a fantastic mother. The twins are great.'

'Yeah. I know.' Eliza waves an embarrassed hand. 'I mean…
*they* are great. Not sure how much that has to do with me. It's not that. It's more…' She trails off, biting her lip. 'But, look…' She leans against the balustrade and folds her arms. 'Are you sure you're OK? Are you coping?'

Lou takes a breath. 'I haven't been amazing,' she admits. 'The lack of sleep, you know. The doctor, he gave me some pills to help me relax.' She checks Eliza's reaction to this, but she doesn't seem fazed at all.

Lou shrugs. 'I don't know. It's harder this time, somehow. With Laila, I mean. Raffy was a breeze in comparison. Girls, eh?' she laughs. 'Much more complicated in every way.'

Eliza gives a rueful nod. 'Well, I'm always here, Lou. If you need to chat. Have a coffee or a walk. Anything.'

An onset of familiar wailing hits Lou like a train. The earlier wine has hollowed her out and pitted her. She has to shower and change and feed the baby, and right then, all of it seems so utterly impossible.

The door to the hut opens.

'Ma'am?'

In the glow of the veranda light, in the babysitter's arms, Laila pauses, mid-screech, staring at them all with wide eyes, her chubby hands spreadeagled in the night air.

'Here, let me,' Eliza says to the babysitter, jogging up the steps to take Laila. 'Why don't you come into my hut with the baby for a bit while her mum here has a nice, long shower and gets ready in peace.'

'Oh really, would you?' Lou feels the burn of sudden tears. 'That would be unbelievable. Thank you.'

When they've gone, she stands underneath the shower, letting tepid water run over her head and down her back. After a while, she realises she has been pushing her nails into her palms so hard there are white crescent shapes scored into her skin. She stares down at her fingers, at the tiny sunspots on the back of her hands.

There's something malevolent about this place. She can feel it. They shouldn't have come. Why did she make them come here? The devils are gathering again, above her. They hover on the roof of the hut, beating their wings. She can hear their drumming. The air turns cold and she is gripped with fear that she is alone and the waters are rising from the sea. The bathroom bulb flickers off and then on again. She screws her eyes shut, gasping for breath, all her muscles tensed, arms raised to ward them off.

There is a knock at the door and that never-ending sound of a baby's cries.

'Lou?' Eliza calls. 'I'm really sorry but I think she's hungry.'

The sound of the crying scratches at the walls until the wood is worn through and the wailing snakes into the hut, crawling along mercilessly, until it's within her and eating at her from the inside out.

Her eyes snap open.

'Coming,' she calls. 'I'm coming.'

# 14

## ELIZA

'No,' Eliza laughs, leaning over the table to take another spoonful of rice. 'It was not love at first sight, was it?' She looks at Noah who lolls back in his chair with a smile. He's more relaxed, but he's drinking a lot, she sees. They all are.

Outside, the threat of rain has passed. The air is cool and Eliza has brought a cream silk shawl to wear over the coral dress. The lights in the restaurant are low, tea lights flicker on the wooden table they sit around. Noah drapes his arm lazily around Eliza's shoulders as he pushes his plate away.

'Man, that rendang was good,' he says. 'You want more?' he asks Eliza, surprised, as she takes another serving from the platter on the table. She normally eats like a bird.

'I don't know what's wrong with me. I'm starving for some reason.'

'It's the sea air,' Adam says.

She notices his eyes drift to where Noah's fingers lie, and then down a little to where her dress gathers at her cleavage. She shivers and pulls her shawl up a touch.

'It always makes me hungry.' Adam grabs a roll from the bread basket and flicks it into the air, catches it and takes a bite, giving Eliza a wink. She flushes, unable to respond, and the table falls silent. Why didn't she just make a joke back? Treat him like any other friend of Noah's who gets a bit cheeky, a bit flirty.

Because it doesn't feel like that.

She's noticed it before this holiday, of course. She's been aware of Adam's gaze on her. The way he often touches her, the flirtatious way he smiles. But it's never been so obvious. Now, she feels as if it flashes neon and it makes her hugely uncomfortable.

She can't get what happened during the explosion out of her mind either. When Adam had reared up – practically on top of her – under the water… Why had he done it? Had he meant to frighten her like that? Or had she read it wrong and overreacted in panic?

But it didn't feel like that. Especially after everything he'd told her about his father and the affairs, his sleazing after women. Was Adam trying it on with her during this holiday? Maybe, under the dark of the waves, away from everyone else, in all the confusion, it was the perfect opportunity for Adam to slip a hand where it shouldn't go, push his body up against hers.

She puts down her fork, her appetite gone.

'So when was it?' Lou asks, sitting forward. Her eyes are bright in the candlelight and her words are slurred. She's also had too much to drink, Eliza realises.

'When was it that you fell in love with each other?'

Eliza glances again at Noah who rubs his thumb along the back of her neck.

'Well,' she says, picking up her wine glass, 'it was actually when my mother died.'

'Oh no, I'm sorry,' Lou says.

Adam's brows are knitted. 'When did she die?' he asks.

He pours more wine into Eliza's glass.

'We were in Chile,' Eliza says, nodding her thanks at him. 'We'd gone backpacking. We wanted to travel all over South America. It was the year after we'd graduated. We'd started going out in our third year at uni. Clearly our future careers as a lawyer and a marketing consultant were predestined by our choice of a history degree.'

'Ha!' Adam exclaims. 'Yep. I did archaeology, of all things. Trying to escape my father, I think. Fat lot of good that did me.' He grimaces at Eliza and takes a gulp of wine. 'Sorry,' he tilts his glass to her. 'You were saying.'

'Yeah, so we'd started going out then. We met in … a civil rights class I think it was, babe? Maybe it was human rights.'

'Civil freedom in the Caribbean,' Noah says. 'I'm the details man,' he shrugs.

'The brains in the partnership,' Eliza says tartly. 'Well whatever it was, when we started going out, I was keen. But, you know, I wasn't *keen*. I liked him a lot.' She turns to Noah and puts a hand on his knee. 'Of course I did. But it wasn't *love*. We weren't going to get married or anything. I mean, I think Noah would agree, wouldn't you? We were so young.'

'Adam and I got together at twenty-three,' Lou says. 'I didn't think it was young.'

Eliza looks at her for a beat. 'Well, maybe it's not for everyone. But for me – and Noah – it was. Anyway, we didn't really talk about it. We booked our flights to Rio de Janeiro and off we went. Boyfriend and girlfriend. Three months travelling there before heading round the world to Australia and New Zealand. Before we had to come home and be grown up. Start living proper lives, earning proper money.'

Eliza takes another drink. Her pulse is quickening. Why is she telling this story? Now she's started, she can't stop. And all the time, she's conscious of Adam watching her. He's leaning back in his chair, one leg over the other, his hair curled and twisted from sea salt, his skin brown and healthy-looking.

She feels as though his eyes never leave her. Those deep blue eyes, on her all of the time. She can sense Noah picking up on it. His thumb on her neck has a pressure that feels like it's indenting her skin.

'Oh shit, sorry!' Lou grabs a napkin and mops up a puddle of wine she's spilt on the table. 'Stupid clumsy me. Sorry. God, Eliza. You'll never get to the end of this story. Come on,' she waves her hand theatrically in the air. 'Let's get to the end of this tale!'

Adam jerks a quick look over at Lou and pours her some water. 'Maybe some of this now?' he says quietly. Lou glares at him but doesn't respond.

'Yes, sorry,' Eliza says. 'It is taking a bit long. I'll cut to the chase.' She clears her throat and takes a breath. 'So there we were.

We'd been in Chile for a month. We were in Santiago. Sitting in this little restaurant on our last night.'

'We had this wicked pasta,' Noah says. 'Clams and garlic—'

'No,' Eliza cuts in. 'On *this* my details are accurate. We had mussels, don't you remember? We treated ourselves to mussels and a glass of champagne each because it was our last night. We had no money,' she explains. 'But we decided we deserved it,' she laughs, 'after all our hard work travelling.'

Eliza looks down at the table. For a second, she is terrified she is going to cry.

'You're right, babe,' Noah says, squeezing her neck gently with his hand. 'We had mussels...'

'And we were sitting there, drinking champagne, thinking how pleased we were with ourselves...' She shakes her hair back from her face. 'And then the manager of the restaurant came over. He... came over, and, and... he looked so sad. So terribly, terribly sad. And I just knew.' She stares up at them, eyes glistening. 'I knew that Mummy was dead.'

'But how?' Lou puts her head on one side, her pupils large and round.

'It was a good restaurant,' Noah says. 'Pretty high-end to what we were used to. We'd had to ask our backpackers' place to make a reservation because our Spanish was OK but limited. Our parents had a list of everywhere we'd booked to stay. We were just kids, you know? We'd planned the entire trip in advance on cardboard coasters in pubs after our exams. We had a whole itinerary. Nothing spontaneous about it. But that was us,' he shrugs again.

'So Noah's dad, he knew to call the hostel. And they knew we were at that restaurant.'

'And so the manager of this place in Santiago is the one who...?' Adam asks.

'He was the one who told me, yes.' Eliza shifts in her chair. 'Massively surreal. I sat there. He said it first in Spanish and then in English. And I sat there. And he was crying, you know. He had real tears in his eyes. And he tells us to go. That we don't have to pay anything. Just go, back to the hostel. Collect our things and go home.'

'Oh, my...' Lou murmurs. She pours herself more wine but Adam doesn't notice, he's so fixated on Eliza.

'And we did as he said.' Eliza sounds surprised at this, as if she still can't believe that they managed it. 'It all happened exactly as he said. We went back to our room, got our stuff, got a taxi to the airport and caught the first flight back to Heathrow.'

'Gatwick,' Noah says.

'But when was it?' Lou stretches her hands over the table as if to grasp Eliza's in her own. Her teeth are a little stained with red wine. 'You started this story talking about love. Talking about falling in love with Noah. When was it?'

'It was on the flight. As the plane came down into... *Heathrow*.' Eliza looks sharply at Noah.

'Sorry,' he mumbles.

'He took my hand and I looked out of the window. It was night-time and all the lights of London were gleaming. You know that sight, right? As you come down. That bend of the Thames. We hadn't been home for three months. And now we were descending into London. The place where I'd grown up. A place I loved. A place that was my home. And I started crying, because at that moment, it didn't feel like home. Because my mum wasn't there any more.'

Eliza halts and lifts her eyes to the ceiling. She bites her lip and then continues.

'But then I held Noah's hand and he was just looking at me. Staring into my eyes with all that love. And the plane dipped down and we circled over the city. And he bent his head into mine, and we gazed out the window together, at the lights growing brighter and brighter. And I could feel his breath on my face,' she laughs a little. 'And his hand on mine, and his heart beating at my back. And I thought that everything would be OK. Because I had made another home. Without my mum. I had made another home with Noah.'

She stops and laughs again, embarrassed.

'So that's the story of us falling in love.'

'That's the most romantic thing I've ever heard,' Lou says, shaking her head. She drinks from her glass and swings it in Adam's direction. 'Isn't that the most romantic thing you've ever heard?'

Adam says nothing for a moment. He looks at Eliza until she raises her head and meets his gaze.

'And how did your mother die?' he asks.

# 15

## NOAH

He is a sucker for Eliza.

Always has been, since the very beginning. She's an addiction. She knows it too. She knows how to play him, always has.

But something's shifted in her. She's been uptight for a while, but here – on the island – it feels to him like she's tipping off balance. What was she doing, telling Adam and Lou about her mum? She knows he hates that story, what it does to him.

The way she had described it: she had made it sound almost *romantic*. The whole Chile thing. The plane back to London.

She forgot to say that she didn't speak to Noah for a year after her mother killed herself. Completely cut him off. Wouldn't answer his calls or emails. Nothing. Wouldn't even let him go to Anna's funeral. A few months after they'd buried her, he'd gone to the flat and she'd slammed the door in his face.

Eventually, he'd given up. Met someone else. Nice girl, she was – Rachel. He was just starting to get happy again and forget about Eliza. And then who should pop up in the local pub?

The tassels of that shawl thing she's wearing trail along his arm as she moves past him to join him on the beach. The moon spins lazy shadows through the warm night air and, as she crosses her legs in the white plastic chair opposite him, he can see the outline of her breasts under her dress.

He is filled with an immediate ache for her, regrets the plan to have a nightcap with the Carters. Eliza smiles at him as if reading his mind. She knows what she's doing. She has always been able to turn him on.

'You're a sexy woman, wife,' he says, his voice a little hoarse. 'And you know how to use it.'

She straightens a long, tanned leg and runs her toe along his calf.

'You're drinking too much, baby. Don't let's have any trouble tonight, hey?'

He tuts, considering his drink. 'A man can have a holiday.'

'Yes he can. But we don't want you passing out, fast asleep, do we? I might have plans for you. For later.'

He leans forward and grabs her ankle.

'Let's go inside.'

'Hi guys.'

The call comes from the direction of the huts and there is Adam wandering over, a bottle of gin swinging from his hand.

'Hey there,' Eliza says, releasing her foot with a soft laugh. 'Everything OK?'

'Yeah, all good. Lou's crashed out, though. Too much sun today. Oh, thanks,' he says as she hands him a plastic glass. 'Nice one. Twins OK?'

'Out for the count, mate,' Noah answers, downing his drink in one before pouring himself a finger's-worth more. 'They're only just there, anyway.'

He gestures towards the semicircle of huts, lit by the glow of the few solar-powered lights that mark out the accommodation block. Most of the huts are swathed in darkness, but the Fishers have left their veranda light switched on and it illuminates a heap of brightly coloured beach toys piled into the inflatable kayak at the bottom of their stairs.

'Oh, that's good,' Adam says, bringing a chair and sticking it in the sand in the middle of them both. 'Hey, I'm really sorry about before,' he directs to Eliza. 'About your mum. Speaking out of turn like that. I am sorry. Sometimes I don't think before speaking,' he gives a sheepish grin.

The clouds part and a full moon dazzles the beach into near-daylight. A few lone crabs scuttle past on the shoreline, side-stepping the reach of a lazy incoming tide.

Noah watches Adam carefully. He sees the other man's eyes drift down her body and it makes him shift ostentatiously on his chair, causing the legs of it to sink into the sand. He pushes up the sleeves of his T-shirt, hoping Adam notices his heft.

He drinks some gin, feels the pleasant numbing along his gullet. Where is this going? he wonders. When is Adam going to give this whole caring-and-sharing routine a rest?

'I didn't mean to make you go through the whole story.'

'It's OK, really.' Eliza shakes her head. 'It was a long time ago. I mean, it still hurts, obviously. I miss her every day. But sometimes it's nice to talk about her, actually. She was an amazing woman.'

'She was a poet.' Noah begins to tip his glass from side to side, this way and that. 'A good one. Not that I know anything about poetry. But I like her poems a lot. They're kind of wacked. In a good way.' He shoots a look at Eliza, who's dreamy, staring at the sea. 'Kind of offbeat, you know?'

'Yeah,' Adam says, although he sounds unconvinced.

'Let's talk about something else,' Eliza sighs. 'How did you and Lou meet? We've bored you all night with our story. What's yours?'

'Ah. Nothing as interesting or romantic as you two, unfortunately. We grew up in the same village. I got a weekend job in the local pub. Her mum managed it and Lou was the fit blonde barmaid. We started going out and that was it.'

'Love at first sight?' Eliza asks.

'Yeah, I mean, I suppose so. Lou was very hot when she was younger.'

'She still is.'

'Yeah, yeah. Of course.' Adam looks from one to the other as if he's refereeing a tennis match. He's jiggling his leg as if he's on edge, Noah thinks. As if he's trying to push the night into a certain direction.

'We're all getting on a bit.' Noah leans back in his chair, resting his glass on a bicep. 'Been a while since I bench-pressed more than sixty kilograms.'

Adam pauses for a second, as if taking this on board, before clearing his throat and rubbing a hand over his hair. He gives Eliza the kind of conspiratorial smile that would normally accompany a wink.

'Weightlifting's a bit of a mug's game, though, isn't it? I'm more of a runner myself. There's a few good half-marathons coming up in the next few months. Sign up, mate,' he says to Noah. 'That's the way to shift the puppy fat.' Adam pats his stomach and smirks. 'You too could look like this physical specimen.'

Noah manages to offer a nod in response. He has to keep it cool. The booze is bringing shit up to the surface and that kind of comment just winds him up. He imagines himself behind his desk, tries to get in the frame of mind where he takes people apart with his words, with his brain.

I'm keeping it cool, he repeats like a mantra. Just keeping it cool.

They drink, looking out on the sea striped with moonlight.

'Well, I think I'm going to go to bed,' Eliza says after a little while. 'I'm tired. You're right, Adam. I think it's the sea air. It's knocked me out.'

'Oh, really?'

Noah can hear the disappointment in Adam's voice and it sneaks into his coolness. Adds a little heat. The bloke's not even trying to hide his interest in his wife. Doesn't even have the respect to try and tone it down in front of her man. Out on the periphery of his composure, Noah can feel hot fingers of rage prodding him in his side and in his chest. Adam's goading him, that's what he's doing.

He drinks more gin to quell the heat.

But the fact is, this Adam is a fool.

'Are you sure? Don't fancy one more for the road?'

'No, not tonight. We've still got tomorrow. Thank the gods for the invention of a long weekend. Night, babe. I'll leave the balcony light on for you.' She leaves them, the tassels of her shawl curved around her waist, her plastic tumbler dangling from her fingers as she goes.

Noah can hear in her tone what she's asking of him. She wants him to come with her. To stop drinking and go back with her to their hut. She'd even sleep with him now. As a reward for doing it. And yet…

… He doesn't honestly feel threatened by this little pickney. If Eliza was going to fuck around, God help him that she'd choose this mop-haired idiot. But it's about respect.

So Noah keeps his eyes on Adam, who watches until Eliza has disappeared into their hut. When he turns back to find Noah intent on him, his face twitches. He's anxious, Noah can tell.

'You all right, mate? What's up?'

Noah considers his answer.

'You need to stop looking at my wife,' he says quietly.

In a rapid move, he uncoils from his seat, and pushes his face into Adam's for a full three seconds. Then he backs down, grabs the gin bottle from where it's been twisted upright into the sand. He pours neat gin into his empty glass and downs it before becoming once again still in his seat.

He sees Adam swallow and run his tongue over his teeth. He's deciding how to play it, Noah thinks.

'Looking at her? What do you mean?'

Noah pinches his nose with two fingers and gives a long sigh. 'I know guys like you, Adam. I've met hundreds of your type. Sleeping with women to forget your own insecurities. It's pathetic.

'Eliza's vulnerable. You're raking through her past, and it's dark, man. Doing it just cos you like what you see when she's in her bikini. Do you get what I mean?'

Adam's mouth falls open. 'No. Uh, I don't. What are you suggesti—?'

'I'm *suggesting* that you're sharing your little stories with my wife. Swapping tales of "my dad's shit, tell me about your fucked-up mum", because you're hoping it'll get her into bed. Am I wrong?'

'Yes. Absolutely and utterly wrong.' Adam swivels round as if appealing to an audience on the beach. 'Properly offensive, actually. We've just been talking. And I'm sorry if asking about her mother was inappropriate—'

'You know it was,' Noah cuts in. 'And I'm just warning you. That's all. I see you, Adam. I see who you are.' He points a finger in the air. 'So be careful.'

'This is ridiculous.' Adam stops and looks up at the sky. 'Shit. Look, can I have some of the booze?' He takes the bottle and drinks straight from it. 'Come on, Noah. What is this? A scene from *Goodfellas*? Remember that? "D'ya think I'm funny? I'm a funny guy." Eh? Do you?'

Noah says nothing.

Adam peters out, his American accent trailing in the air.

'Look, OK. Well… can you blame a bloke for trying? She's an attractive woman. But it's harmless,' he says in earnest. 'Just banter. There's nothing in it. You're my mate. Right? I'll back off.'

'Yes, I'm a shit. I'm sorry. I do this and I should know better. And, rightly, you've warned me. Come on, mate. We're on a beach in Malaysia. The moon is shining. We've got booze and life is good. Yes?'

He holds up the bottle of gin.

There's a clank further up the beach and someone shouts a laugh.

Noah looks at him. Such a cocky fool.

He pounces forward and snatches the gin from Adam's hand. He lurches, getting up out of his seat, and then he's weaving. He can't stand straight. Fuck, he's hammered. Why hasn't he noticed this before?

'God, you're pathetic, Adam,' Noah slurs, slicing his hands through the air, gesturing at him. 'Get up. Come on.'

Adam doesn't move. Noah leans down and grabs hold of his T-shirt, panting hot, gin-soaked breath in his face.

'All right, mate,' Adam says, pushing him off and standing up. 'Take it easy.'

They face each other in their shorts, their Hawaiian shirts, bare feet stuck in the cold sand. 'You've had too much to drink. Just stop it, yeah? Let's just call it a night.'

Noah laughs. 'Haven't got a fucking clue, have you?' He peers at Adam, head lolling side to side. 'Have you? It's sort of funny.' He steps forward and he stumbles and trips.

It embarrasses him.

He sees the look on Adam's face and all the cool just melts away. He cracks the punch on Adam nice and square. The force of it renders Adam speechless, propelling him backwards, making him stagger in a mirror image of Noah the minute before.

He bends over, holding his head.

'What the fuck?' Adam's voice is thick with pain. 'What was that for, you prick?' He feels his teeth with his tongue, prodding his face delicately with his fingers. 'You could have broken my jaw. Are you insane or just really pissed?'

Noah watches the swelling appear next to Adam's lip. His knuckles throb. He's always been in awe at the ability of the body to cause pain to itself. Or others.

'Yeah, well. Maybe weightlifting's not such a waste of time after all.'

'Go and sleep it off, you twat.'

Adam springs towards him as if to hit him back, but Noah doesn't react. He's been told. The damage is done.

'I'm going to get some ice.'

Noah doesn't respond as Adam pushes past him.

He just watches as Adam moves up the beach towards the bar, his hand fixed to his jaw as he goes.

# 16

## ADAM

In the bar, Lars is alone.

The music is off and only a few lights remain. As Adam comes in, Lars glances up and springs into action.

'Jesus, what happened to you? I'll get some ice. Come. Sit down. Here.'

He goes behind the bar and pours Adam a whisky. Then he grabs some ice out of the freezer, wraps it in a towel and hands it over.

Adam clamps it to his jaw and downs the Scotch before taking a stool. He pushes the glass back to Lars who refills it.

'What happened?'

'Had a fight with a door. It's nothing,' Adam mutters.

'Let's see.' Lars adjusts the bundle of ice and inspects the injury. 'Can you move your jaw from side to side like this?' He nods when Adam does so. 'Yah, it's not broken I don't think. You'd be screaming in agony if it was. You'll live, buddy. Your *door* has a mean right hook, though.'

Adam raises his eyebrows and blows out his cheeks in frustration before wincing with pain. 'Yeah. Whatever.'

Lars lights two cigarettes and passes one across. 'It's late.' He exhales a stream of smoke above their heads. 'Maybe you should turn in?'

Headlights roam the ceiling before a car engine is silenced outside leaving only the hum of cicadas. Another car late at night, just like the night before when he'd been sitting in the restaurant with Eliza and Noah.

'I'm no mechanic,' Adam says, flicking ash on to the floor. 'But that motor sounds like it's on its last legs.'

'*Hai...?*'

A car door slams. A tall Malay ambles in and folds himself over the bar. He's skinny. Adam can see the outline of his ribcage above the neckline of the lime-green vest he wears. His cut-off jeans are baggy, weighed down by the contents of his pockets, and he's got a line shaved round the back of his hair like a train track. He reaches over the counter and takes a jar of maraschino cherries. Using a flick knife from his back pocket, he prises open the lid and pops one in his mouth.

'*Apa khabar?*'

'I'm good,' Lars replies, pouring clear liquid into a shot glass and sliding it over.

'Evening.' Adam's split lip makes him sound like Rocky Balboa but despite the punch to the head, despite the gallons of booze, he's wide awake and alert. Lars doesn't want him here, he can tell. His bare-chested hackles are up.

The other man raises his head slowly, barely taking Adam in. His eyes are crêped and hooded, the skin around them dark as if he hasn't slept for months.

'We're closing now, Adam. Sorry about that.' Lars wipes the bar with a cloth, then gets the whisky bottle. 'Can I give you a roadie to take back to the hut, mate? Have one on the house. Ease the pain of that lip.'

Adam stands up, flinching at the pain shooting from his head down throughout his body. 'Sure. Why not?' He tilts the refilled glass towards the men. 'Here's to codeine and long weekends.'

'Absolutely!' Lars says, clapping his hands. 'Night, Adam. You rest up now, OK?'

The Malay doesn't acknowledge Adam as he leaves. He reaches into the jar and helps himself to another cherry.

Adam can hear them murmuring as he goes down the steps on to the beach. He doesn't think they're paying him any attention, but to be careful he walks out of the light and into the shadows before doubling back to the atap. He squats down beneath a window ledge, clutching his glass of whisky to his chest, trying to hear what they're saying. The beach is empty. Noah must have stumbled back to his hut.

*What a prick.*

Tenderly, he rests his cheek against the slatted wood, feeling rough splinters on his skin. Adam's pride hurts more than his jaw, if he's honest. What is it with this place? Everyone seems to want to attack him.

Earlier, Lou had bollocked him for asking Eliza about her mum's suicide. They'd gone back to their hut after dinner to freshen up and he'd wandered into the bathroom to brush his teeth. Lou had been sitting on the toilet wearing her nightshirt, glaring at him.

'Are you going to bed?' Adam asked, noticing what she was wearing. 'Aren't you coming down to the beach?'

Lou had been scathing. 'And the children?'

'They'll be fine. We're only a few feet away. We'll be able to hear Laila if she cries. She's like a bloody klaxon.'

'No, Adam. I'm not doing it. I'm not going to be some Malaysian version of the McCanns. We're on an island in the middle of nowhere with jungle all around us. Anyone could walk in and...' She'd stood up and flushed the toilet. 'Well, you know...'

Adam had spat toothpaste into the basin and rubbed a hand over his mouth. He'd looked at himself in the mirror. Two days' worth of stubble grazed his chin and he'd caught the sun on the dive trip. He was looking OK, he thought. Not bad.

And then, in seconds, she'd ripped that little piece of self-confidence from him.

'As usual, Adam,' she'd said, pushing past him and marching over to their bed, 'your selfishness continues to astound.'

'What do you mean?' he'd asked, genuinely confused by the hatred in her voice.

She'd sat down, giving him a withering look. 'Earlier on? With Eliza? Why on earth would you say that? Ask: "How did your mother *die*?" What the fuck? There's everyone else, all lost in the romanticism, thinking how lovely and how sad it is. And then you... just...' She'd shaken her hands away from her body as if she was trying to rid herself of him. 'You made the poor woman sit there and have to tell us that her mother committed suicide. I mean… for fuck's sake!'

Adam's mouth had dried.

It had indeed been a fuck-up. Lou wasn't wrong. He shouldn't have asked Eliza about her mother.

But he had been so curious. How in God's name had she fallen in love with Noah in bloody economy class when she'd just heard about the death of a parent? And when she'd said – when she'd admitted – that she hadn't actually been that bothered about him before then.

'I don't have the energy to argue with you,' was all he said to Lou in the end. 'You should come to the beach. The kids will be safe as houses in here. We can lock the door and everything.'

Lou had rolled over, turning her back on him. 'You don't care. Not really, Adam. As long as Eliza's there, you'll be happy.'

'What's that supposed to mean?'

'You can't take your eyes off her. It doesn't matter. I don't actually care. Just piss off and let me get some sleep.'

Adam had tried to catch the outrage inside his head and pummel it into words. He was so maddened, he'd had to do a little dance on his feet while clenching and unclenching his hands in order to release the frustration and rage. The injustice of it.

'*You* were the one who chose to come here. I wanted to go to Bali,' he hissed. 'This was all *your* idea.'

'Oh, fuck off.'

Adam had stared at her shape, rigid on the bed. She said nothing. He waited. She said nothing.

Finally, he blew a long breath out of his mouth.

'OK, then. I will fuck off, if that's what you want. Goodnight.'

He'd gripped the door to slam it shut as he left but, just in time, remembered the sleeping Laila. He had hovered on the veranda, almost winded by the argument. He had stood there for a minute, controlling his breathing, and by the time he got to the beach where Noah and Eliza were sitting, he was calm. It was all fine. One gin and tonic and off to bed. No drama.

He had given an internal shrug and put Lou in the compartment of his brain marked *tomorrow*.

But then, down on the beach, Noah had been even worse with his self-righteous haranguing and his outrageous temper. What was wrong with everyone? Christ, what's wrong with a bit of flirting? He's not harming anyone, is he?

Adam sneers and looks up at the moon.

Noah clearly reckons he's God's gift to the world because he's a lawyer.

Taking the piss earlier, comparing Roman McFee to the Bond books. It's bullshit. Adam's books clearly aren't *intellectual* enough for him. Adam isn't intellectual enough, full stop. Which is why Noah doesn't back him up with his theory about Lars and the dynamite trading and then, adding injury to insult, he lamps him.

*Fucking prick.*

Noah probably thinks the same as all those dickheads: that *coming from such an illustrious background,* Adam writes books that... *merely squander his talent and make a mockery of the craft.* Which wouldn't be quite so hurtful if it hadn't also been what his own father had told him.

And that's what Benjamin had actually thought.

It's so unfair. Because meanwhile, here's Lars – an utter deadbeat – doing fuck all with his life, and everyone's treating him like a total hero. They *love* him. *Adore* him.

What's the point of being a millionaire? Adam finishes the whisky and tosses the glass away from him, on to the sand. What's the point of living in a bloody amazing house with a beautiful wife and children? When all you need to do is put on a pair of board shorts, not bother having a shower for your entire life, rip off every person you meet, and literally *everyone* will think you're the greatest thing to ever walk the earth.

'It's un-fucking believable,' Adam says out loud to himself.

'*Apa tu?*' the Malay asks from inside.

'Nothing. Just a wind chime on one of the huts.'

Adam freezes. He hears footsteps approach the window and flattens himself against the wall, bringing his knees in tight to his chest.

'Maybe that guy...'

'He's gone to bed. He's just a pissed-up tourist... You're early anyway, Che. What do you expect if you come before I've even locked up? I don't want to be over at the kampong yet anyway. If they see us together, there'll be trouble.'

There's the sound of a shot glass being slammed down.

'Let's fucking go.'

'Wait outside. I'll tell you when we go.'

Adam barely breathes as he hears the footsteps retreat, then the scrape of a stool. The pools of light on the sand are extinguished one by one and then the bar is silent. He can hear only the slow and steady brush of the tide on the shore and, after a few more minutes, the thud of a door, the mechanical rumble of the car engine.

As the sound of it recedes, he uncoils, collapsing on to the sand, his legs sticking out in front of him. The moon is lower now than when they were sitting on the beach, but still it streams out over a dark sea that stretches and yawns with far-out waves.

Shadows hop and swirl in the eddies and he can just make out the circle of chairs where they'd sat earlier. His vision is blurred from the whisky, his skull throbs with pain. He shuts his eyes, listening to the sea, breathing in the warm tang of salt.

For some reason, he thinks about Raffy, his son. About the time he'd gone to New York on a work trip last summer and had bought him the same Yankees cap as his own. When he flew back, Lou and Raffy had come to meet him in the arrivals hall. Adam had taken the cap from his bag and pulled it down on Raffy's head, saying: *There. Now we're two men about town.* He doesn't know why he's suddenly thought about this, or why he now has tears running down his cheeks. He grimaces, rubbing a thumb gingerly across his jaw, and then his eyes open, and his breath stops and he thinks he's going to have a heart attack.

A face looms into his. Pale as the moon, staring at him through the darkness.

It's a girl he recognises but can't place. His head's messed up and all he can focus on are her smoky eyes and long, long eyelashes, and wavy blonde hair tied up in a ponytail. She smells like soap made out of pine trees.

'Well, hello there, sleepyhead,' she says. 'You look like you might need a helping hand.'

# 17

## Eliza

She can't sleep.

Noah still hasn't come to bed and she feels the empty space next to her like a chasm.

Giving up, Eliza climbs out of bed and goes outside on to the veranda. The beach is empty but for the shadows of palm trees stretching over the sand in the moonlight. She breathes in the smell of the ocean. It's still so warm even though it's so late.

She decides to walk to tire herself out. She doesn't change, setting out in her pyjama shorts and vest top, her feet bare. She stays away from the waterline, sticking to the fine white sand, higher up the beach. The restaurant is closed now, the shutters are down and the interior dark.

She wonders again where Noah has got to and half-scouts the beach for him as she walks. She worries about his drinking. In London, he was just about managing to keep it under control. But over here in Asia, the lifestyle is fuelled by alcohol. Everything revolves around it, both work and social life. They seem to start drinking earlier and earlier every day and it's blurring boundaries for him, she can tell. It's not helping their relationship either. She tries to rein him in, but look at tonight. Even the promise of sex hadn't stopped him. And the more he drinks, the more it cements their secrets, increases their distance from each other.

She stops and looks back along the beach. She hasn't missed him, has she? Failed to spot him, passed out and snoring under a chair somewhere?

Then she hears voices and turns, thinking it must be him and Adam. She moves towards the sound. It's definitely Adam. She can hear the timbre of his voice. He rounds one of the huts nearest to the bar and appears on the beach, caught in a halo of moonlight. Seeing him, Eliza pulls back immediately, ducking behind a tree trunk.

He's not alone.

He's with a blonde girl. She's young. Ridiculously young.

It's the kid from the restaurant, isn't it? One of the backpackers? Zoe, she thinks her name is.

Eliza can't tear her eyes away as they walk off. She hears Adam laugh, sees they're holding hands.

She wants to be sick.

Phrases spin through her head: *apples don't fall far from the tree*; *philanderer*; *betrayal*; *heartbreak*.

She gulps in air and pushes herself off from where she's leaning against the trunk of the palm. She has to move. She strides up the beach, adrenaline quivering through her.

What an absolute shit.

All the time he's been mooning over Eliza, gazing at her adoringly, all of it has been false. She could be anyone. He'd have anyone. He's just like his father. Literally, exactly the same. Unfaithful, incapable of remaining true to one person.

Poor Lou, she thinks, as she starts to move faster and faster. The poor woman. Fast asleep and totally unaware of what's happening right under her nose.

Eliza is so angry, she doesn't know what to do with herself. There doesn't seem anywhere she can put this rage. It's like an engine inside her and the ignition's been started and now she has to run it out.

And so she does.

She runs. Sprints barefoot up and down the beach until she can't breathe and her muscles are on fire. The way she feels right now, she could keep running like this till morning.

# 18

## ADAM

He follows her, of course he does.

The girl takes a bottle of rum and a litre of Coke from behind the bar and mixes an impromptu cocktail before they leave.

'The jeep's just up the road,' she says, passing it to Adam as they walk out of the resort. It's not really a road, just a dirt track, and he can barely see a metre in front of his face. A tiny voice inside his head taps in time with the thud of the pain in his jaw, saying: *Why are you going off with a girl who must be half your age? What are you doing, you ridiculous, drunken fool?*

And yet, his feet keep moving, tracing her footsteps, even as they make a turn and have to cut through the damp undergrowth of the rainforest. She takes his hand and he drinks more rum. Feels the pressure of her thumb on his palm, the effect on his groin. She smells so good, so clean. It's like a sensory black hole, as if they're floating out of time and space, and he can do anything and no one will ever know.

This was becoming one of those infamous nights. A tale he'd spin at the club – with just the right amount of information – to the guys after a round of golf. A crazy fucked-up night where he'd drunk too much, got smacked in the jaw, and headed deep into the jungle with a sexy blonde.

Lou was going to kill him.

'So where's this party?' he whispers.

'Not far, baby,' she squeezes his hand. 'Aren't you glad I rescued you?'

He laughs and it sounds like an explosion in the darkness.

Then they're in her open-top jeep, flying over the potholes in the road as if they have wings, warm air hitting his lungs until they're full and he can't breathe. They round a corner and lights twinkle along a wooden jetty stretching out into the water. The bright of the moon gives the sky a strange pale sheen that silhouettes a line of fishing boats. They climb out of the jeep and walk past them, tipsy, hearing the creak and jostle of the prows, nudging each other like old friends on their moorings.

'Hey, where are we going?' He reaches for her hand, and they link fingers again as if they've been a couple for years.

'We're going to a party. Ssssh.' The girl stops and puts a painted nail to her lips. She totters a little on her feet and it occurs to Adam that she must be very drunk.

It dips his mood a little. Because her inebriation could be the only reason that she's coming on to him like this.

So he pushes the thought away.

'He never lets me come here normally. So we're going to surprise him,' she giggles, butting her breasts into his chest provocatively. 'We're going to give him a little surprise.'

'OK.' He gives her an indulgent smile. She's not that drunk, he doesn't think. Maybe she's heard that he's an author. He gets this sometimes. Girls like hanging out with writers, taking them to parties. It makes them feel important.

Ahead of them is what appears to be a village, or a collection of thatched huts on stilts. Most are in darkness but some windows are lit. As they walk through the settlement, Adam can hear the murmurs of roosting chickens, the heavy breath of a horned cow standing chained to one of the huts, its head bowed.

'What is this place?'

'Ssssh,' the girl whispers. 'I gotta find the right one.'

After a minute, she stops, hands on hips, screwing up her face at the hut closest to them. 'It's this one,' she says and – without warning after her previously soft murmuring – shouts out a loud hello.

The door bangs open revealing a rectangle of artificial light.

'Zoe, is that you? Why the fuck are you here?'

Adam starts. He peers up into the darkness.

'You didn't say it was Lars's party,' he says.

'Hey baby,' Zoe calls. 'I tried phoning. I brought Alex.'

'Jesus, keep your voice down. You'll wake the whole kampong.'

'Adam.'

'Huh?'

Adam prods her elbow with a finger. 'I'm not Alex. I'm Adam.'

'Oh. Yeah.' Zoe swigs from the Coke bottle. 'So, we coming up, or what?'

A smattering of lights begins to flicker on throughout the village. A conversation starts up in the next-door hut. Close by, someone shouts angrily in Malay. A rooster hollers.

'Babeee,' Zoe sing-songs, oblivious to the reaction at her arrival. 'You said you were having a party. I brought Alex. Cos he looked so sad.'

'I did not look sad,' Adam says, outraged.

'Shit,' Lars is saying angrily to someone in the hut. 'She's got a voice like a fucking foghorn. It's waking everyone up... Yah, well obviously I didn't ask her over here. What am I, an idiot? She's hammered.'

*No longer the easy-going surf dude.* Adam's observations are licked with schadenfreude. *Away from the guests, his mask slips.*

Nevertheless, he turns to Zoe, irritated. Lars is right. She's totally drunk. She sways next to him, her eyes blinking slowly like a cat's. She's nearly asleep on her feet. Whatever party she'd thought she was bringing him along to is obviously not going to happen.

Then, like the twist of a cold wind, he notices the atmosphere around them shift. He looks to one side and sees a group of men coming out of the shadows. They're circling him. Moving and melding around him and the girl.

'Hey,' he mutters from the side of his mouth as Lars goes into the hut and shuts the door. 'Zoe. What's going on? Who are this lot?'

Then he grabs her hand. 'Come on. Let's go. Where are your keys? I'll drive.'

'Is that you, Mr Carter?'

Adam whirls round, squinting to try and see who's speaking in the gloom. 'Who's that? Oh... Alif?'

It's the elderly boatman from their transit over from the mainland to Pulau Kalah on Friday.

'Hello there!' Adam swallows, hearing how drunk he must sound. 'Well, how nice to see you.' He clears his throat. 'And is this where you live?'

*Fuck*. He sounds like Prince Charles or someone equally royal, on a tour of a local primary school. But he does not need news of his trip over here getting back to his wife and friends.

'Yes, boss,' Alif replies. 'Are you OK, Mr Carter? Shall I take you back to Turtle Cove?'

'Oh no, Alif.' Adam makes a sweeping gesture with his hand as if he couldn't possibly expect such a kindness. 'Zoe here,' he glances over at her and is relieved to see she has at least now opened her eyes, 'has very generously offered to return me. Now that she has... uh... finished her... uh... *tour* of this side of the island. Isn't that right, Zoe?'

Zoe ignores Adam entirely and, noticing the now-closed hut door, starts to whine. 'Lars, baby, are you coming down? You promised, baby. You said we were having a...' She leans back and the effort nearly knocks her off her feet. 'Oh, hello Alif,' she says, righting herself.

Alif whips up his head to where Zoe is looking. 'Mr Lars?' he asks. 'He is in there?' He talks in rapid Malay to someone behind him and then spits on the ground, his expression crumpling in disgust.

Adam's mouth hangs open drunkenly. Is it wrong that Lars is there? What the fuck is going on? Zoe yells up again, and this time the door opens.

'Zoe, for Christ's—' Lars stops and peers down at the group of people at the foot of the stairs. 'I can't see down there. Hang on. Alif, is that you? Hi, man. You're up early.'

Alif doesn't answer immediately and, when he does, his voice is low. 'You're with bin Jalal?'

Lars hesitates. 'Che?'

Alif waits for the answer.

'Yes, I am.'

Adam watches as Che comes out and stands behind Lars, his lime-green vest visible even in the murky light. What's going on?

Adam can physically feel the fury emanating from Alif that Lars is with this other man, but why?

'We had an agreement. You were to give *us* the...' The boatman pauses with a fleeting glance at Adam. 'For me and mine. Not for him. Not for bin Jalal. An agreement only between us,' Alif continues, his voice tight with anger. 'We had an agreement. We did.' He puts his hand to his chest.

'We still do, Alif,' Lars says. 'You're talking out of turn here. I know what's going on. You don't.'

The old man laughs. 'On the land you step on, there the sky is...'

Lars shrugs.

'These are our ways,' Alif spits again. 'Bin Jalal should know better.'

Adam's eyes dart back and forth. What are they talking about? What agreement? Something between Alif and Lars that this guy Che is muscling in on? What is Lars playing at?

'Be careful, Alif,' Lars says. 'We talk later, yes?'

In his peripheral vision, Adam can see a soft ribbon of light, far out on the edge of the horizon. Daylight is soaking through the air and melting the darkness.

At once he is overcome with exhaustion and pain and, frankly, pissed off that Zoe has brought him here and led him into this awkward situation. He is annoyed with himself that he let himself be brought. He grabs the Coke bottle and takes a long swallow, feeling the rum burn through his veins.

God, she's made this cocktail strong. So much so, he actually doesn't care any more about any of it. 'Come on, Zoe. Let's go.'

It comes out louder than he'd wanted. Not that he's hiding from Lars, but he just wants out of here now. This is all getting bloody painful.

'Who's that?' Lars asks sharply.

He steps forward. 'Adam,' he says. 'Adam Carter. One of your guests, Lars.'

And then he hears a click. An unmistakable sound from a million Hollywood films.

He stares up and realises that they have to leave right away.

102

The gun that Che is holding rests casually at the top of his thigh. His face is deep in shadow. Even Lars seems shrouded by the dark.

'It's the guy from the bar,' Che says. 'I told you to watch him.'

'Get out of here, Adam,' Lars says. 'Go, now.'

Adam isn't going to argue. He grips Zoe by the arm. She seems to have collapsed like a toy that's run out of batteries and comes without resistance. How he finds the jeep, let alone drives it back to the resort, he doesn't know. But somehow he does, skidding into the lay-by where they'd found it at the edge of the forest and jumping out, heart pounding in case they were followed. It's a ridiculous thought, given that Lars knows exactly where they are. But if he and Che had wanted to frighten Adam, it had worked.

As he stumbles with Zoe through the forest and eventually trips into the clearing by the restaurant, he looks up at the moon and gives it a little prayer of thanks. Thank God he's safely back and able to think about things from the comfort of his rum cocoon.

He almost wants to laugh. He doesn't know how he does it. No matter how bad the shit he falls into, he always manages to climb out of it smelling like pot fucking pourri.

When Eliza hears about the fight and Noah hitting Adam, maybe she'll finally realise that her husband isn't such a stand-up guy. That actually he's a Neanderthal.

And after tonight's little jaunt to the kampong, Adam's got the proof that Lars is not the golden surfer boy he makes himself out to be.

He's clearly been shagging this Zoe girl. Adam shakes his head self-righteously, conveniently forgetting his own designs on the backpacker. And hanging out with guys with guns, for fuck's sake? Standing by while one was aimed at his face? A client of the resort?

And what's the agreement he's got going with Alif that the boatman was so furious about? Lars has got so many fingers stuck in so many holes all over this island, you literally couldn't make it up.

Zoe has staggered off, leaving him with the rum. He thinks about following her, maybe checking she's OK. He starts to walk in what he thinks is the same direction but it's so dark, he doesn't see the dustbins put out at the back of the restaurant and crashes into them, sprawling head-first on to the ground.

The noise of it is extraordinary as the metal lids spin across the patch of concrete behind the kitchens. He lies, mentally scanning himself, wondering if he's broken anything. He seems OK, so he calls out to Zoe to let her know.

Only the cicadas answer him. After a moment, he gets on to his hands and knees. He feels around until he makes contact with the Coke bottle and takes a good long drink before he crawls over to one of the plastic chairs the kitchen staff use for their break-times. He hauls himself to his feet, pats himself down. He's OK. No harm done.

He swings round towards the beach, swigging from the bottle as he weaves back to the hut. He's swaying with the booze, but Lou will put him to bed. She'll look after him. She puts up with a lot, he knows. She's a wonderful wife.

I'm a lucky man, Adam thinks.

Truly very blessed.

# 19

## LOU

She wakes with a start, hands scrabbling across the sheets to find the travel cot, feel the slumbering warmth of the baby.

Laila is there in the moon-streaked dark under the mosquito net.

She's there and she's breathing.

Lou leans back on her pillow for a moment to calm her heart rate then reaches for the water carafe on the bedside table and pours herself a glass. It's only then she notices that the bed is empty of Adam. She puts down the glass, flushed with weary anger. Tapping her Apple watch, she sees it's gone 4 a.m. Where the hell is he?

Almost without thinking, she takes a pill out and puts it in her mouth. Swallows it with the water. She hovers a hand over Laila, checking that her breath is steady, and gets out of bed. She opens the door of the hut and slips out on to the veranda. The moon is high, the sea and beach illuminated by its sharp light.

She looks around. The air is warm and the sky clear. The clouds that banked the sky during the day have gone, scuttled by the breeze that brushes across the bare skin on her arms. Shapes familiar to her in the daylight take on new meaning in the moon-hued shadows. Under the palm trees fringing the beach, she can make out the contours of some beach chairs. She thinks they're chairs but, as she stares at them, is it her imagination or are they moving? Are they in fact filled with two people, heads bent together, close enough for their shadows to have melded into one?

She should walk down the steps and go on to the beach. See if she can find Adam. See if it's him sitting on one of those chairs. But the fear won't let her. She shivers in the breeze as she notices, again, the patter of crabs along the sand. She hates this place, she realises. Hates the resort. She should never have suggested they come.

She doesn't trust anyone here. Not even Eliza. She doesn't know her, not really. And what about Noah? Thinking about him, about the way he put his hands on Eliza so proprietarily over dinner. There's a latent violence about him, she thinks. She doesn't trust either of them.

She stares again at the lumpen blackness of the chairs under the trees. Is anyone there? She clenches the balcony rail, twisting her hands around the rough wood, standing on tiptoe, not knowing what to do.

She hears a crash from inside the darkness of the trees to her right. A faraway bang, the violence of it shocking in the otherwise calm of the night. The crunch of feet over gravel and a shout from somewhere. A call that sounds faintly alien. A tribal greeting, its final note lasting long and high as it careens on the wind across the trees.

She feels odd. As if the world has tilted. It's a common feeling at the moment. The devils swooping in, wings beating, directly above her. A constant grip of anxiety wrapped around her heart. She takes in a shuddering breath, tries to calm the pounding in her chest. Banish the fear that sits inside it, heavy and black and cold.

Time seems to stop. She doesn't know how long she stands there.

Lou screws her eyes shut tight, stuck in fear and indecision.

Then, her hands are grabbed roughly. She lets out a small cry.

'Lou!'

It's Adam. He leers at her from the sand at the bottom of the veranda, greedily reaching up to her. His hair is mussed and he stinks of rum.

'Lou! Where have you been?'

'Sssssh!' She recovers quickly from the fright and hisses at him. 'Keep your voice down. It's past four in the morning.'

'Lou! I've been looking for you.'

'No you haven't. You're drunk, Adam. I've been asleep. Here in the hut. Where have you been?'

Adam shakes his head. He touches his jaw with his fingers. 'Lars gave me drinks. Had to get ice,' he mumbles, looking back in the direction of the bar. 'Cos of Noah. Cos he hit me...'

'He hit you?' Lou asks, amazed. 'Jesus Christ. What's been going on? Get up here and into bed.'

Adam weaves his head up and down like a lowing cow. 'There are things going on here,' he whispers, 'that you do not know about.'

'What things? Adam, seriously? I can't deal with this. Just get to bed. Go into the other room. You're an embarrassment.'

'I mean it,' Adam insists. 'Larry... Larn... Lou... LARS. Fuck!' He wipes his mouth, shaking his head. 'He's dodgy. Must tell someone... Saying things to me... too much to drink, yes.' He peers over his shoulder. 'So dodgy. Need to see about it all...'

'Adam. Get to bed. I've had enough.'

'No. Wait. Is serious. So dodgy. Tried to kill me. Had a gun.'

'What?' Lou stares. 'Are you bullshitting me?'

'No, no, no.' Adam waves a hand from side to side. 'S'true. In the kompan. Kampan. Fuck's sake. What they call it. Where they live.' He swallows, squeezing the veranda rail with clammy hands. 'Think Lars playing them off. He's not what you think. Is what I said.'

'But a gun?'

'Yes, yes. Gun. Had to drive back. Got away.' He tries to snap his fingers together but they miss and he merely cleaves the air with his fist.

Lou narrows her eyes. 'Drove back? Like this? What did you drive?'

'Jeep.'

'What jeep?'

'Red one. Zoe gave me keys.'

Lou takes a breath. 'Oh, I see.' She folds her arms. 'Bloody hell.'

'Huh?' Adam is still looking at his fingers as if they are broken.

'You went off with that kid Zoe? From the kids' club? The kids' club? Jesus Christ, Adam. When are you ever going to learn?' She laughs. 'When am I ever going to learn? A gun. Fuck. Yeah, right. You must think I am an absolute idiot.'

'Oh, fuck off,' Adam slurs. 'Sick of getting shit all the time.'

'We're finished, Adam.' She can hear the strength in her voice and it takes her by surprise. She thought she'd be more afraid, more broken. But she's not. She's as calm as the sea she faces.

'We're over. When we get back to Singapore, I want you to move out. We can deal with the legalities later, but I'm telling you now. I'm done. Our marriage is over.'

He lurches and staggers up the stairs, stumbles past her, knocking blindly into the closed door of their bedroom with his shoulders.

'Shut up! Wait . . .' Lou grabs his collar and pulls him back. 'You can't go in there. You'll fall on top of the bed. You're smashed. It's too dangerous with the baby. You'll roll on top of her. You have to go in the other room.'

'Put her . . . the floor.' Adam is swaying on his feet, his eyes rheumy and glazed.

'For God's sake, Adam. I'm not putting her on the floor. You can go in Raffy's room on the bottom bunk.' Lou swivels him around to face the door into the adjacent room. She pokes him in the back with an index finger. 'There. Go.'

'You're such a bitch,' Adam says to the door. 'The whole lot of you.'

When Adam smashes his fist into the door, it's as if she is watching it on screen. As if a cell door has slammed shut, leaving her out cold, on the other side of her feelings, all of her emotions. She feels nothing as he turns to her, his eyebrows raised as if daring her to challenge him.

'Everything I do is wrong, isn't it? Everything, everything, everything. And now you want me to sleep in here like a little fucking child? You have to be fucking joking, Louise. Miss fucking Louise.'

She wipes away the spittle he has aimed at her cheek and, still, she says nothing. She feels nothing. Only the heaviness. It's as if she's looking down from above at them both. She thinks about what she'd believed was love. Had she ever really loved Adam? Looking at him, standing here, watching shame spread and flush over his face like a drop of ink into water, she can't remember loving this man.

Somewhere inside of her, she feels the impulse to lift her arm. She sees it – her own hand – travel through the air and make contact with his face. She wants to laugh. Two hits in one night. That's a bad evening by anyone's standards. The diamonds on her eternity ring catch him under the eye. He's too drunk to dodge it, his reflexes marred by booze. He looks at her in disbelief as a scratch of blood flames red on his face.

And then, the darkness wins. She just wants to sink into the ground. Slip through the wooden slats of the veranda and soak into the sand like the coffee she spilt earlier. Was that only this morning? It feels like months ago. Above her, the devils are laughing. She stands motionless, unable to do anything except witness the heaviness that washes over her with the rhythm of the tide.

She feels nothing.

Not even as he pushes her to one side and half-falls down the steps to the beach.

She feels nothing. She looks on with curiosity as he lurches away, halting at something he notices next door, underneath the Fishers' hut. Under the glow of the balcony light, she sees him fumble at the bottom of their steps. He tips out a pile of something and the effort causes him to fall backwards on to the sand. He scrabbles around his feet then manages to get up and sets off again, tugging this thing, low and cumbersome, behind him.

Still, she watches detached, as if observing a set piece in a nature documentary. It's only as Adam gets to the shore – under the direct glare of the moon – that she realises he's carrying a paddle. That he's taken Noah's kayak.

Still, she feels nothing as he pushes it into the ripples of surf at the edge of the sea. As he falls heavily into it, the oar across his lap, his chin lifted high as his head lolls, facing up towards the stars.

She feels nothing as she turns and slowly enters the hut and climbs back into bed. Lifts Laila to her breast and feels the pull of her rhythmic suckling. Afterwards, she lays the baby back in the bassinet and lies on her own pillow.

Her clock says that it's 5.10 a.m.

Still, she feels nothing.

# 20

## ELIZA

*Sunday*

'The Carters are late for breakfast,' she says, wiping yoghurt from the tabletop with a napkin. 'It's gone nine a.m. You haven't seen Raffy, have you, Sam?'

He shakes his head, spooning cornflakes into his mouth. 'Their door was all broken. I knocked on it but no one answered. I had to play basketball with Chloe.'

He looks in disgust at his sister who ignores him, playing with her Shopkins in amongst the breakfast things on the table.

'What do you mean their door was broken?' Eliza asks.

Sam shrugs. 'All splintered and stuff in the middle.'

'Hey guys.' Lars comes up to them, sunglasses pushed through his blond hair. He's wearing a ripped T-shirt and board shorts. 'Big night last night, hey?'

Noah nods ruefully, indicating his coffee. 'Bit dusty, yeah,' he says.

'Ha, yeah, Adam looked a bit worse for wear, you know? He came in here around one, I think? We were clearing up. Had to get him some ice. Said he'd cracked his head on the door of his hut.' Lars makes a sympathetic face and then laughs, ruffling a hand over Sam's hair. 'Poor guy looked like he could do with a lie-down.'

Eliza lifts her eyebrows towards Noah. 'Seems like it was a big night for everyone. I didn't even hear you come in.'

'Yeah, well. Did my old trick of falling asleep on the beach. Don't know about the door, though. Adam must have done that after we separated.' Noah finishes his coffee in a single gulp.

'Right, Chlo. Shall we go and have a snorkel? We can head out to the little reef in the kayak?'

Chloe nods eagerly as Sam protests. 'What about me?'

'You're next in line, buddy. Weather looks better today,' Noah directs at Lars.

'Oh, yeah. It's OK. Hate to tell you it's going to get worse this afternoon, though. Looks like the storm might finally break.'

'Such a shame when we've got so little time here,' Eliza says. 'We've had such bad luck.'

'Well, make the most of the morning. It's beautiful now,' Lars says, turning towards the kitchens. 'I'll catch you later, guys.'

They stand up and Eliza gathers Chloe's toys together into a little canvas bag. 'I'll go and check on Lou,' she says. 'I hope they're OK and not sick or anything. Sam, you come with me to find Raffy and let Daddy and Chloe go and have some time on the beach.'

They leave the restaurant and walk back together to the huts. At the basketball court, they diverge with Noah and Chloe going to their hut and Eliza and Sam climbing the steps to the Carters'. At the top, she studies the damage. Sam was right. The middle of the right-hand door into Raffy's room is dented inwards, the wood splintered and riven with cracks.

She knocks on the other door, and waits on the veranda, resting against the balcony rail. After a moment, Lou appears in her nightshirt, holding Laila.

'Oh, hi,' she says. 'Sorry. We missed breakfast. We had a really good sleep for once and now we're just being lazy. This little champion slept for six hours last night.'

'Amazing,' Eliza says. 'I was checking you were OK as Sam knocked for Raffy but there was no answer.'

'Oh, he's in with me. Got his headphones on and watching his iPad.' Lou opens the door further to reveal Raffy on the bed with his stuffed monkey, plugged in to his device. 'How are you guys anyway? All good?'

'Yes. We've just had breakfast and Noah and Chloe are going out on the kayak.' Eliza smiles at her before glancing across at the door damage. 'What happened there?'

Lou's eyes follow her gaze. 'Oh, that. Adam had a bit too much to drink. Idiot bashed into it without realising. Don't worry,' she laughs. 'He came off much worse.'

'Oh right.' Eliza gives her a sympathetic smile. 'Lars said he'd had a late night. Was that where he hit his head? Apparently he needed some ice?'

'Um, yes. Must have been,' Lou answers. 'Was he down at the restaurant for breakfast?'

'Adam? No.' Eliza sounds surprised. 'At least, we didn't see him. Maybe he was there before us?'

Lou looks over Eliza's shoulder in the direction of the restaurant. 'Yes. Maybe,' she says.

'Uh, well... I'm sure he's around. Maybe he's gone for a run or something,' Eliza says.

Lou comes out on to the balcony. Laila gurgles in her arms as Eliza tickles her under the chin.

'Hello, Miss Laila. And how are you this morning?'

'El?' Noah calls over from their hut. 'Have you seen the kayak?'

She looks over to where he's standing at the bottom of their steps. Sam has left the Carters' veranda and is playing tag with Chloe, the pair of them running in and out of the palm trees that circle the huts.

'What do you mean? It's under the stairs.'

Eliza trots down the steps and over to Noah who gestures underneath the hut.

'Well, it's not there now.'

'Would someone have taken it?' Eliza puts her hands on her hips and looks around. 'Maybe someone took it by mistake? Or borrowed it?' She gazes out to sea. 'Can you see it out there?'

They peer at the horizon but the water is flat and empty. There are only a few people swimming, further up the beach towards the restaurant.

'I'll go up and ask Lars. See if anyone's got it up at the bar,' Noah says. He reaches through the veranda rail to get a baseball cap lying on the deck. 'Some idiot's probably taken it and then not been bothered to bring it back.'

113

'Are you all right, Lou?' Eliza has turned to see Lou sitting heavily on the top step. Her expression is hollow, her skin a white mask. 'What's the matter? Do you feel ill?'

Lou shakes her head, her mouth opening a little as if she's trying to find the words. Laila stares out at the beach, jiggling in Lou's lap, her hands in the air. After all that sleep, the baby is the happiest Eliza has ever seen her. Her bright eyes and peachy skin contrasts horribly with the waxen pallor spread across Lou's face.

'Lou, what is it?' Eliza hurries over and kneels on the step below. She touches Lou's knees, trying to get her to focus, to look at her.

Lou frowns, rousing herself as Laila emits a laugh, tapping at Eliza's face and blowing a bubble of spit from her mouth. 'Adam...' she says.

'Yes,' Eliza nods. 'What about Adam? What is it? Lou, you're starting to really freak me out.'

Lou swallows and looks at Eliza. 'Last night. I saw Adam... we had a fight. He was drunk. The door, you know. And he went...' Her eyes move to the hut where Noah is standing, staring over at them from under the brim of his cap. Eliza can hear Sam and Chloe laughing as they run down to the waves, shrieking as the surf splashes over their toes.

'He went where?' Eliza says. 'Lou, concentrate. Last night. Adam was drunk and... where did he go?'

Lou hands the baby over as if in a dream. Eliza manages to take her without losing balance, as Lou gets to her feet and comes down the steps, gazing out towards where the children are playing. She lifts her hand and turns to point at the Fishers' hut.

'He took it. He went out with it. And I saw—'

'Took what?' Eliza says, hoisting Laila on to her hip. Then she freezes. 'Wait. Do you mean the kayak? Lou, are you saying that Adam took the kayak out last night? When he was drunk?'

Lou seems to float over the sand in her white nightshirt, her dark hair streaming across her shoulders. She looks like a deathly bride; a spectral waif. She squints into the glare of the sun, at the diamonds of light that sparkle on the surface of the water.

Eliza can't help it. It's so idyllic, she thinks. Even now, as Lou confirms what she's realised. Even now, when everything is about to turn into a living nightmare, it still looks like paradise. So utterly, perfectly beautiful.

'Yes,' Lou says slowly and then she begins to cry and rake her hair.

'Yes, he took the kayak. And I let him.' She begins to sob and hiccup; she can't catch her breath. 'I stood here and I let him. And now, he hasn't come back, has he?'

They stand – Noah and Eliza, holding the baby – staring in horror as Lou's face takes on the silent scream of a gargoyle.

'*Has* he?' she cries. 'He's dead, isn't he? Oh!' She clamps a hand over her mouth as she catches sight of something behind Eliza, who turns to see what it is.

There is Raffy on the balcony, his headphones dangling from his hands, his hair mussed and sticking up from where he's been lying on his bed.

'Raffy...' Lou sobs. 'Oh, Raffy...'

He stares at them all looking at him, a little frown creasing his forehead.

'Where's Daddy?' he asks. 'Where's my daddy?'

# 21

## LOU

She can't sit still. She keeps pinching her lips between her fingers over and over again. Every one of her muscles is rigid with tension.

They are sitting in the restaurant. Sara the waitress has turned off the music and the silence there is strange to Lou. As if she's looking at someone without any make-up for the first time.

Lars was immediately reassuring. Without any visible panic, he radioed over to the neighbouring resort of Timba and coordinated staff in both resorts as well as any guests who wanted to volunteer, to search the beach and around the headland.

'It is most likely he has been pulled in by the early morning current and is just beyond the reef in that direction,' he'd pointed to the north. 'Zikri and I will take the tender out now and scout the perimeter. We will find him, Lou. Please don't worry.'

Before he left, he arranged for the children to be taken to the kids' club with Julie and they trooped off dolefully, Sam and Chloe either side of Raffy, taking an arm each as if he had been wounded.

The other guests have backed off, headed down to the beach or into their huts, not knowing how best to help. There is nothing left for Lou to do, other than sit and wait.

'This is a nightmare,' she says, her hand over her mouth. 'A nightmare. I can't believe I just let him go. I knew he was drunk. But I... I don't know. I don't know what I was thinking.'

Worry scores her face and she beckons Eliza close. 'I told you about the pills the doctor gave me. Sometimes they make my head fuzzy. Not clear. I shouldn't have drunk anything last night.

It made me... not myself. If I'd been myself, I never would have let him go.'

'I know,' Eliza soothes, rubbing Lou's back. 'Please try not to worry. Adam's a strong swimmer. He's fit. And it was starting to get light when he left, wasn't it? Or not long after anyway. He probably beached himself on a sandbank around the headland and he's fast asleep there. Massively sunburnt and massively hung-over.'

Even as she hears it, Lou knows it is a lie. The likely truth is that Adam did indeed fall asleep or pass out in the kayak, and he's been drifting slowly out to sea for the last five hours.

The sound of the waves moving in and out across the sand, the tick of the ceiling fan above her, have a soporific effect. She and Eliza stare at the grain of the wooden table where they sit, and Lou feels her eyes droop, even as she fights sleep. She knows it's a defence mechanism. A way to try and deny the reality of what is happening.

Noah comes into the bar and she jerks back into life, searching his face for information.

'Anything?'

He grabs a chair and sits down. 'Nothing. We went all the way up and down the beach. On to those bits where you can climb over the rocks either end. He might have gone inland, I suppose. But it's sensible for Lars to check the coastline first, given he was in the kayak.'

'Can they take out the bigger boat? The one we came in? Go back across that stretch to the mainland? Because maybe he's floating in the channel there?' Lou's knuckles are white where she presses her fingertips on to the table.

'I've spoken to Lars. He's doing everything that can be done,' Noah says. His skin is slick with sweat and his eyes are heavy with exhaustion and hangover. 'He's called the coastguard. And he's reported it to the Malaysian police. They'll be here in the next couple of hours, he says.'

'The police?' Lou's eyes flash, panicked. 'Why? Because they think he's dead?'

'No, no,' Eliza says, shooting Noah a look. 'It's probably just procedure. They have to be informed.'

'If Adam took the kayak all the way round the island, he could easily be lost or wandering through the jungle, trying to find his way back here. We just don't know. It's better – it's *good* – that the police come. They can organise a proper search party. They know the terrain much better than we do.'

'You were the last to see him, weren't you? On the beach. Well...' Lou glances down at her eternity ring '... before me, I mean. But how was he?' She weaves her head in order to catch his eye. 'Noah? Hey. He said you hit him. When he came back to the hut. He told me. What happened? Did you have a fight?'

'You hit him?' Eliza turns to Noah. 'What do you mean? Why would you hit Adam?'

Noah rubs the back of his neck with his hand. 'No, no. I didn't *hit* him. It was just a bit of a, you know, like a ... friendly shove...'

'A friendly shove?' Eliza looks incredulous.

'I was pissed off with him,' Noah appeals to her. 'All those questions he asked you. Making you talk about your mum like that. I didn't like him upsetting you.'

Lou scans his face. There's a hollow pitch to his tone. Something about it doesn't ring true.

'I think that's up to me to decide, isn't it?' Eliza says, folding her arms. 'So, what did you do? Have a scrap on the beach after I'd gone to bed, like two little schoolboys?'

'No, no, it wasn't like that. El. Come on. I told him he was out of order. He must have told me to ... eff off. He wanted more booze. I said he'd had enough. He tried to get past me and I blocked him...'

'With your fist?' Eliza is disdainful.

'No. He was pissed, El. He fell over. I couldn't even really see, it was so dark. He just staggered off. Came up to the bar. Look, I was drunk,' Noah raises his palms. 'I admit it. But then I came to bed. Didn't I? El?'

'I was asleep, Noah. I told you. I have no idea...'

'Well, I didn't see him again.' Noah turns from Eliza to Lou. 'I swear. I didn't see him. I went to bed and the next thing I knew it was morning and Sam was on top of me, waking me up to go to breakfast.'

'He was totally drunk,' Lou concedes. 'When he came to the hut, he could barely stand. He was rambling about some conspiracy on the island. Telling me again how Lars was a criminal mastermind.'

Eliza flicks a sideways glance at Lou. 'There is one thing...' she says.

'What?' Lou searches her face.

'I don't know what time it was. I don't wear a watch and my phone was off, but I came out and went down on to the beach. It was late. The beach was empty. The restaurant was shut.'

'Why?' Noah asks.

'Why what?'

'Why did you come on to the beach that late?'

Eliza shrugs. 'I couldn't sleep. You hadn't come back. I think I was looking for you, or trying to tire myself out. I don't know.' She looks at them both. 'Anyway. I walked up to where the bar is and I saw Adam. And...'

'What is it?' Lou asks in a small voice.

'Well, it's nothing really. It's just he was with a girl. They walked off over there, in that direction.' Eliza gestures towards the clearing in front of the kids' club. 'And, um, well, the girl was one of the backpackers that works here. The blonde one? Zoe?'

Lou puts her head in her hands. She can feel pity from the other two flooding her in a deluge. It makes her hate Adam so much in that moment. That he would put her through this. 'I know,' she says. 'He let it slip that he'd been with her. Said he'd been driving them around the island in a jeep, for God's sake. I mean, they could have been killed.' She halts, realising the weird irony of what she's said. 'Well, anyway. Then he made up some story to cover it up. About Lars having a gun and threatening him with it. It was all bullshit.'

'A gun?' Eliza asks, sitting forward. 'Why would Lars have a gun?'

Lou looks at her. 'I don't think it was even true,' she says wearily. 'Just another one of Adam's stories to take the heat off him messing around with yet another girl.'

'But we have to tell someone about it, don't we?' Eliza says. 'We have to tell the police about it.'

'Yes of course,' Lou says. 'But it doesn't really mean anything,' she adds bitterly. 'Even if something had happened with Lars, even if Adam was going to fuck that girl, I saw him get in the kayak, didn't I? That girl isn't to blame, is she? I'm the only one that's to blame.'

There doesn't appear to be any response to that, so they say nothing.

'Is it possible he didn't actually go into the water with the kayak?' Eliza asks as the thought occurs to her. 'Maybe he sat in it for a while in the surf. The tide was out. It would have been really shallow. Maybe, after a bit, he got out and just wandered off? Then whatever happened with Lars – or Zoe – is actually massively relevant.'

'Then, where is the kayak?' Lou says dully.

'It got swept out to sea with the current,' Eliza answers. 'It doesn't mean Adam was in it.'

'That's true,' Noah says.

'Oh stop.' Lou bangs her fist on to the table. 'What's the point of this? We don't know. We have no idea. We were all too pissed or weird or whatever to know. We *can't* know. All we know is, he's gone. He's not here. And… we have to find him.' She places her fingers slowly down on the table, one by one. 'We have to find him because I'm not sure I can cope. If Raffy… and, Jesus, Laila… ?'

'She's fine, Lou.' Eliza takes hold of Lou's shoulders, preventing her rising up in a panic. 'Don't you remember? The babysitter from last night – Tita? She's watching Laila over at the staff quarters. She said she'll come and find you to feed her when she wakes up.'

'Wouldn't you know it,' Lou gives a horrible laugh. 'Kid loves to sleep on this awful island.'

She can't stay there any more. She can't listen to these two go on and on with their theories about what's happened. She can't breathe. She needs to walk. To look at the ocean and see if she feels Adam out there. If she can be quiet for just a minute, maybe she can hear him. These two don't even know him. She hates them. Hates this place.

They never should have come here.

'I need to get out of here,' she says.

'I'll come with you.' Eliza moves to follow her.

'No. Please. I just want to be on my own.'

She leaves the restaurant, bare-footed. Wet sand sticks to her toes as she walks in time with her breath. She goes down to the shoreline and watches the foam melt on to the sand. It's hot. Midday and the sun is high. She can feel the burn on her skin as she turns to the horizon and puts her hand to her eyes, seeking out Adam on the flat, still ocean.

There is nothing but glassy water, stretching as far as she can see. Only one puff of cloud and a bird soaring in the distance.

*Adam*, she thinks.

She calls silently to him, twisting her ring around and around.

*Adam. You shit. Come back. It's not supposed to end like this.*

At the edge of the world, she sees a fountain of water growing bigger and bigger.

It's a boat approaching the shore. Lou's hair is caught by a breeze and she pushes it from her eyes, trying to make out the occupants. As it comes closer, she can hear the blare of a horn.

She remembers then, the noises she heard last night. The bang in the forest. That call across the wind.

Where was Noah? Why wasn't he with Adam? Why can't he remember where he was? And why was Eliza wandering along the beach so late? Had she been with them? Why was she then on her own?

She stares out at the boat biting its course through the waves. Why are they blasting the horn? Have they found him? Is he lying in the bottom of the boat, unconscious but alive?

She starts to wade into the sea. She's still wearing her nightshirt. The water rises up and over it as she goes deeper. The boat veers away from her, skidding wildly into the shallows up the beach and near the bar. Seawater reaches her waist; her nightshirt sticks to her legs. It's heavy now and see-through.

She can see Lars jump out. Just as they did two days ago when they arrived. She can see Adam then, as he leapt from the boat. Filled with confidence and the pleasure of a long weekend stretching ahead of him. Slapping Noah on the back, looking over at her and smiling as he raised his cocktail glass.

*Adam.*

Lou begins to swim, her nightshirt dragging through the water as she lifts her arms to call for him.

But Lars is out of the boat and now he's talking to Zikri. And their faces are dark, filled with worry and stress.

Adam is not on the boat.

Adam is still missing.

# 22

## ELIZA

'You can see, this is a map of the island.'

The few guests staying at the resort are picking at a late lunch of chicken curry, muttering amongst themselves in low voices. Only the adults are present at lunch. Given the situation, Lars had decreed that all the children should be fed over at the kids' club. There was no need to worry them unnecessarily, he had said. Keep them active and happy, and out of the way.

He stands in front of the buffet table in the restaurant. He's stuck an enlarged map of Pulau Kalah up on a whiteboard and points at sections of it to show them as they eat.

'You observe it's not big at all. Six kilometres long and only one kilometre wide. We're at the top here, in the north. Around the headland to the west a short way is Timba. Carry round a little further and you reach the local village where the jetty is that we use to get off the island in bad weather.' He taps at the place on the map.

'How long does it take to walk round the headland to Timba?' Noah asks.

'About an hour,' Lars answers. 'Maybe more. It's a jungle trail so it's not straightforward. If you know it, it's not too bad.'

'Can you swim round to it?' Eliza asks.

'Yah,' Lars shrugs. 'A strong swimmer could. But you'd need to avoid the coral on the reef if you didn't want to get sliced to ribbons.'

'Are there beaches along that bit of coast?' she queries. 'Places Adam might have landed the kayak to rest?'

'That's where Zikri and I searched earlier,' replies Lars. 'And unfortunately didn't see anything. I'm going to go back out on the tender.' He gestures behind Eliza to the elderly boatman she recognises from their journey to the island from the mainland.

'Alif and I will go round the entire island and search again. I might have missed him the first time if he was asleep. So... we'll do it again.'

'What about the south of the island?' the groom of the newly-weds asks, pointing towards the bottom of the map. 'It's so small, he could have kayaked around it and be down there, on a beach or something?'

Lars shakes his head. 'We'll look, but the only place you can land is a tiny campsite, not even a beach as such. Otherwise, it's mangroves and jungle. My feeling is Adam's at the top end of the island. He was hung-over, by all accounts. We're not sure he had any water and it's a decent kayak to get all the way down there.' Lars shrugs. 'It's not impossible, but I'd be surprised.'

'Well, we should look down there anyway, shouldn't we?' the man persists.

'For now, let's stick to where it's most likely Adam would be. If we don't find him in the next few hours, we can reassess,' Lars says.

Eliza takes him in, thinking over what Lou said: about Adam's story of Lars and the gun. She gnaws a chipped nail, considering him. Does he look like the kind of guy who'd hold a gun to someone? She can't see it. In all honesty, he just looks like a beach bum.

He has an authority about him. He clearly knows the island, the water. The kids who work here obviously hero-worship him.

But... a gun? He hardly seems Michael Corleone.

If she was pushed, she'd say it does look as though he's aged in only a few short hours. The tan lines that crease his face seem leathery and his eyes are watery, bleached by the harsh light from the beach. But then again, he's probably hung-over himself.

And it's entirely reasonable he'd be stressed, given a guest of the resort is missing.

Nevertheless, why would Adam make up something like that? Yes, he'd taken an irrational dislike to Lars. But to say he had a gun? It's such an outrageous allegation. Which kind of suggests that it might be true.

Eliza sinks her head into her palms. What can they do about it, though? They can hardly ask Lars about it direct. If he is in possession of a firearm, asking him about it could be dangerous. And if Adam has been bullshitting, the news will royally piss Lars off – just when they need him most.

No. They'll have to wait until the police arrive and take it up with them.

The humidity is sluggish, leaving them bleary-eyed and sleepy, barely bothering to swat the flies that land on their dinner plates and rims of water glasses. Eliza flicks breadcrumbs off the table in frustration. The atmosphere should be taut, buzzing with tension, crackling with the energy they need to search the island and find Adam. She tries to catch Noah's eye, but he's deliberately ignoring her. Everything feels wrong somehow. As if they've all been drugged, as if they're suffocating under a weighted blanket of some kind.

Her mind returns again to last night when she'd left Adam and Noah on the beach. Had there been any sign of violence between them? Any hint that they would fight, that Noah would hit Adam? Has he been secretly jealous all this time? He had mentioned something about Adam being interested in her, that first night when they arrived – when Adam had been talking about his father. So maybe it's been festering inside? But then, why hasn't he spoken to her about it instead of getting drunk and behaving so stupidly?

And what was Adam doing with that girl? Does Noah know about that? Had he been with them before going AWOL on the beach?

She closes her eyes momentarily. It would be so easy to go to sleep right now. To rest her head and pretend that none of this was happening.

'So we'll reconvene here this afternoon.' Lars is clapping his hands as if he's about to leave.

Eliza forces herself to straighten, to snap out of her listlessness. 'But when will the coastguard get here? It must be soon, surely?'

Lars sighs. 'This is Malaysia. Things happen on island time. We've made the call. They'll come. But we must be patient.'

He turns towards the Lancashire family's table. 'Hey, guys. How about an afternoon of snorkelling for the kids, yah? We can arrange for them and the others to go out to the reef near the bluff up the beach?'

This provokes a prolonged murmur of dissent amongst the parents.

'I don't think that's a great idea,' Noah says. 'Wouldn't it be better to keep everyone in one place for now?'

Lars narrows his eyes for a brief second. 'Sure, sure,' he says. 'I'm just thinking of ways to keep the youngsters happy and occupied.'

'I'll help Julie out with the kids.' Eliza gets to her feet. 'Then everyone else can join in the search.'

'That's very kind, thank you.' Lars clips her a smile. 'OK, well let's go then.' He moves towards Lou who sits at a table looking at an untouched plate of food. 'Let's find Adam, yes Lou?'

When she doesn't answer, he places a hand on her back and then walks briskly out of the restaurant.

'I reckon they've only got another two hours to find him, tops,' Julie whispers to Eliza with more than a little relish as they gather the children to them like chicks and begin setting up a crafting table in an annexe off the restaurant.

'Why? It's not sunset for at least another five hours.'

Julie shrugs and raises eyebrows under her bluntly cut fringe, but won't say any more.

Eliza decides to ignore her, cutting round a stencil of a *PAW Patrol* character for Raffy.

'There we are,' she says, handing it to him. 'Now you can colour it in, and we can stick it on the picture with the others.'

The mural is Julie's idea. A long white roll of paper where the children can glue cut-outs of their favourite cartoon characters and draw cityscapes or space scenes around them. Unhelpful comments aside, at least Julie's here, making an effort with

126

the kids. Zoe is nowhere to be seen. Sleeping off her hangover, most likely.

'Where's Daddy?' It's the third time Raffy's asked her this. He drops the stencil, uninterested. Ever since he'd heard about the fish bomb yesterday, Raffy has been obsessed with discovering ways to protect the marine life. He's been collecting rubbish from the beach and instead of cartoon characters, now he's drawing endless pictures of different kinds of fish that live on the reef. He doesn't seem overly upset, Eliza thinks. But the insistence of his questions makes her concerned he's not as relaxed as he appears.

'Daddy's out on the kayak,' she answers. 'He'll be back soon.'

Eliza doesn't know if lying to him is the right thing to do. Judging by her heavy sigh, Julie disagrees with the strategy. But what else can she say? That Daddy got really drunk last night and went out into the waves with a potential head injury and hasn't been seen since?

Eliza bites her lip. Surely it's up to Lou to explain to her son what's going on?

The problem is that Lou is a mess. She hasn't changed out of her nightshirt and has been sitting alone since the morning with wild hair, her eyes panda-ringed with mascara. She veers from fits of sobbing to manic laughter and, glancing over now, Eliza sees that the Dutch woman from the dive yesterday has given her a glass of whisky.

Lou needs to keep sober and calm. Eliza should go and see if she's OK. Check it's only the one drink she'll have. But she doesn't want to leave Julie alone in charge.

'Where's Zoe?' she asks, irritated, moving out of earshot of the children. 'Can't she come and help out? I really should go and be with Lou.'

Julie's face darkens. 'Haven't seen her all morning. Zikri says she was at a party last night.'

Eliza feels the muscles in her shoulders tighten. 'Oh yeah? What time did she make it back?'

Julie glances up at her. 'She does it a lot,' she says.

'Not show up for work?'

'Not with the kids, no. She doesn't mind working with Lars.' Julie's bottom lip sinks so low with disapprobation, she gives herself a double chin.

Eliza thinks about Zoe, remembering what she's seen of her. It's true, she hadn't immediately struck her as the Mary Poppins type, with a flat stomach as hard as the expression in her baby-blue eyes. 'You two don't get on?' she surmises.

Julie squints as if thinking deeply about this. 'She's OK, I suppose. She's the usual type Lars employs for the season. Always likes his own little revolving harem.' She bitterly scissors round the Little Einsteins' spaceship. 'All perky boobs but no heavy lifting, frankly. He only gets me back every year cos he knows I'll actually do the work. I don't think Zoe's helped unload a dive boat once since she's been here.' Julie sneaks a look at Eliza. 'Sorry. I probably shouldn't be saying this to you.'

'I'll take it with me to the grave,' Eliza says, her gaze shifting back towards Raffy.

The more she hears about Lars, the more chipped and faded his charming veneer becomes. Whether Adam had been telling the truth about a gun or not, he obviously thought he knew something about Lars's business on the island. And Julie has just implied a rather sordid HR policy. It's all starting to feel a little grubby here at Turtle Cove.

'I'm going to check on Lou and get the kids ice creams, OK?'

She wanders over to the fridge by the bar and leans her forehead against it for a moment.

Something has to happen soon, she thinks. Something has to break. Because right now, it feels like they're stuck in one of those snow domes. Except it's hot and stifling and the glass burns your hand to the touch. She turns and puts her back against the cold of the door.

Beyond the fringe of the atap roof, there is nothing. Nothing but blue, blue sea up to a bleak horizon with a sun that sears white heat across them, slowly cooking them under ultraviolet light.

She used to love the ocean.

But now it feels like a trap.

They're stuck like insects in this dome, caught between the heavy tide with its rising waves out in front, and the dark volcano that glowers over them, curling its shadow from out of the sky.

And there's no escaping any of what lies ahead.

No way out, for any of them.

# 23

## NOAH

After Lars leaves on the tender with Alif, Zikri coordinates a search party made up of staff and groups of guests and they fan out in all directions from the resort.

Noah is tasked with searching the track through the section of rainforest that runs parallel to the beach. Zikri has paired him with one of the kitchen staff, a tiny-framed twig of a boy who speaks no English, shouting only *Manda* as he thwacks giant leaves of banana plants with a hefty piece of sugar cane as they go.

Noah follows as best he can, sweat dripping in his eyes, his hangover causing his belly to gripe and growl as he puffs uphill, his feet dragging. Zikri had explained that the path leads all the way to Timba, but Noah and his companion focus on a section of tangled roots and buttresses only a few hundred metres from the resort.

In the canopy above them, birds squawk, and the screeching flays his nerves. He keeps replaying it. That stumble on the beach. Adam's laugh seems to stalk him, echoing through the jungle. That hot wind of rage shunting through him like a train in a tunnel, taking his breath away, light shuttering, flickering, until all he can see is Adam's grin hardening, blood swelling, his own fist jangling and ringing with the pain.

He can't hold it in. He bends over and vomits on to the rainforest floor. The kitchen boy watches him, impassive. Noah lets out a moan as he straightens, wiping his mouth with the bottom of his white T-shirt.

'Fuck.'

'*Manda*.' The kitchen boy comes over. He flattens both palms towards the ground. '*Manda*,' he says kindly.

Noah has no idea if this is a Malay word or what the boy thinks Adam is called. He decides to interpret it as an invitation to sit down and sinks to his haunches, running his hands over his head.

What an absolute fuck-up.

He drops fully on to the ground.

He hadn't been able to look Eliza in the eye at lunch today. He knew she would be… what? Furious with him for lamping Adam? Frustrated with his constant jealousy? Exhausted by his drinking? His temper? On and on it went. The list of ways he always got it wrong. It didn't seem to matter that he never meant any of it. That these episodes always came from his best intentions. From his devotion to her.

The boy leans down and hands him a water bottle and he drinks from it gratefully.

'I'm going back, yeah?' He gets to his feet, scuffing earth over the mess he's made on the ground. Then he points along the track towards the resort. 'Back down.'

He sets off and the boy follows. Adam isn't here. Why would he be? What would he be doing, hiding under a freaking bush? Noah shakes his head and rolls his shoulders, tries to ease the tension in his muscles.

He gets to the bar and buys two full-fat Cokes. He hands one to the boy who grins widely before darting off to the kitchen.

Noah asks for a little rum to be added to his glass. He drinks it, then shakes the ice in the cocktail, sucking the liquid through his teeth, feeling the hair of the dog work its soothing magic.

In the reflection of the mirror behind the bar, he sees Eliza come to the fridge for ice creams. For a minute, she leans her head against the cool of the glass and he watches, admiring her. She is so beautiful, his wife. No wonder men flirt with her. Why would Adam be any different?

Looking up, she sees him and lifts a hand. Chloe skips over on bare feet to grab the lollies and Eliza hurries to join him at the bar.

'No sign?' she says.

'No, not yet. It's just a Coke,' he says, noticing her raised eyebrow at his glass. 'Want anything?'

She shakes her head. 'What were you doing last night, Noah? Why would you hit Adam? I don't understand you.'

'Babe, it wasn't that bad. You're overreacting.'

'Uh huh.' Eliza tightens her mouth.

Noah takes a long swallow of Coke, thinking of his endless walk last night. Wandering on the outskirts of the rainforest in the dark, trying to figure things out, work out how to make things better. Trying to sober up. What an idiot he's been.

'It's the truth. Fact is, Adam was being a cock. He was flirting with you.' He holds up a hand to stop her protest. 'Yes he was. I'm not an idiot, El. I have eyes, and I see when a man is making a play for my wife. He needed telling. Plus, all this Lars nonsense with his dynamite-trading shit. Adam was causing trouble all over the place.'

He swings round on the bar stool, arms folded. Still, he doesn't mention what he'd overheard Lars say about the fish bomb and the dynamite in the admin office.

'Maybe he was right, though?' Eliza lowers her voice, checking no one behind the bar is within earshot. 'If he found out something, maybe it meant he had to be kept quiet?'

He doesn't answer immediately. 'That seems really unlikely,' he says at last. 'If Adam is dead, it's a shitstorm for the resort. Think of all the bad publicity. And if there is some kind of dynamite trade going on here,' he makes a dubious face, 'Adam's disappearance brings in the authorities – authorities that will presumably interfere with it.' He laughs briefly. 'The whole thing is way too outlandish.'

They turn sharply at a familiar clap of hands and there is Lars. He's standing at the entrance to the bar, his hair and T-shirt soaked with rain that Noah hasn't even noticed has begun to fall.

Alif the boatman is behind him, along with Zikri and some of the other staff. Julie has wandered over from the restaurant although the kids are still occupied with their crafts. The newly-weds have also come into the bar, wiping splatters of rain from their faces and arms.

The resort manager looks grim, his lips pressed tightly together, a deep frown creasing his brow.

'Sorry to interrupt, guys, but I have bad news,' he says.

Noah reaches for Eliza and pulls her into him, his arm round her waist.

'Is it Adam?' she asks.

Lars shakes his head. 'No, no. It's not that. Alif and I didn't spot him. He's not anywhere on the shoreline of the northern section of the island. We've searched it twice now. So he's either over on the other side somewhere we can't see, or he did go south.'

Or he's drifted, Noah thinks. He's drifted so far now, that he's gone.

'Well, the coastguard will be able to—' Eliza begins.

'No,' Lars cuts in. 'Look,' and his head jerks in the direction of the beach. 'Look at the rain. Well, yah, rain doesn't matter so much. But we checked the radar.' He leans against the bar, reaching for a towel to dry his forehead. 'I'm sorry, but the monsoon is on its way. It's coming. The swell is too big now. The boats can't sail.'

Noah glances behind him where a grey tide is overlapping and pushing in on top of itself. 'It doesn't look so bad,' he says.

'Yah, but the reef breaks up the waves. Half a mile out, though, it's impassable.'

'Impassable?'

Noah turns and there is Lou standing by the ladies. She's still in her nightshirt, her hair tangled and knotted.

'What do you mean, impassable?'

Lars rubs along his jaw before continuing. 'The coastguard, the police. They can't come. Not at the moment. They wouldn't be able to moor the vessels. They couldn't land.'

Noah stares, feeling Eliza stiffen in his arms. 'For how long?'

'What?'

'How long? Until they can. Land,' Noah asks again.

'Not long.'

'Hours?' Lou barks. 'Days?'

'It's hard to give a definite time frame. We'll know more from the radar in the morning.'

'In the morning…' Lou sounds strangled, her voice a near-whisper. 'So he'll be another night out in the open? And in this? If he's injured…? Got hypothermia?' She shakes her head at the rain bouncing off the waves.

All at once, Lars's face is overcome with a dozen tics and muscle spasms. Seemingly embarrassed by it, he begins to massage his cheeks with his hands. 'We just need to keep calm. Adam is a sensible guy. If he's on the island, he'll have sought shelter. It's what anyone would do. Find a cave. Some water. It's not cold. He won't have hypothermia. Please try not to get hysterical. It won't help.'

'Hang on,' Noah says, straightening on his stool. 'You're saying boats can't land, yes?'

Lars nods.

'Where are the two tenders you'd use to take us off the island the day after tomorrow? When we're supposed to be leaving.'

Everyone is fixated on Lars.

'They're secure. Tied up on the other side of the island. By the kampong.'

'Yes but if boats can't land, can we still leave? Can the tenders make the journey to the mainland?'

'It wasn't exactly plain sailing on the way over here, was it?' Eliza says, her voice rising a notch in panic. 'And that was supposedly normal weather.'

'Can they?' Noah repeats. 'Can the resort boats make the journey back to the mainland?'

Lars takes a breath and exhales and they hear the *no* before he actually says it. 'It would be too dangerous at the moment.'

'Dangerous for how long?' Eliza puts her hands on her hips. 'We have children here, Lars. We can't stay here indefinitely. If the weather presents risks, we need to get the children off the island.'

'Yeah, no kidding. And I've got a lot of money riding on the fact I have to be back in the office by Wednesday.'

'Jesus Christ, Noah,' Eliza says sharply.

'I'm just saying.' He angles round to her. 'It's a consideration.'

'Yeah, right.' She gives a nasty laugh.

'Monsoon is only at its peak for a few days,' Zikri says.

134

The guests begin to murmur and the noise of the dissent is increasing.

'I'm just making the point that we need to get off the island,' Noah says to Eliza.

'Maybe you could actually do something, though? Yeah?' Her eyes are on fire as she glares at him. 'Instead of thinking about yourself and your own needs?'

Noah drains his glass. 'Whatever.'

He turns back to the bar as Eliza marches off. Then he hears Lou sob and run outside, calling the name of her baby. He stares at the grain of the wood of the bar top as he taps his fingers. Hears the reassuring crackle of ice and the old familiar smell of his dad and home as the glass of amber liquid is put under his nose.

Just two doubles will see him right. Set him up so he can go and look after his woman and children like a man's supposed to do.

Two doubles and it won't feel like it's raining.

# 24

## LOU

She has to find Laila.

Fat drops of rain fall on her head as she hurries over the clearing towards the staff quarters. She can still taste whisky in her mouth from earlier. Why did she drink it? She knows why. Because in the moment that the woman had held out the glass, she had looked at it and felt the desire for oblivion so strong that she had no control. She had watched her hand take the glass and, before she knew it, felt the peaty burn of it down her throat.

It had been a mistake, obviously. She wasn't going to be knocked out by one whisky and, anyway, she knows that she can't find oblivion until Adam is back and with them all once again. She doesn't deserve it. She is responsible for his death. Or his disappearance. She may as well have pushed that kayak out into the waves herself.

She has to see Laila. She has to feel her daughter's warmth, the blood underneath her skin, her milky breath, soft fontanelle pulsing. Her daughter is so *alive*. She has to feel that life in her arms.

By the time she reaches the hut where Laila is being looked after, Lou is soaked to the skin. The monsoon arrived only a moment after Lars announced that it was coming, but that the police were not. No help was on the way. No coastguard. No search party. No one. Nobody can make the crossing from the mainland in this weather.

They are stuck together on this island in the middle of nowhere until the storm plays itself out.

She bangs on the door, shivering in her wet nightshirt. Still, she hasn't changed. Still, she carries the shame of last night. It's a reek that hangs off her, an indelible stain that no amount of washing or scrubbing will ever remove.

How could she have let him go like that? Drunk and paralytic. Barely able to speak, stumbling around in the dark. Yes, in her mind, their relationship was all but officially over. But he was the father of her children. How *could* she have let him go? What had she been thinking?

The door opens and she's inside, grasping for Laila, pulling her into her chest, breathing in her smell, putting her cheek to hers, feeling the gentle heat of her. She lays a hand on Laila's head and sways gently with her, crying silently.

Tita watches her from the shadows. She sits on her usual wooden chair, polished with time, her broad thighs lapping its sides. Wringing her hands, she hums the songs of the sea, of the underworld and the legends of the moon, as Lou rocks back and forth in the middle of the room.

After a moment, Lou lifts her head and meets the old woman's gaze.

'I didn't mean to do it.'

Tita offers her a white-toothed smile.

'I didn't know he would go off like that. When I hit him, I didn't think...' Lou shivers, and not only from the cold of her damp nightshirt clinging to her frame. 'He doesn't love me,' she whispers. 'I'm a piece of sky that you look at every day. A tree at the bottom of the garden that you stare at as you have a glass of wine. It's comforting. *I'm comforting*. He can never be alone.'

Lou's voice turns hard. 'He wouldn't know what to do. I knew this was our last holiday together. I knew I was going to tell him I was leaving, with the children. I knew it would take a long, long time for it to sink in, for him to accept it. But I meant to do it anyway. Does that make me cruel?' She beseeches the woman, rain droplets running down her face. 'The fact that I don't need him? I love him. I really do. Just not in the same way, not like that. Not any more.

'But he needs me. He wouldn't know what to do without me. He'd die . . .'

She breaks off, aware of what she's said.

'I didn't want him to die. You have to believe me.' She stares wildly at Tita. 'Did I curse him? By coming here? I wished for him to be gone and now he is. Oh God . . .

'But I didn't mean *completely*. Just not with me any more. No more hurt. For *me*.'

She backs away from any judgement in the woman's eyes. The pills and the whisky curdle in her stomach and she feels a sudden wave of nausea. She turns, searching for space, needing to get out from this place. Laila's fingers on her collarbone feel like sharp and tiny vices.

Tita noisily expels air from her nose and shifts, edging fat fingers to her knees to gain purchase for standing. She is a head shorter than Lou and, in the gloom of the hut, her features blur, only her irises gleam. It's so dark in here, it's hard to breathe. The walls begin to bend over Lou. The ceiling flattens. White snow fills her vision.

Strong arms propel her until she is sitting in the chair. Laila is removed from her with a surprising gentleness and placed in the bassinet, before Lou's head is pushed down between her knees.

'Stay there,' Tita says softly. 'Must get blood to your head.'

She stays like that for a few minutes, the woman rubbing slow circles on the centre of her back. After a while, the nausea and panic passes and Lou feels able to sit up.

'Thank you, Tita. I'm sorry. I felt a bit . . .'

She passes a hand over her face and lifts her head to the noise of the barracking of rain on the roof. She glances up to see Tita staring at her and feels suddenly embarrassed. The woman must think she's insane. Rambling about Adam and her marriage and then nearly passing out while stinking of whisky.

Tita hums atonally, folding her arms over her huge bosom. 'I see many things here,' she says. 'Many things.'

'I should go.'

'Baby hungry soon. Bring her back when sleep time.'

'You're very kind. But we'll be fine. Thank you.' Trying to muster some dignity, Lou gets to her feet slowly and picks up

Laila. Not able to see the door handle fully in the low light, she fumbles, muttering under her breath. She hoists Laila further up on her shoulder, then remembers the bassinet and change bag and turns back to get them.

Tita is there. She hooks the bassinet's handle over her wrist and hangs the bag over Lou's shoulder. She smells of cloves and anti-septic cream. It's pungent in the thick humidity but it's comforting. All at once, Lou doesn't want to leave. She wants to stay and be cared for by this woman, here in the warmth of her cabin.

'Rain,' Tita says philosophically as they consider the down-pour between the hut and the shelter of the bar. She pats Laila on the hip. 'Must run.'

From out of nowhere, Lou hears Adam's voice and it stops her dead.

*It's just motherhood, Lou, not rocket science.*

Lou doesn't answer. She grips her baby to her chest, tugs the bag more securely on to her shoulder and does as the woman says. She sprints fast across the clearing, the bassinet handle cutting into her wrist, hard rain like needles dashing into her face.

# 25

## ELIZA

'This rain is crazy.'

She peers in between the slats of the blinds battened down against the storm, almost having to shout to make herself heard. Rainwater mists her face through the gaps. The force of the wind is like nothing she has ever experienced. It body-slams the bar and restaurant, a violent intruder on the attack.

The emergency generator has kicked in but its power is low and extra hurricane lamps have been lit, licking tongues of light across the bar. The air is filled with salt and damp. As night fell, the search was suspended. They returned to the resort, soaking wet and dog-tired, grabbing bowls of rice and beans from earthenware vats set out by the kitchen staff.

Lars pours shots of dark rum for Eliza and Noah. In the shadows of the back pantry lurks Zikri.

'You two are inseparable,' Noah says, tipping his glass in Zikri's direction. Eliza frowns, hearing his words steeped in booze. She hasn't spoken to him since Lars's announcement earlier that the monsoon was coming. Has Noah continued drinking since then?

By unspoken agreement, Lou had not joined in the search. As the heavens had washed through the resort, and the palm trees on the beach flattened under the gale, Lou had stayed with the children. She seemed suspended underwater, as if she couldn't hear properly. Her pupils were pinpricks, tiny dots, Eliza had noticed. How much of this medication was she taking? An hour ago, she had made Lou drink a pint of water and go to bed, all the children piled on top of her like something out of Roald Dahl.

The wheels are falling off, Eliza thinks, turning her glass round slowly in a circle. Adam's disappearance has destabilised them and they're toppling, crumbling separately, when they should be holding each other up as a team.

Lars laughs lightly. 'Oh, Zikri is my right-hand man. He's been here since my old man started this place.'

'When was that?' Eliza forces herself to ask. They have to maintain some semblance of normality, even if the reality is that their friend could be lost at sea, or injured, or dead; that this man they are speaking to may very well be involved; that they are barely speaking between themselves; and all of them are utterly exhausted by stress.

She keeps talking, giving careful, brittle smiles to Lars, but she feels her pulse quick and anxious. A cold, clammy sweat covers her skin as if she's keeping a fever at bay with every hour that Adam isn't found. Her brain seems incapable of forming a single coherent thought. Adam going missing has so many consequences. It's like the childhood game, except she can't work out what any of the endings actually mean.

For any of them.

Still, what can they do? They are stuck. They have to wait out the storm, wait until the seas calm and the police can reach them from the mainland. But even then, she's nervous. The idea of foreign policemen frightens her. How can she trust the process here? How does she know that things won't get misinterpreted?

She still can't understand what had happened down on the beach after she went to bed. Were they fighting about her? Had Noah accused Adam of something? Or was it to do with Zoe? Did Noah know about her, that Adam had gone off with her? They have to talk to each other properly. But he's doing what he always does when the shit hits the fan, and diving into the bottom of a bottle.

She keeps nodding at Lars, forcing herself to concentrate.

'Dad was a dive freak. I grew up here with my sister, Helle. Mum home-schooled us.' Lars shrugs. 'He was an adventurer. He built that,' he waves a hand at the dive shack. 'That was our house for a long time. Then...' he swigs rum, glancing upwards

141

as thunder pounds the sky '... five years after we came here, he was killed on a dive.'

Eliza looks up sharply.

He smiles at her. 'Yeah well. Even in paradise, shit happens. I was ten. Helle was twelve. Mum was... she became like a warrior. She changed everything. Turned our little idyll into a business. From ecstasy to e-commerce, right?' He gives a short laugh and holds his hands up. 'Although the Wi-Fi is non-existent, I will accept that. But, you know,' he says without irony, 'we only want the best for our guests, that's all.'

'Where's your mum now?'

'On the mainland. She comes over every so often.'

'And your sister?'

'She's in New York. Helle escaped as fast as she could. Went to college in the US. Now she trains F&B staff for a massive hotel chain. She got lucky. Got the golden ticket out of here.' Lars doles out more rum. 'Mum didn't want this place run by another girl. It had been too hard for her. It's a more male environment, you know?'

Eliza studies him as he pours the drinks, looks at his strong forearms, blond hairs turning amber in the muted light of the lamps. He sounds bitter, she thinks. Even angry.

'Did you want to stay here forever?' she asks. 'Keep it running for your mum?'

He leans on to the bar with his elbows and presses his glass up to his cheek. 'Did I? Do I? It's a question but... who knows? We don't know, do we? What the future has in store for us?'

He holds her gaze and it's so intense that, after a minute, she has to look away. She sips at the rum, feels it burn her throat and settle hot into her stomach. 'Yeah, agreed.'

She glances at Noah, staring with glazed eyes into the middle distance, and puts her hand on his shoulder, digs in her fingers to rouse him. He twitches in response as the blinds shake, as he comes back to the present.

'Can Adam really be alive out there?'

Lars turns to him. 'It's not impossible. I've known people survive worse things. Adam's a tough guy. If he can find shelter, get out of the wet and the rain and he hasn't been hurt. He can go this long without food, that's not an issue.'

'But water. He'd need fresh water.'

'There are many natural springs all across the island.'

Eliza hears the power of the rain outside, thinks about the sea tossing their little kayak around in the waves. 'But in the ocean in this storm? It's been so long. Too long without water, without medical assistance.'

'We have to be positive, guys. What else can we do?'

A shotgun explodes deep within the forest.

'Jesus.' Noah jerks back. The lamps flicker in and out, sweeping their light up to the atap roof, down to the deck dusted with sand.

'It's just thunder, Noah,' Lars says.

Eliza shakes her head and briefly shuts her eyes. She puts her hand over her glass as Lars goes to pour more rum. 'No. Not for me. I'm going to make a run for it and check on Lou and the kids.'

'She'll be sparko,' Noah says. 'She took a sleeping tablet, didn't she?'

'Did she? I didn't know that.' Eliza hops down from her stool, suddenly uneasy for Lou – and for the children. Sleeping tablets on top of everything else? 'All the more reason to check on the kids, then.'

There's a momentary lull in the hammering of the rain on the roof and the sound of a shout from outside. Zikri disappears from his post in the shadows. Lars pushes himself up from the bar and goes out, his movement easy as a cat's.

There are raised voices, whether in anger or because of the storm, Eliza can't tell. It's impossible to hear over the resumed clatter of the rain.

'Staff problems?' Noah suggests, his question a little slurred.

'Please, no more, babe,' Eliza says, moving his glass away.

Lars is back behind the bar. It's eerie, she thinks. The way he magically materialises; his long, muscular frame, his sleek blond hair.

There's movement behind her and she starts, whipping round as heavy footsteps thud into the bar.

He walks in as if he were Indiana Jones himself, water dripping from the brim of his brown hat, his khaki shirt sodden from the rain. Eliza thinks she recognises him. Hadn't he been drinking here last night? The night that Adam went missing, in fact. That actually now feels like a week ago, or some kind of mirage before hard reality kicked in.

The man wipes his face and casts a quick look at Lars before coming over, palm outstretched.

'Harry Wells,' he says. 'I work over at Timba.' He nods in its vague direction. 'Over at the turtle sanctuary. Did you tell them?' he directs to Lars.

'These are guests. It doesn't concern them—'

'Tell us what?' Eliza interrupts.

'One of the men that works there,' Harry says, 'he's gone missing, can't be found. We've tried everywhere, been over to the kampong—'

'The kampong?' Eliza asks.

'The local village. It's about a kilometre away on the other side of the island. Che – that's the guy – he walks across to us like clockwork every day. Gets to the sanctuary by midday. Except today he didn't show up.' Harry rubs a thumb over his mouth. 'It's out of character, first. Now, with the weather kicking up a stink, I like it even less.' He takes off his hat and drops it on to the bar.

'Someone else has gone missing?' Eliza says, turning first to Noah and then Lars. 'What's going on? Our friend Adam went out on our kayak early this morning,' Eliza tells Harry. 'He hasn't been seen since.'

'I know,' he says. 'That's why I'm here. Wanted to come and check. See if they're connected.'

'They're not—' Lars says.

'Have you called the police?' Eliza cuts in. 'Lars says the police can't come. They can't dock or moor or whatever... on the island in this weather.' She stops. 'It *must* be related, mustn't it? The fact that both these men have disappeared?'

'You're jumping several guns here. Let's calm down and take things one at a time. Come on,' Lars argues. 'Adam went off in the kayak. He never even met Che, who's a local man and probably gone off with his mates for a bit of a party. OK? It's not unheard of for people to skive off work, Harry.'

'He's never skived before,' Harry says to Lars. 'And I've told you, he's not in the kampong.'

'Maybe they're not telling you, buddy. You're not exactly popular over there.' Lars lights a cigarette, lifting his eyebrows.

'It's not relevant.'

'Isn't it?' Lars blows a plume of smoke at the ceiling. 'A lot of people would disagree.'

Harry frowns. 'You're saying Che going AWOL is to do with the problem the kampong has with the turtle sanctuary?' He looks up. 'Is Zikri here?'

The barman emerges into the dim light from the room behind the bar.

'Have you heard anything about this? Has something happened over at the kampong that involved Che or the sanctuary?'

Zikri shrugs and shakes his head.

'What are you talking about?' Eliza asks. 'What has any of this got to do with Adam? Did anyone look for him at this kampong place today? Noah,' she prods him in the back of the neck, 'are you listening to this?'

Noah clears his throat and shifts on his stool. 'Sounds like they're separate issues,' he says with a frown. 'I don't know.'

'Adam wasn't at the kampong,' Lars says. 'Have you tried calling Che?'

'Yes, of course,' Harry answers as if Lars is stupid. 'He doesn't pick up.'

'There's no mobile phone signal anyway,' Eliza says.

'There is at Timba,' Harry explains. 'We need it to send our data. We have a different set-up from here. The point is... I know Che wouldn't just go off. He can't afford to lose this job.'

'Have you got power over there?' Lars asks.

Harry shakes his head. 'Even the emergency gen's down.'

Eliza shivers.

They are in the middle of nowhere. Surrounded by thick, dense jungle and overlooked by a volcano. Her chest tightens. She's watching Harry and Lars talk. Their mouths are moving, busy with rapid speech, but she can't hear them. Noah's face comes in close to hers and then shrinks to a pinhead every few seconds. The blinds slam on the wooden joists, the lamplight throws shadows on the walls. She can feel the forest outside moving in closer and closer, its tendrils creeping over wet sand, in amongst the mud crabs, the sharp elbows of the lightning splitting the sky, the moths rising out of the lamp, blackened and shrivelled by the flame...

And then the lights go out.

# 26

## LOU

*Monday*

She's in the water and she can't move.

Waves wash over her head and she gulps in sea. She tries to lift her hands to the surface, to drag herself upwards and out of the water so she can breathe, but they won't work. They float alongside her like bloodless cut-offs from a cadaver.

She is drowning.

Then she sees Adam. He's standing on the shore in his cobalt-blue board shorts, his Oakley sunglasses reflecting the glare. He waves at her, beckons her in. He's smiling, calling to her, but she can't answer. There's so much water. It's filling her lungs and she tries to yell and beg him to rescue her. She's drowning. But he doesn't hear her, or he doesn't understand, and she's getting tired, so tired.

She starts to sink, her lips parted on his name.

And the water keeps on coming.

She wakes covered in sweat. She flings her hand to the other side of the bed but meets only the travel cot.

No Adam.

She sits up, pushing her hair out of her face, looking down at Laila who is awake but smiling, moving her hands in and out of the early sunlight dappling through the shutters. She puts the baby to her breast. Next door, she can hear the other children murmuring to each other as they play on their iPads.

She feels spacey. Looking at Laila suckle, it occurs to her she shouldn't be feeding her on the sleeping tablet she took last night.

But surely it's gone through her system by now? She looks over at the bedside table, at the foil strip of tranquillisers. She can't remember how many she took yesterday. No more than three, she thinks. That's the maximum dose. And anyway, these are exceptional circumstances.

Her head pounds. She has that empty, absent feeling she gets when she goes too long without coffee. She leans back and closes her eyes. After a minute, she opens them and looks again at the foil packet. She can take one this morning. And then one in the afternoon. That's only two. Less than the doctor recommended.

She swallows the tablet and, after she's finished feeding Laila, climbs out of bed and goes to see the children who had begun the night starfished on her bed in a tangle of hot, sweaty limbs. They'd pretended it was because they wanted a 'sleepover', but Lou knows it was really because they wanted to be with Raffy, sensing the sadness in their friend at the absence of his father.

At some point in the night, they must have traipsed through to Raffy's room to try and cool down on the top bunks under his fan.

'Raffy?' she says.

'I'm Sam,' says Sam.

'Oh, sorry,' she replies, peering into the room, gloomy with its still-closed shutters. 'You're wearing his top.'

Sam looks down at the bright orange T-shirt he's got on and shrugs.

'Where's Raffy?'

'I thought he was with you.'

'No. Did you hear him leave?'

Chloe's iPad makes a series of beeps. 'He's probably gone to breakfast already.'

'Yes,' Lou agrees, thinking of her independent son and his constant need for Frosties. She looks at his bunk and sees that Monkey is missing. Raffy must have taken him to the restaurant.

She needs a shower. She hasn't had one since Saturday. She checks that Laila is asleep before diving into the bathroom for a wash in record time. She throws her nightshirt to one side.

She has to change – she's been wearing it for about thirty-six hours, including her impromptu wade into the sea. She comes back into the bedroom and stops short.

There is Adam's holdall on the floor by the bed, his clothes spilling out of it, his boxers, his T-shirts. Next to the bed on the table is the bottle of water he had drunk from on Saturday.

*Saturday.*

A lifetime ago.

Lou drops on to the mattress, almost winded by the sight of these things. These items that are so *Adam*. It seems impossible that someone as alive as him, as forceful a person, could just disappear. Vanish into a puff of smoke.

Adam has been in her life since she was a teenager. Even though their relationship was going to morph into a different shape, she had never considered a life where he would be entirely *absent*. The idea that she might never be able to share moments about the children they had together with their father...

She grabs at the T-shirt he last slept in and brings it to her nose, inhales the familiar tang of his soap – Adam never wore after-shave, declaring it for pussies – and that smell that was uniquely him – whatever it was – his skin or his sweat or his DNA seeping out of him. Tears roar into her eyes and she buries her face in the shirt, sobbing into the material.

After a moment, she lifts her head and breathes in sharply. She drops the T-shirt on to the bed and gets up, wiping her face. She goes round to her side of the room and pulls on a pair of shorts and a T-shirt. She dresses and straps Laila into the papoose, hesitating for a moment before snapping another pill out of the packet and swallowing it down quickly.

'I'm just going to the restaurant,' she calls to the twins. 'Come with, if you're hungry.'

They follow behind her across the clearing, hopping bare-footed to dodge the pine cones. The sun is still low and the air is cool. There's no rain but the ground is boggy and the skies brood. Black clouds perch on the top of Fire Mountain.

Wanting to see her boy, Lou breaks into a near-jog to get to the restaurant. And she knows it's ridiculous, but she can't help imagining walking in there to see Adam at a table, coffee in hand, regaling everyone with the tale of his adventure.

He is not there.

And neither is Raffy.

She grabs at the waitress, Sara, as she passes holding a coffee pot.

'Have you seen my son?'

Sara stops and thinks for a moment. 'I'm not sure,' she says anxiously. 'Is he not with you? Maybe you'd better have a look in the kids' club?'

Lou turns to the twins but they're off before she can say anything. She goes to follow them, to check on Raffy. At the top of the steps leading back outside, Zikri finds her.

'Ah, ma'am Lou,' he says. 'How are you this morning? Can I get you anything?'

'Oh, I'm just going to see Raffy at the clubhouse. He's playing...' She trails off.

'Ma'am Lou?'

The world seems to roll on its side. She holds out a hand to steady herself but there is nothing there.

'Please,' Zikri says. 'Please sit down here.'

He pushes her gently into a chair and Sara brings her a glass of water. She drinks and her mind clears a little. Across the clearing, she can see the blond heads of Raffy and Chloe running away from her to the ladder that leads up to the treehouse.

'Thank you,' she says. 'I'm so sorry. Just felt a bit dizzy. Maybe the heat.'

'Let us take the baby, miss,' Zikri says, gesturing at the papoose. 'She is an oven on you.'

Lou giggles. 'Yes, she is. Good idea.' She unclasps the carrier and lifts Laila out, passing her to Sara. 'There you go, Bun in the Oven.' She starts laughing, holding her stomach. 'Ah. Huh. That's funny.'

Zikri looks down at her as Sara jiggles Laila.

'Sorry. Bit hysterical maybe,' Lou says with a tiny snort. 'Stress.' She gazes up at them and her cheeks turn pink. 'Sorry.'

Zikri waves a hand. 'No, no. Quite understandable.'

Sara takes Laila for a little walk around the restaurant and Zikri pours Lou a coffee. She finishes her water and tries to breathe, peering at the sea.

'The weather's calmer, isn't it? The rain's stopped. So the police can come today?'

Zikri shakes his head. 'Look further out, beyond the breakwater.'

He's right. The water is grey and angry, and spitting with foam. Even here, on the otherwise idyllic beach, small waves tug back and forth across the sand. On the horizon, Lou can just make out a swell that grows into heights a small boat would struggle to climb.

'The rain comes and goes,' Zikri shrugs. 'Monsoon is like this. The rain stays in the clouds, it moves in the sky. It's the wind that's the problem. Monsoon wind is very strong.'

'So not today.' Lou wraps her arms around herself.

Zikri puffs air through his lips. 'Maybe,' he says, but his face says otherwise.

Outside, a wind chime clangs.

'Be strong, madam. We will find him.'

Lou clears her throat as if shaking off her earlier moment of hysteria. 'Where is Lars? I need to know what happened last night. What the plan is for the search today… Is he out looking for Adam already?' Something passes over Zikri's face that she doesn't understand. 'What is it? Where is he?'

'Oh Lou, there you are!'

Eliza comes into the restaurant with Noah just behind her and heads straight over. 'How are you? I put my head round your door last night but it was so dark, I couldn't really see.'

'Yes, that tablet knocked me out,' Lou nods, still gazing at Zikri. 'But now… I feel foggy. I'm not sure… I must speak to Lars.' She turns to Eliza. 'Was he with you last night? Has anything happened? Is there any news?'

'Yes, Lars was here,' Eliza says, taking a seat. 'Where are the children? Oh thank you.'

Sara brings a bread basket and glasses of juice to the table.

Zikri gives a little bow and leaves them.

Lou looks at the breakfast and then across at the Fishers who are spreading napkins across their laps and helping themselves to croissants. 'Wait, why are we doing this? Having breakfast?' She pushes her coffee cup away so it clatters in the saucer. 'I don't want this. We need to be out there looking.' She stands up, her voice shrill. 'Sara, where's Laila? Can you bring me my baby?'

'Lou, it's OK.' Eliza reaches for her hand. 'We're going to start looking right away. It's only just light. It's barely seven a.m.'

'I'll bring baby, ma'am. She's right here,' Sara says, backing away. 'The children are at the kids' club,' she says to Eliza, casting a worried look at Lou.

'We have to eat, Lou,' Noah says. 'I'm literally just going to have this and then I'll be out again.'

'Thank you,' Eliza says as Laila is brought over to Lou. 'Don't worry, she's fine. Aren't you, Lou? Come on. Let me tell you what happened last night. Please.'

Lou lifts the baby to her shoulder and rubs her back as she begins to grizzle.

'They're just doing their jobs, you know? They don't know what else to do in a situation like this. They're only carrying on the routine.'

After a minute, Eliza continues. 'So last night. We stayed up when you went to bed. The storm got so bad that the power went out. The emergency generator crashed and we were in total darkness.

'But, hang on, I'm getting this the wrong way round. Sorry. Before that happened, someone came into the resort from the place around the headland. That Timba place? He's a marine biologist staying there studying the turtles or something. Anyway...'

Eliza stops uncomfortably and turns to Noah.

'Uh, well, he's going to help with the search,' he says. 'He's got students staying with him over there. Interns and volunteers. They're all going to pitch in and help. If we have more people looking, able to go into the mangroves and look further round the coastline, I'm sure we'll find him today, Lou. I really am.'

'Why did he come over here? Has he heard about Adam?'

Lou's eyes dart between the Fishers. She feels unaccountably paranoid. Noah's shoulders are so tense they are nearly up to his ears, and Eliza has a fixed expression on her face, a stern sort of stoicism.

'What's going on? What are you not telling me?'

'Nothing, nothing at all,' Eliza soothes. 'I'm downplaying it, but it was actually bloody terrifying last night when all the lights went out. The guy from Timba came over because they'd lost power. Then the emergency generator packed up here. The wind was rattling. It was all very Hitchcock, *Psycho*. Stranger turning up during the storm, you know… Honestly, that's all that happened. The lights went out and we felt our way back to the hut. I tried to check in on you and then we went to bed.'

'The main landline phone is also down,' Noah says. 'We tried it last night and I went over to the admin hut just now but there's nothing. And obviously we've got no signal on any mobiles. Harry – that's the biologist bloke – he reckons we'll get signal at Timba, though. We're going to head over there now to call the police again. See what the prognosis is on them getting here, when we can expect them and the coastguard. Getting a proper search organised.'

'I feel like you're shutting me out,' Lou says in a low voice fringed with tears. 'You're not telling me everything. Like, what really happened on the dive trip. Something could be important. Something that might affect Adam's chances…'

Eliza gets up and puts an arm around Lou. 'I know this is incredibly hard,' she says. 'But you *have* to try and keep calm. Keep strong. For Raffy, and Laila.'

She halts as Harry stomps into the restaurant and comes over, giving Noah a grim nod.

'Ready?'

'Yep. I'll just grab some water.'

'Harry, this is Lou,' Eliza says. 'Adam's wife.'

She looks up and her cheeks flame. It's the man from the bar the night that Adam went missing. The man who smiled at her. She feels another inexplicable urge to giggle. What's happening to her? God, she's losing control. She has to rein this in.

Harry holds out his hand and Lou shakes it.

'Do you think he's dead?' she asks him without thinking. She can't help it as more hysteria bubbles up inside her and she laughs again.

Harry glances at Eliza, who bites her lip.

'I'm not *mad*, you know,' Lou snaps, noticing the exchange. 'You don't need to look at each other as if I'm *mad*. It's entirely possible that Adam is dead. I just wish someone would be honest with me.'

They look at her but say nothing. Why is no one talking? The silence feels deafening, with only the sound of those bloody wind chimes rattling inside her skull.

She scratches at the inside of her arm. Eliza's giving looks to this Harry, her skin stretched tight across her face. What do they know? What aren't they saying?

The pills aren't working as well. The beating of the devils' wings has started overhead again. They're getting louder so it's hard for her to hear.

When will they leave her alone?

'Oh what's the point?' Lou says. Laila hiccups a small cry and she glances down, loosens her grip on the baby's back. 'None of you are going to tell me the truth.'

'What do you mean? What truth?' Eliza asks. 'We're not hiding anything from you.'

Lou stares at her and then over at Noah. And something clicks round; a cog of mistrust.

'I don't believe you,' she says. 'I need to sort this out myself. Something's going on. Where is Lars, for a start?'

Eliza looks at her nonplussed. 'I... genuinely don't know. I thought he'd be here for breakfast. Isn't he here?'

'No. He isn't. So I'm going to have to find him. I told you what Adam said. About Lars being involved in something bad. I didn't believe him then, but now... Well, now I need some honest answers.'

'Lou,' Noah interrupts. 'I think you're making more of this than you need—'

'Oh, do you? Making more of the fact that my husband has vanished and no one's really looking for him?'

'We are, Lou. Please.' Eliza is on the verge of tears.

'Stop.' Lou hoists Laila further on to her shoulder and holds up a hand. 'Raffy is in the kids' club with Julie. I'm going to give Laila to Tita. And then I'm going to go out and find Adam myself.'

# 27

## NOAH

It's over an hour's hard hike to Timba.

Noah follows Harry through the thick of the jungle, up and then over the foothills of Fire Mountain. As they go higher, Noah can see glimpses of the turquoise of the sea below, hear the wash of the tide against the volcanic contours of the land. It's been over twenty-four hours since Adam took the kayak. If he beached it somewhere below where they're walking, could he have hauled himself up the side of the island? If he was injured, could he have found help from someone?

The sun is hot. He can feel sweat pooling in his armpits, the bottom of his back. The storm of the night before – the monsoon coming in that Lars described – it all seems a fabrication. It doesn't make any sense.

'Weather seems OK now,' he calls up to Harry.

'It's changeable. A patch of sun doesn't mean the storm has blown itself out.'

'Maybe Adam found shelter over here last night. You haven't heard from Lars this morning?'

Harry shakes his head as they begin to descend to Timba. 'Haven't heard anything,' he says.

'So this is where you watch for the turtles, is it?' Noah asks, adjusting his cap to the glare of the sunlight.

'We monitor them, yes. They nest along the beach and, when they do, we remove the eggs and hatch them. Then we release the babies into the sea.'

'Why don't you just leave them?'

'They get eaten. Monitor lizards. Other animals. People steal them.'

'What do they steal them for?'

'They're considered a delicacy. An aphrodisiac. It's a tradition going back centuries.'

'So what's the issue with the locals, then? What you talked about last night,' Noah asks, his pace increasing as the downward slope steepens right before it flattens on to the beach. 'The locals are hating you cos they need the eggs to get randy with their wives?'

Harry turns back to him and rolls his eyes.

'Sorry,' Noah apologises. 'I'm being a dick.'

The Timba beach is pristine with pure white sand and completely empty of people.

As they jog down on to it, the land curves back from the beach into a sheltered clearing behind the dunes. They carry on a little way up and then down again, into a natural bowl where several thatched wooden huts have been erected in a round. Further up the hill is a modern-looking building with a satellite dish on an exterior wall, and a generator in a purpose-built shelter outside.

'It's hard to change people's minds when they don't see anything wrong in what they're doing. *And* when it can make them money at a time when they have very little,' Harry says. 'Monsoon season's tough for the Orang Laut. Fishing's impossible for tiny boats like theirs in rough seas, big waves. Plus, stocks are getting massively overfished by big corporates. So they look for other means of survival. Selling the eggs makes them pennies. Less than pennies. But that's better than nothing, right? He shrugs. 'Some locals – like Che – agree with us. They want to improve things. The old guard, though...

'Truth is, the turtles are dying out. So we're trying to teach sustainability. Tourists will come and watch the hatching. They can help in the process. And money from tourism will be a damn sight more than any ringgit earned from a market trader.'

Noah wipes at the perspiration at his temples, along his upper lip.

'You must all know each other quite well. On Pulau Kalah, I mean? It's so small.'

Harry nods. 'I s'pose. The younger kids go over to the bar at Turtle Cove every so often. It's still a trek, though, even though the island's not big. Not that much fun to do this in the dark, trust me.'

'There's a road across the island, though?' Noah asks, pointing at several mopeds and a red jeep parked under the trees.

'Yeah, yeah, there is. It follows the coast round to the other side but it's pretty shitty. It's quicker to cut across on foot. That's what our local guys do. They walk over from the kampong like Che did. During the monsoon, you can only get on and off the island on that side. The jetty there means the boats can moor out beyond the reef.'

Harry walks past a fire pit, underneath some hanging washing, giving a wave to a young Malay boy. It's bizarre, Noah thinks, that this little community exists less than an hour's walk away from where, in Turtle Cove, they swan around drinking cocktails and reading Jack Reacher novels. It's like walking out of a film set, past the crew and the lighting rigs and the scene flats, and back into reality.

They head to the modern-looking building that they call the bunkhouse but which, Harry explains, is actually the research centre. Inside, it's chilly from an air conditioner that hums above the door. Noah shudders, gazing round as the interior is inherently creepy. An ultraviolet light shines from two interior windows at the back of the room which he assumes must be the hatcheries, imagining reptilian legs cracking through giant eggs, poking bloody heads out of shells with half-closed and sleepy, ancient eyes.

'Here again, Zoe? Did you come over with Lars?'

Harry appears to be addressing an empty room but then a blonde girl emerges from behind a computer.

'Oh hi, Harry. No, I drove over myself. I haven't seen Lars all morning. I should get back, actually. Just wanted to see what was happening over here with the search.'

Noah stares at the girl, trying to remember where he's seen her before.

'Zoe, this is Noah.' Harry waves a hand between the two of them as an introduction. 'Just wait here a sec, OK? I'll go and find Simon. He's the main volunteer coordinator. He can get them organised into search groups. We can start back down at the beach and head inland.'

Noah nods impatiently.

Zoe paces the length of the room, staring at her iPhone.

'Oh of course. You have signal here, don't you?' Noah asks, taking off his backpack.

'Uh-uh,' the girl replies without looking up.

With the lack of Wi-Fi at the resort, Noah had switched his phone off to save battery. Turning it on, it bleeps loudly, as over a hundred emails crowd into his inbox and endless WhatsApp messages arrive.

For the first time in his life, he ignores all of them. He just sends Eliza a quick text to say he's OK but he has no news as yet. He has no idea whether she'll be able to receive it but at least he's tried.

'Do you have the number for the police?'

Zoe freezes, whipping up her head and fixing her gaze on him like a startled rabbit. 'What?'

'The number for the police? Or the coastguard? Could we search for it on your computer? I need to get hold of them urgently. Our friend is missing.'

She doesn't reply, her mouth a little open as if words have got stuck in her throat.

'Yes,' he explains. 'A friend of ours has gone missing. Adam. He went out on the kayak . . .'

Noah frowns. When was it? Time seems to have transformed into something impossible to pin down. The dive on Saturday feels like it happened only hours ago but, at the same time, a world with Adam in it seems unbelievably far away, as if he's actually been gone for years.

' . . . very late Saturday night. More like Sunday morning. What day is it now?'

'It's Monday.' Zoe swallows. 'Uh, you do know the emergency services run a skeleton service on Monday?'

'What?'

'Uh-huh.' She rubs a freckled nose with her palm. 'It's a religious thing.'

'Is that a joke?'

'No.' She looks surprised. 'Not at all.'

He clicks his tongue against the roof of his mouth, considering her. 'Maybe we just wait for Harry,' he says at last. Outside, the skies have opened. It sounds as if bullets are hitting the corrugated roof. 'Actually, I think I'll go and find him.'

'Oh, OK,' Zoe says, sliding her phone into the back pocket of her shorts. 'I'll come too. I'm starving.'

Noah bites down his intense irritation and goes to the door. Already the rain is transforming the brown earth into rivers of mud. Peering out, he is hit by a nauseating smell and recoils involuntarily, covering his nose with his hand.

Harry is on his way up the hill, uselessly trying to wipe his face free of the rain that tumbles from the sky. He's with – presumably – Simon, a gangly boy-man wearing a Homer Simpson T-shirt. Even without the British accent, Noah would have guessed his nationality from his lobster-red sunburn.

Noah re-enters the bunkhouse and they follow, standing by the open door, their clothes wet through and clearly mid-conversation.

'No sign of Lars,' Harry mutters to Noah.

'What's that smell? Has the wind changed?' Noah asks him. 'Why have I only just noticed it?'

Harry nods but ignores the question, clearly distracted, as Simon carries on.

'Harry, that's what I'm trying to tell you. There was a ruckus in the kampong in the early hours of Sunday morning. An argument between the families. They said Lars Van Graan was there.'

As Noah hears this, his uneasiness intensifies.

What is this place, where they've come? It had seemed so idyllic when the Carters had suggested it. An island paradise so close to the buzzing city life of Singapore. Within the hour, they were driving through endless kilometres of palm plantations, through thatched villages, zipping past kids playing on the side of dirt roads. Watching it all from the comfort of their air-conditioned Hyundai seven-seaters.

But that luxury and security is fracturing with every moment.

This island seems less a paradise than a place of tension and conflict.

The locals are clashing.

Two men have disappeared.

And where is the reassuring presence of Lars? He's a sort of bridge between the two cultures – a halfway man. Not entirely local, although he's trusted by them. But not a complete expat either.

Lars understands the locals, and he understands the tourists.

But he isn't here, at Timba, as they'd thought. Where has he gone?

'You were there too, apparently, Zoe?' Simon's question breaks into Noah's thoughts.

Zoe looks up from her phone. 'Huh?'

'Over at the kampong,' Simon repeats. 'You were there with Lars early Sunday morning.'

'Nope,' Zoe says lightly. 'Negative. Sunday, I was working all day. I was looking for your friend, actually,' she says to Noah. 'Driving round the island off-road, seeing if I could spot him in the bush.'

Harry scratches at his chin and goes to the open door, considering what they can see of their surroundings in the downpour as water spatters off the rim of his hat. 'You're right. What is that stink?' He scowls into the distance for a minute. 'Can you come with me please, Simon?' he says before striding off towards the rainforest boundary.

'Where are you going?' Noah asks, jogging to catch up with him as Simon brings up the rear.

'To the septic tank. We have one for sewage. It's upland, for obvious reasons.'

'What do you think the smell is? It's rank.'

Harry gives a grim shake of the head but doesn't answer.

The intensity of the odour increases as they go further into the rainforest. The rain has stopped. It's quiet but for the drips that fall from the leaves, the occasional rustle, the beep of a bird, the sound of their feet scuffing the earth.

After an indeterminate time walking through soaking-wet foliage, they reach a glade where, under balloons of mosquito clouds, is a large white tank with two red metal wheel valves on its lid. Harry goes immediately to one and in silent agreement Noah and Simon take the other. They spin them slowly, cranking them round until they loosen and turn easily. Nobody speaks, but it's clear from Harry's expression that the possibility of them finding Che here is real and very concerning.

'On three,' Harry says, once the valves are open. They lift the lid, setting it down on the ground before hurriedly pulling their shirts up over their noses and mouths.

The stench is almost visceral. Noah gags. The smell isn't just of turds and piss and all the fluids that come from animal disintegration, but something sickly sweet. A fermented, eggy stink that seeps into his very pores. It's pungent and it's disgusting but it's more than that. Whatever the gases and vapours are that are rising up from inside that tank, they're filled with something *mournful*.

At that moment, Noah feels a part of him shut down. It closes off and puts this memory somewhere hidden, to be dealt with later. Right then, he has to pretend that he's fine with this, that he can handle it. Because the thought has suddenly and horrifically occurred to him that the body in the tank – for that smell can only possibly be coming from a dead body – might not be the body of the local man, Che.

That the body might, in fact, belong to Adam.

# 28

## LOU

Sod the lot of them, Lou thinks, slamming one foot in front of the other.

She ignores the hammering of her heart and her lungs screaming for lack of air as the path wends steeper and steeper uphill. Fat leaves bow down above her, pregnant with the weight of rainwater. More than once, she is splatted in the face by a deluge as a leaf snaps clean from a branch due to its watery load.

On she goes. She just has to follow the path. She'd heard Lars talking about it the other day. The route leads uphill, right through the jungle, up one side of the foothills of Fire Mountain, and straight down again, into Timba. She'll get there and make enquiries herself. She'll see the beach and try and work out if Adam had kayaked around the headland. Yes sure, Lars had told her they'd searched there yesterday. But she doesn't trust Lars any more. Where the hell is he anyway? She has to find out what's been going on in this place. Because something bad has happened, that much is clear.

As she treks on, she runs over it all again. Standing on the veranda. Adam, drunk and belligerent. Her cheeks flash with heat remembering what she'd done. How she'd let him go. Why had she let him go? She shakes her head, beating herself up. Stupid, *stupid*. It's a bad dream made real.

She'd known when she married Adam that he would be disloyal. She'd weighed it up and decided, though, that the fun of him, the energy and wide-eyed enthusiasm he had for life, would counter it. His philandering was part of that, somehow. He couldn't say no to things, to new experiences, to new people.

She laughs now at her naivety. How all of her thoughts and considerations had been about *him*. Never about her, and what *she* might need. And so, was it his fault? That he took more than she actually wanted to give? When she hadn't set any limits? Not until last year, when she'd finally realised that she was enough. Even on her own. That she had the strength to leave him.

But life is cruel, isn't it? And when Laila was born, she lost that sense of herself. She's been floundering as if she's untethered, spinning into space. That feeling – as if devils are surrounding her, beating their wings – it's defeated her for all this time, weakened her. But for some reason – here in this dense jungle – she can feel that sense returning. It's alert and alive again, coiling inside her, calling her name and telling her to act.

She isn't going to take the Valium any more. It's killing her, dulling her senses, fogging her brain. The doctor had told her she only needed it for a little while. Just to tide her over the first few months of Laila's life. But what did that even mean? She scoffs in the direction of her audience of brush and vegetation as she walks. What does she need to *tide over*?

She is a mother and she has to care for her daughter. That's it. She has to care for her family. She has to put them first. Over and above everything else. Raffy and Laila have to come first. Why hasn't she realised this before?

The pills have been drowning her natural motherly instincts in a wash of chemicals. She needs to be clean. Needs to get rid of all these drugs and compounds and whatever else it is that she's pumped into her system. She can see it now. Around her, everything suddenly seems so clear, so *alive*. The colours in the forest are suddenly so vivid. Bright emerald greens; ochres; maroons and charcoals.

She stops.

At her feet, the ground is a rich, red colour. The path she followed out of the resort was dull and brown and mulched with leaves. Around her, the vegetation has become dense. It feels too close, as if it reaches for her with its fingers.

She has strayed.

She is in thick bush. She takes in her surroundings, breathing hard. A black and yellow myna bird hops along a branch at her eye level. Its own eye is beady and considers her intently. Then the bird flits, off and gone from the branch, giving a piercing whistle as it goes.

Lou snaps round, trying to assess her position, work out the way she's come, how to retrace her steps. But it's as if the jungle has opened up to invite her in, and then closed the gap behind her. The brush around her is impenetrable.

She begins to panic. She has no phone. She has no water. She feels her pocket for the reassuring shape of her inhaler. It's there, thank God. She swallows. *OK. Stay calm.* This is an island. She is surrounded by water. She has been trekking uphill for all this time. So then, if she heads down, she will reach the coastline. Once she's at sea level, all she needs to do is follow the coast around to either Turtle Cove or Timba.

She steps forward. The heat feels like a wall she has to push through. Far away, thunder cracks, but it's claustrophobic down in the jungle. Ridged ropes of vine twist and block her way. Instinctively, she moves in the direction she thinks is towards the sea. She pulls back a knot of branches.

Immediately she freezes.

Hanging off a branch less than a metre ahead of her is a writhing slash of neon green. It's a whip snake. She's seen one at Singapore Zoo. It's so close, she can see the white dots speckled on its back; the deep black of its eyes, and its tongue, darting and flickering in the air towards her. She inches backward as it bends and waves, its muscles taut with tension as it curls outwards from the branch in a gravity-defying gymnastics display.

For a long moment, the snake seems to sniff the air in front of her face and hover there, its eyes holding her in its sights. It is beautiful, she thinks, and her heart rate steadies. She can't tear her gaze away as it weaves up and down her chest, smelling her, taking her in, reading her. She breathes in the silence of the forest, her feet planted on the earth, hands by her side, feeling the humidity swirl between her and the snake, spiralling its heat from one to the other.

Like a flash, she ducks and she's running, scrabbling through the undergrowth, tripping, sliding, down, down. She spies a scrap of blue through the trees. And thunder rips the sky again.

As she descends, the rain sweeps down the mountain like an avalanche, flattening the treetops horizontal, propelling her forward.

Down, down, she goes. The jungle is helping her. She feels it in her bones. It's carrying her downwards, scooping her over the gnarled branches and twisted roots.

And then she's at the beach. At the top end, away from the restaurant and the bar, but she can see the resort buildings through the sheeting rain. She runs along the waterline towards the lights and the sound of the music in the bar.

She has to find Raffy and get Laila from Tita. Whatever happens from now on, they mustn't be separated.

She will never be separated from her family again.

# 29

## ELIZA

Glancing up, she moves Mrs Peacock into the study.

Lou shivers in a chair next to their table. The waitress, Sara, had rushed to fetch blankets and towels as soon as Lou had burst into the bar. She was drowned, utterly sodden, sucking at her inhaler: her eyes fixed on some point on the horizon.

The rain was coming down too hard to take her back to her hut so they'd gathered her inside and wrapped her up with a mug of hot tea and now she sits, rocking Laila's baby seat with a listless hand, staring out at the waves pounding the beach.

Nobody cares now that children are in the bar. Eliza is playing Cluedo with Chloe while Sam and Raffy remain at the kids' club with Julie. The winds whip through the blinds as time ticks on. Eliza hasn't heard from Noah since this morning. She doesn't know when he'll be back or what he's discovered, if anything. The skies are dark with storm and rain. She feels skittish, at bay. Her fingers tremble as she rolls the dice.

'Mummy? Look.' Chloe tugs at her arm. 'I've got the candlestick, see?'

Eliza flinches, bringing herself back to the bar. 'Oh yes, so you do. OK then. Your roll.'

Chloe throws the dice and Eliza sips at her Diet Coke.

'Did you know that I was going to leave Adam?'

Lou has sat straight up in her chair like a corpse banging out of a coffin. She stares at Eliza, her expression grim.

'Were you? But...'

'He'd had so many affairs in Singapore, I think he'd probably been around the island twice without even realising.'

Chloe's hand hovers in the air, her Colonel Mustard counter dangling in her fingers.

'Did he ever try anything on with you?'

'How about a hot chocolate, Chlo?' Eliza says brightly. 'Why don't you pop to the restaurant and see if you can find Sara and ask?'

'OK,' Chloe says uncertainly. 'Shall I get one for Sam and Raffy?'

'Sure, why not?' Eliza watches Chloe trot off, biting down on a knuckle. It leaves the imprint of a half-moon, a sheen of her saliva. She wipes it away. 'You can't mean that, Lou. It's an awful thing to say.'

'Did he?' Lou persists, her hands clasped over her knees, eyes fixed forward on Eliza.

'No. Of course not. And even if he did, I would never… Anyway,' Eliza shakes her head back, frustrated, 'he didn't. You're my *friend*. I would never hurt you like that. I swear.'

'There was *something* between you, though, wasn't there? I could sense it. A closeness or something. You… you were *weird* with him. Like, you had all these feelings…' Lou revolves a hand in front of her stomach to demonstrate what she means '… all these *emotions* coming out of you, and you didn't know what to do with them. Like,' she pulls a strand of her hair and twists it round, confused, 'you didn't know whether you loved him or hated him.'

Eliza feels her pulse thump heavy in her throat. She can't speak.

'I'm right, aren't I?' Lou hitches her chair closer. 'Aren't I? What was it? I mean, look. I know Adam was an arse. Jesus – *is* an arse.' She halts and takes a breath. 'People *do* either love him or hate him. He provokes things. Sticks his fingers into wasps' nests. He likes causing trouble, I know he does. But with you… what was it? It was different with you.'

Still, Eliza says nothing. She can't even deny it. Everything seems to be unravelling within her, and she can't find the start of the words. Doesn't know how to explain it. Find the beginning of the piece of thread.

'If he's dead, it doesn't matter any more, does it?' Lou reaches for Eliza, lets her fingers rest on her arm. 'But if he's alive, I have to know. I have to know what happened that night on the beach.'

'Oh God, *nothing* happened!' Eliza manages to blurt. Then she inhales deeply. 'Nothing happened. I went to bed. Adam and Noah… I don't know. They had a barney or something. Noah says that was all it was. Adam came to the bar and then he left. Went to *your* cabin. You obviously had a fight. The door,' Eliza bends her head, forcing Lou to meet her gaze, 'the door was smashed and broken. Adam didn't walk into it by mistake, did he? You'd had a big fight, hadn't you?'

She tries to quell her breathing. She knows this is cruel but Lou can't be allowed to shift the focus on to her and Noah. They're all in this together. She's not going to let Noah take the blame. And, God help her, neither will she.

'You had a fight, and that's when Adam took the kayak. So what did you fight about?' She passes a hand over her face. 'I don't blame you, really I don't. Adam has been a shit husband and a shit father. I've seen it on this holiday. More than I ever have before back at home in Singapore.

'I've wanted to help you. I know you've been struggling. With a lack of sleep. With the baby. Taking those pills—'

'Enough.' Lou holds up a hand. She sits for a moment just breathing, her eyes closed. 'Yes, it's true. About us fighting. Adam was out of control.' She lets out a painful laugh. 'I hit him. He hit the door.' She shrugs. 'Not our finest moment.'

Eliza bites her lip. 'Were you fighting about me?'

Lou looks at her for a beat. 'Yes, you. And every woman like you. Every woman Adam's flirted with or made a pass at, or kissed or fucked when he thought I didn't know. Like I'm an idiot. Really?' Lou arches an eyebrow. 'All my money is my own. For most of our marriage, Adam has depended on me financially. And yet, he seems to think I'm a complete fool. Thinks he's the alpha male beating his chest.'

A swell of nausea curls into Eliza's throat. Hot, rough bile that makes her cough. She reaches for some water and the sensation passes. They sit silently under the whirring fan that sends gentle pulses of warm air across their skin.

'You said… you were going to leave him? With Laila so little?' Eliza asks, after a while.

'I'm stronger than his own mother,' Lou nods. 'She stayed with Benjamin until his death. And for what? Neither of them were happy. What did they do it for? Duty? Fear? I don't want to live like that—'

'Mummy?'

Sam and Chloe stand at the entrance of the bar, both wet from the rain, hair stuck to their foreheads.

'Hi darling.' Eliza paints a smile on her face as she turns to them. 'Have you come to get the hot chocolates?'

'Where's Raffy?' Lou asks. 'Is he coming over too?'

Sam looks confused. 'Raffy's here, isn't he?'

Lou pushes the blanket off her lap. 'Raffy's been in the kids' club with you and Julie. Hasn't he?'

Sam flashes a look at Eliza and his cheeks turn red, as if he might cry.

'It's OK, darling,' Eliza goes to him. 'When was the last time you saw Raffy? When have you seen him today?'

Sam shakes his head, and turns to his sister for help. 'We… haven't, have we?'

'What?' Lou's voice is paper thin. 'What do you mean you haven't seen him?'

'He was gone when we woke up. We told you when you came in. You saw he was gone.'

Lou claws at her hair, trying to organise her thoughts. 'Yes, yes,' she says. 'But then we came over here and I saw him go to the treehouse. I saw him in the clearing with Chloe…'

She turns slowly in a circle, thinking it through.

'Sara!' As the waitress comes into the bar, Lou leaps on her like a drowning woman grabbing hold of a life raft. 'You! You were with me. We saw Raffy go to the kids' club this morning, didn't we? Right before I went funny and had to sit down.

'Remember?' she insists. 'He was there. Over in the clearing. In his orange T-shirt…' Lou's hand points in the direction she saw her son walk.

Sara's expression ripples from blank to terrified. 'The blond boy? The little one. Like him but different?' She gestures to Sam, frowning, and then shakes her head. 'No, no. I saw *him*. This boy went to the treehouse.'

'That's not right.' Lou goes and grabs her by the shoulders. 'You saw *Raffy*. My son. He went over this morning. You said you saw him go. You *said*. Didn't you? I'm sure. Because Zikri was there, and...'

She spins round, pinching the bridge of her nose. 'OK well, look, just think. *Think*. What about lunchtime, then? Eliza, you must have seen Raffy at lunch when I went looking for Adam.' Her voice cracks, desperate. 'Didn't you?'

Eliza swallows down a cold spike of adrenaline. 'The kids weren't at lunch. Were they?' She stares round wildly for support. 'I don't know, Lou. If I'm honest, no. I was looking for you anyway then. And also, I thought... he was with Julie. I mean, I just assumed...'

But Lou is gone, racing down the steps of the bar and out into the rain, running under the dark skies towards the kids' club, screaming Raffy's name into the thunder.

# 30

## LOU

She stands in the ladies off the restaurant, soaked to the skin. Her T-shirt clings to her body, her hair hanging like rat's tails around her face. She breathes hard, staring at herself in the mirror, turning her wedding ring round and around on her cold, wet finger.

This is the moment.

All the rest of it: Adam going missing; her exhaustion and depression; her battle to find herself again after having Laila. All of it dissipates now like the steam rising off her in the humid warmth of the bathroom as lightning flashes at the window and the wind bangs against the wall.

Raffy is gone.

Her boy. Her Raffy.

Stupid, *stupid*. When will the list of her fuck-ups ever end? She'd just assumed the boy she'd seen walking across the clearing was Raffy because of his orange T-shirt; his tanned skin; his ruffled, curly, blond hair, and because her head was so messed up with those tablets.

How could she? She'd mistaken another person's child for her own son, and now he was gone.

He has been missing for *hours*. No one has seen him all day.

She meets her own gaze. Her pupils are round with adrenaline. *Good.* Adrenaline is good. It will give her strength and courage and the energy to keep going.

OK.

So she has made a very, very bad mistake. But, now, she has to keep very, very calm. She cannot lose control. Every single thing

172

she does from this moment on will be crucial. She has to push aside all the panic and all the fear and put it down, somewhere else inside of her. She has to think, think, *think*.

Even if the resort staff have had no luck in finding Adam, Raffy is a child. Everyone will want to help. She has to mobilise them. Be methodical. Send them off in groups. Split the island into sections. Go over each of those sections, one by one by one.

She needs maps, and torches.

She needs Lars.

Lou bangs out of the ladies and hurries into the bar. Eliza is sitting on a rattan sofa, an arm around each of the twins. Sara and Julie stand off to one side, twitching with nerves, anxiety scratched across their features. As usual, Zoe is nowhere to be seen. Zikri is behind the bar, a reassuring beacon of calm.

'Where is Lars?' Lou's voice is level and clear. It cuts across the racket of the storm and causes the other guests scattered through the bar to immediately turn to her.

'My son Raffy is missing. You will have seen him around here. He's only eight years old.' She pauses for the briefest of seconds before continuing. 'We think he has been missing since early this morning. I need your help. I need you to help me search the island for him. And I must speak to Lars.' She turns to Zikri urgently. 'Where is he? Nobody's seen him all day.'

'I'm so sorry, Ma'am Lou, but I cannot help you on this. Mr Lars is not answering his phone. Earlier, he did ask me to look after things. It may be...' Zikri says and lowers his eyes as if ashamed '... it may be that Mr Lars has left the island.'

'What?' Eliza exclaims from the sofa, leaning forward on her knees, her hands blotchy with pressure. 'What do you mean he's left? You said *no one* could leave. Or arrive. You said the weather was too bad. That we were trapped here.' She gets to her feet, visibly shaken. 'Are you lying to us, Zikri?' She turns to face Lou and the other guests. 'I think he's lying to us. What's going on here?'

'Please, miss,' Zikri comes out from behind the bar, shaking his head, 'this is not a lie. It is too dangerous to leave. For anyone to come.' He shrugs. 'But Mr Lars... he knows the water. He may have gone to the other side of the island where the jetty is. It's easier to navigate the waters from there.'

'But why?' Lou asks, her hand flat on her forehead. 'Why would he leave? He's supposed to be helping us. He's supposed to be finding Adam. He's... oh my God... Raffy!' She turns to Eliza, eyes flashing wildly. 'Do you think he's taken Raffy?'

'No, no...' Zikri says.

'Why would he take Raffy?' Eliza asks at the same time, taking in the terrified stares of Sam and Chloe perching on the sofa cushions. 'Shit, Lou. We've got to get out of here. Once Noah gets back, we'll go. Find a boat, whatever you say about the weather.' She holds a hand up to Zikri who has stepped forward to argue. 'No. I'm sorry. If he can go, why can't we? They're trapping us here, Lou. I can't deal with it.' She starts to scrabble at her neck as if she can't breathe.

Lou has, with effort, swallowed down the terrible thought that Lars may have abducted her son. It won't help. She has to think clearly. And hell will freeze over before she'll leave this island without her boy.

Even if she does leave it without her husband.

'This isn't helping. Calm down, Eliza,' she says firmly. 'Just... look, just sit down, can't you? Even if we do leave the island, we're not doing it now, in the dark, with the storm at its peak. We have to wait until morning. At least we can see where we're going then.'

'I agree.' The father from the newlywed party gets up from his chair, doddering a little on creaky knees. 'There's no need to panic unnecessarily. First thing to do is devise a strategy for finding the child.'

'I'm with you on that,' says the dad from the Lancashire family. 'Let's divide people into groups and then we can at least search this side of the island methodically.'

'Look, Lou.' Eliza pulls her friend over and away from where the men are suddenly galvanised, pointing fingers and trying to look authoritative. 'I think we really have to find Lars. Where's he gone? Can we trust Zikri? Lars said it himself in the bar the other night. Told me he's his right-hand man. How do we know

174

they're not in it together? That they haven't kidnapped Raffy for a ransom?'

'Why would they do that? It doesn't make any sense. Apart from Lars going AWOL, the staff have done nothing except help us.'

'What about the gun, Lou? Think about it. Can we really trust them?' Eliza asks. Her eyes constantly dart to the horizon. 'How do we know they're not all involved in this scheme?'

'What scheme? You mean what Adam was talking about?' Lou frowns.

'I don't know,' Eliza hisses. 'And where the hell is Noah?'

'Don't collapse on me, El. I need you,' Lou says, taking in Eliza's rapid breath, the sheen of sweat across her forehead. It feels as though the tables have turned and where, before, Lou had been the one in danger of breaking down, now she feels in control, where Eliza seems to be completely falling apart.

'Let's just take this one step at a time, OK? I'm sure Raffy will have gone to look for Adam. Let me go out with this group and see what we find. You stay with the children. Keep them safe here.'

'I'm not going anywhere now,' Eliza replies, sitting back down and hugging the twins tight. 'But I don't care what you say. Once Noah's back, we're gone.'

Lou looks at her, astonished.

'You'd leave me? Alone? To deal with all of this? What's wrong with you?'

Eliza's jaw tightens. She doesn't reply. Her eyes refuse to meet Lou's.

'Fine. I don't have time to argue with you about this,' Lou's voice shimmers with tears. 'You suit yourself.'

'I'll swim it if I have to,' Eliza calls after her. 'You just watch me, Lou. I'll fucking swim it.'

# 31

## NOAH

They stare down at the wild pig carcass in the centre of the clearing.

It's vast. Noah sucks at his teeth. He can still feel the sensation in his palms of its wiry hair, the heft of its split and gnarly trotters. They'd dragged it out of the septic tank, grunting with the effort, staggering backwards before dropping it unceremoniously where it lies now.

'About a hundred kilos, I'd say,' Harry pants, bending over to catch his breath. 'He's been shot. See there?' He points to one hole in the boar's head and another in his shoulder. 'Your common and garden Eurasian wild pig. This one's seen better days, though, to be fair.' He takes off his hat and wipes his brow.

The carcass is already disintegrating.

'Lividity's set in already,' Harry goes on, prodding at the pig with the toe of his boot. 'You can see how the abdomen's bloated and opening up. The skin's slipping. This chap was killed over a week ago, I'd say.'

'Yeah, but what's it doing in your septic tank?' Noah asks, curling his lip at the boar's glassy eyes, the thick layer of blood crusted along its monstrous nostrils, its stubby whiskers. 'Why would anyone put a pig there? It's rank.'

'I don't know,' Harry mutters, glancing around. 'Maybe a message of some sort.'

'Something to do with Che?' Simon asks, looking decidedly green around the gills. 'Has anyone got any water?'

'I'm not sure yet,' Harry answers, passing him a bottle. 'It's possible. Maybe something to do with that fight down at the kampong,' he sighs. 'I don't know.'

'So what do we do with it?' Noah asks. 'Just leave it here?'

'Not if we want Eau de Dead Pig hanging round camp for a month,' Harry says. 'We'll have to burn it. Let's go back and get the buggy. He's too heavy to carry.'

'And slippery,' Noah remarks. He pours some water on his hands and rubs them together as relief sinks in that it wasn't Adam's body that they'd discovered.

Harry bends to grab his hat, glancing up as he straightens. He freezes and peers into the trees for a few seconds. 'Ah, OK... that's not good news.'

Noah peers up in the same direction. 'What isn't?'

'We're going to be in for a ripper of a storm in about twenty minutes, half an hour, I'd say.'

'Jesus. This place. It's only just stopped raining,' Noah says. 'How can you tell, anyway? The sky's totally blue. Not a cloud in it.'

'Look at the tops of the trees.'

Noah adjusts his glasses and stares above. The trees are filled with birds. He shakes his head and shrugs at Harry.

'They're perching on the leeward side. See that? Birds can hear infrasound. They're very sensitive to barometric pressure. If you ever see birds huddling together on the side of a tree furthest from the direction of the wind, you know you should find some shelter too.'

Noah looks up again. 'Huh. Good knowledge, I guess.' He sniffs, trying to smell the approach of rain but there's nothing beyond the reek of the pig.

'Harry, the bird whisperer,' Simon says as they make their way out of the clearing and head back in the direction of the research camp.

'Skills,' Noah admits, although privately he thinks he'll reserve judgement until he actually sees evidence of this incredible storm. He looks at his watch. He's been gone from Turtle Cove for hours. He needs to get back and see Eliza and the kids.

'Given your expertise on the island and its natural inhabitants, then,' he asks Harry, 'what do you think's happened to Adam? I mean, I'm losing hope, to be honest. Thinking we need to prepare ourselves. Prepare Lou and the kids psychologically.'

'Well, I don't know your friend. But if he's got his wits about him and he's not injured – that's vital – it's possible he's alive.'

'Even out at sea?'

'Could be, yeah. I've heard loads of stories of people floating for days in inflatables. I know he'd been drinking, though, so the dehydration's a problem. But if he gets out past the swell, and sees a bigger boat, a trawler or container,' Harry pushes a branch out of his way, 'it's a possibility. I wouldn't give up all hope just yet.'

'Such an idiot. Going out in the boat like that. Pissed up. Angry. Adam can be a complete prick sometimes.' Noah cuts himself off, hearing his tone. 'Don't get me wrong. I'd still prefer him to be alive.'

'I get it, mate. Don't worry.'

The jungle is quiet. The birds have stopped their whistles and cheers and observe their progress silently from their posts in the sky. There's no wind, not even a breeze.

Noah coughs, just to hear the sound of his own voice. It feels utterly surreal, he thinks. Trekking through the jungle with a couple of complete strangers, having just hauled the carcass of a wild boar out of a septic tank. His mum was always on at him to go and spend time with his family in Jamaica, learn about island life, his roots. What was he going to do there, he'd tell her? He's a south London boy, got the city in his veins, not the ocean.

He feels a surge of sudden mania. He's in a parallel universe. Somewhere back in Singapore the real Noah Fisher is sitting in his law office doing what he should be doing. Not playing Crocodile Dundee with these two.

They walk on. He tries to quiet his anxiety. He's sick of the sound of his own voice asking Harry all these questions and he can tell Simon just wants to be left in peace to concentrate on not vomiting.

OK, so he'll think of something to distract him. He'll think of his children. Nope, can't do that. Just makes him agitated he can't get back to them right away. Work? Even more stressful because he hasn't sent the report to Lena, and Germany will be wondering what the fuck is going on.

Good. So this is going well.

A shadow falls over them. The men halt on the path and lift their heads in unison.

The birds rise as one, the screech of them like an ancient, rusted lid releasing and spitting venom and all the nightmares of hell, their wings beating the air, swooping down, down, towards them. Then the sky turns black and the air in front seems to shimmer. It bends and refracts away, and then it comes up close, curving into his chest.

He doesn't know what it is but he knows he has to get out of there.

He bends low and he runs. Sprints from the vacuum and heads for ground level. It doesn't matter where, just down – down to the beach and the ocean and space.

As he tumbles and freewheels over his feet down the path, the only thought he has is that Harry was right about the birds.

That a storm for Armageddon has come and that God must have made the mountain explode.

That God has woken up Fire Mountain.

Noah lands hard on the ground and he runs.

# 32

## LOU

'What was that?'

She stops on the beach, whips round into the wind, peering into the sky for evidence of the source of what can only have been an explosion.

'Thunder?' her search-party companion says, the groom of the newlyweds.

'That wasn't thunder,' Lou answers, turning inland. 'Look.' Inside the forest, flames are licking the tops of the trees, sparks whirling dangerously in the violent wind of the storm. 'It's a fire. Shit. With this squall, the trees will catch. It'll be an inferno.'

'It's too wet,' the man calls after her, his shouts lost on the gale. 'After all that rain, the bark's too damp. It'll be OK.'

But Lou is running back to the resort to find a staff member, someone who understands this terrain, this country. Someone who knows this place as their home. Because the terrible thought has come to her, that the noise she heard – a sound as if the planet were being ripped in half along its seams – might just be the sleeping Fire Mountain waking up.

She dashes up the steps and bursts into the bar.

'Hello?' she calls out. 'Sara? Zikri?'

Zikri emerges from somewhere, staring at her penetratingly as she garbles at him.

'What was that bang? That noise? Is it Fire Mountain? Is the volcano exploding?' She stands in front of him, hands on hips, chest heaving from her run.

When she's finished, he gives a low chuckle. 'You think the sound was Gunung Api?' His eyes crinkle with mirth. 'Ma'am Lou. Gunung Api sleeps. Nobody can wake Gunung Api. Only God can wake him. He sleeps.'

Lou feels a rush of temper, as if she might explode in common with the volcano. 'What was it, then?' she snaps. 'There are flames. There was a hell of a bang. It sounded like a bomb going off. There are sparks in the air. It's dangerous. The trees could catch fire...'

'Don't worry, Ma'am Lou,' Zikri tuts. 'We will look after the sparks. Most likely the generator backfiring.' He holds out a reassuring hand. 'Monsoon makes many things strange.'

'Why do you open the resort when it's the monsoon, then? Why do you bring people here to get stuck, and frightened, and lost? Jesus Christ. *You people!*'

She takes a breath and looks down on herself, bug-eyed and trembling with anger. She's an *ang moh*, all right – the name that the locals give expats in Singapore.

It's not a compliment. It means 'red-haired'. Sunburnt, gin-soaked colonials, wild with heatstroke, screaming unchecked at their native servants. This is who she has become. She is just as bad as the family who humiliated her in this bar when Laila was howling. She is making this situation all about her; treating Zikri as if he's just there to provide her with information, as if his only role in life is to serve her.

'Let me help you, Miss Lou,' Zikri says.

She hasn't thought about her father-in-law for a long time, but now Benjamin Carter's face swims into her mind. She and Adam had taken him and Adam's mother, the long-suffering Mary, out for an expensive lunch to celebrate the sale of Lou's business. As they sat in the two-star Michelin restaurant in Mayfair, Benjamin had given her a wry look.

'Be careful, Miss Lou,' he'd said, tilting his champagne flute towards her.

'Be careful of what?'

'It's the root of all evils, as you know.'

She'd smiled then. She liked Benjamin. Say what you wanted about his incessant philandering and his woeful capabilities as a husband and a father, he wasn't materialistic. She was just glad she didn't love him; that she didn't want anything from him that he would undoubtedly fail to provide. Poor Adam – and Mary – lived in an endless state of quivering expectation that *one day* Benjamin would miraculously change and become someone who could openly show them love and care. Which of course he never would.

'But such a useful root, don't you think? That we cannot get by without it, any more than we can potatoes ... I think it was Louisa M. Alcott who said that.' Lou had forked a wedge of dauphinoise as she'd said it, grinning at him.

'Touché,' he had laughed. 'Still,' he went on, cutting into his fillet steak, 'your world is going to get bigger now. You'll demand others grow along with it. Expect things from them that you never considered before, not in your previous life. You may think yourself above them. Just be watchful, that's all. My two pennies, for what they're worth.'

She hadn't thought of this for a long time – probably since that day, in fact. Why is she thinking of it now? Memories reel from the sky like the earlier rain. Adam's disappearance has uncorked all these feelings, these parts of herself she'd forgotten.

Because Benjamin had read her wrong. She never thought herself above anyone. Not like he did, in actual fact. A trait he had passed down to his son.

Lou has always known the value of respect, of treating others well, no matter how much wealth she may have.

She looks over and sees the concern on Zikri's face, hears the kindness in his voice.

'Yes,' she says, holding out a hand. 'Please help me.'

'Remember when you first arrived? *Air dicencang takkan putus*,' Zikri answers. 'Parted water is never severed. Come and sit down. Let me go and check the generator. I'll find out about this bang. Wait here, please.'

She watches him go. She has to keep it together, she *has* to calm down. She remembers the vow she'd made in the ladies. The only way she can possibly find Raffy is to keep everything very clear in her mind.

But everything feels so jittery and out of control. The constant sound of the wind jars nerves that are already shot; this explosion and fire has literally added fuel to the flames; and... she scans the bar and across into the restaurant, only now fully cognisant of its emptiness.

*Where is Eliza?* She's supposed to be here, watching over the twins, keeping a close eye on Laila.

'Lou?' Eliza appears at the top of the steps that lead down to the beach.

She whirls round. 'There you are. How is Laila? Where are Sam and Chloe?'

'Laila's with Tita. I took them all over to Julie's hut. I'm... Look, I'm sorry about before. I was stressed, upset. Let me help you. I want to.'

Lou takes her in, Eliza's anxious expression, the sorrow in her eyes. 'OK, all right. Thanks. Come on then.' She hurries to the bar fridge and grabs two big bottles of water. 'You heard that explosion, that noise or whatever? Zikri's gone to see what it was but I can't just sit here waiting. Adam, and now Raffy...' She pauses and swallows. 'I have to get out there. I have to try and find them.'

They leave the building and hurry across the glade of pine trees, dodging sparks that fly over their heads like fireflies.

'If it was an explosion, I don't know what it was,' Lou says. 'But it didn't seem too far from the beach. You can see where we should head, look.' She points upwards where a line of orange splits the tips of the forest trees from the clouds. 'That must be the fire but why is the sky so dark?' she asks. 'It's only the afternoon.'

'Are you sure we should be doing this? Wouldn't it be better to stay here? Supposing Raffy comes looking for you?'

'It can't be a coincidence. I mean,' Lou checks the sky as she half-walks, half-runs, 'it's got to be connected, hasn't it? Maybe you're right. What you said earlier. What Adam told me about the gun. I don't think I really believed him, just put it down to him being pissed. But now... I mean, where has Lars gone...?'

'A local man is missing too.' Eliza strides along next to her.

'What?' Lou pulls up. 'What local man? Who?'

'We didn't want to worry you this morning. You seemed in such a state. But last night, that Harry who came over? He came because he was looking for him. Said it was out of character. He'd never missed a day except yesterday. Sunday.'

'The day that Adam went missing,' Lou says.

'Yes,' Eliza replies.

They've breached the forest line by now. It's always hot on Pulau Kalah, with a humidity that feels like a second skin. But this is a different kind of heat. Lou can feel its pulse from inside the bush. It's got a heart, a feverish rhythm. Above them, the sky has grown darker still, but it's licked with embers. The smoke in the air chars the back of her throat.

'What I said earlier,' she says, clambering over a twisted junction of roots in the middle of the path, holding a tree trunk to keep her balance, 'about Adam. I didn't mean...' She concentrates on her feet, her eyes dipped low. 'I didn't mean I blame you. I know what Adam's like. Of everyone, I know.'

There is the sudden sound of ripping bark and a heavy thud as something indiscernible lands from a height. They come to halt, breathing heavily.

'There's a clearing through there, I think,' Lou says. 'It looks lighter, easier to see, although... maybe...' Her voice trails away.

'Lou, the thing is,' Eliza says. She's behind Lou, standing on a buttress. 'The thing is with Adam and me...' she begins.

But Lou isn't listening.

She is very calm and very still, her mouth dry, feet fixed. She peers through the forest with its burning trees and the wind lit with flame, and she sees a shape lying on the path ahead.

She moves closer.

She's dreamy as she picks him up and everything beyond him fades.

His button eyes stare at her, as they have done from bed to car to school and back again. He flops in her grip with his brown matted fur, his head lolling back.

She holds him at arm's length. Still, he stares.

She hears a roaring. She turns him upside down by his ankles, shakes him as if the answer will drop out. His arms hang. She wants to rip them off to see inside him. Find out what he knows.

'Lou?' Eliza comes up to her. 'Oh, God, Lou. It's Monkey.'

Lou's fingers curl at her side. Her mouth tightens, her jaw clamps. All the power in her rage turns to strength. When she turns her head, it is as if she is made of steel. She cannot be hurt by anyone, any more. She is untouchable.

'I know it's Monkey,' she says.

And then she goes forward, further into the forest and the flames.

# 33

## ELIZA

As they go deeper into the rainforest, towards the foothills of Fire Mountain, every cell in Eliza's body is screaming at her to turn around, go back to the staff quarters and Julie's hut, lock the door behind her and hold her children tight until the police come and take her off this godforsaken island.

Her legs are welded to the ground. They won't move. They've got bottles of water but that's it. They have no equipment. She doesn't want to be doing this. She doesn't want to have to see Raffy's charred little body lying amongst the debris of this fire, whatever it is. She can't bear it.

Then she looks ahead at Lou as she streaks through the trees and she knows she can't abandon her. She's her friend. How can she leave her to go through this alone?

Eliza leaps back as a hot piece of ash falls on to her T-shirt. As they penetrate a tunnel of undergrowth, they hear the fire before they see it and then the heat comes roaring at them through the heart of the jungle. It's a movie. It's *Apocalypse Now* or something. This isn't real. She staggers back, shielding her face with her arms from the nucleus of the fire.

They are in a sort of clearing, surrounded by burning branches. The wind is goading the fire to lick greedy tongues towards them. They see Zikri pointing and yelling at them, but they can't understand him and then he's gone, dashing off into the dark of the forest. The smell of dank, scorched wood seeps into their hair and clothes.

Lou has skidded to a halt. Even she is awed by the fire's force. In front of them is the blackened frame of a small building, some kind of hut, charred and eaten by the flames. She turns to Eliza and her expression is desperate.

'I have to go in there,' she shouts.

'No!' Eliza yells back. 'You'll get yourself killed.'

'What else can I do? He's my son.'

Lou pushes Monkey at Eliza and rips off her T-shirt and drenches it in water from her bottle. In her bra and shorts, she wraps the shirt around her head, covering her mouth and nose.

'Lou, come on,' Eliza pleads. 'You can't even be sure he's there. And what about your chest? You can't breathe with all this smoke. Just wait for the others to come.'

'He's there,' Lou pants, tying a knot in the shirt. 'And what are they going to do? Bring a fucking hose up here? It's only going to get worse. He could be hurt. He'll be terrified.' She pauses and pulls out her inhaler. 'See? I'm all good.' She takes two long puffs and reaches back to touch Eliza's hand. 'It'll be OK.' And then she's gone, running into the flames without a backwards glance.

Eliza stands, staring after Lou. She moves from foot to foot, tracing the mulched ground with the toes of her canvas shoes. She doesn't know what to do. Should she follow? Or run back and get help?

The decision is made for her by a shout from behind. As she turns to see who it is, she nearly collapses with relief. It's Noah. He runs over with Harry and wraps his arms around her.

'Are you OK? Are you hurt?'

She buries her head into his chest, her voice muffled. 'No, I'm fine. But Lou's gone into the fire.' She stares up at him. 'Raffy's missing, Noah. We haven't seen him all day. Lou found his toy,' she holds it up to him, 'his monkey – just here, so we think he got caught in this... explosion, or whatever it was.' Eliza looks anxiously into the darkness beyond that's lit only by flames, dancing through the tops of the trees.

'We could be in luck,' Harry yells from a few metres way. He's got his hands over his forehead, as if he's searching the horizon for something.

'Harry, we have to get Lou and Raffy,' Noah shouts. 'They're in there.' Hot ash soars into the darkness as a small tree splits and

187

crashes only a few metres away from them. 'Shit, El,' he murmurs. 'They're going to be burned alive.'

'Come on, Noah.' Harry mimics Lou's actions from earlier. He takes off his shirt and drenches it in water, ties it around his face like a mask. 'Do what I'm doing.'

Over the fury of the crackling flames, they hear a burst of thunder.

'Remember the birds?' Harry says, shoving a canister of water at Noah. 'With any luck, we're about to get drenched with a nice long bout of monsoon rain. Follow me in, OK? Keep low. It's easier to breathe.'

Noah nods and takes the route behind Harry. After a moment, they drop to the ground and crawl. There's a prolonged flash of lightning and, in its glare, Eliza can see their shapes disappear into the bush. Then the lightning fades and the image is gone.

How are they going to find Raffy in this? Where there aren't raging flames, it's so dark it's impossible to see, as if the flames have sucked out all the available light. There's no discernible epicentre of the fire – just clusters of bonfires whose fingers reach up and mesh like red-hot cobwebs under the treetops. The explosion has created a bower of heat that could collapse at any time.

And then the strange darkness of the afternoon is explained as the monsoon rain arrives.

The shock of it is electric. As Harry predicted, it's a cloudburst, a powerful detonation of water that feels like a burn on her skin, it's so sharp and present. Within minutes, the largest of the flames have subsided and the consuming heat has evaporated into a cloying dampness. Smoke still lingers but its ferocity is gone; it's put away its knives.

Eliza inches forward in the direction the others took. The quiet after the roar of the fire is eerie, the beam of her torch in the trees feels lonely. She trips and nearly flies head-first over an ancient buttress at the sound of voices, spotting a scattering of torchlights ahead. Righting herself, she flicks her torch upwards.

Her throat is dry and thick with smoke. The world tilts.

Above her hangs a body dripping with black water from the rain. It's been cremated, its face nothing more than a sunken scab

188

with shadowed hollows for eyes. His legs are tied together, his arms above his head. He's blackened; layered with a thick crust of carbon. But, here and there, are terrible cuts of colour. Slashes of bright baby pink scattered down his torso and thighs. Patches that glisten as they weep with pus. This is where his skin has been flayed clean by the fire.

Whoever hangs there looks nothing more than a stick of charcoal.

Hanged to burn above the flames of the hut as if he were strung up to be barbecued.

Everything is opening up. All the things she's locked away, banished forever in that box of hurt. They're coming out now, screaming memories that bloat the flame-filled sky.

Her mother swings by the neck in the garden.

Her skin bleached white: the brittle sheen of frost on car bonnets. That silence of an early morning. The gift of being awake when others sleep.

Hearing is the final sense to fail when unconsciousness comes.

Eliza can hear the shouts of others as she falls.

*She's out cold. Put her on her side.*

Her mother dangles wordlessly, she circles round and around. The rope is twisted, it's knotted and frayed.

Still, she turns.

Eliza drops to the ground, her cheek on hot leaves singed with fire. The heat is her rage, searing up from the earth. It winds around her, round and round, just as her mother slowly turns.

*I'd lost count of the women he'd messed around with by the time he entered the pearly gates...*

The rage closes in: a lion circling a camp. The steel-tipped analysis of a hunter, watching her prey.

*How did your mother die?*

*Splish-splash. Parted water is never severed.*

Now it comes. Closer still.

*Blood is thicker than water.*

*Blood...*

*Blood...*

# 34

## LOU

He's kissing her. He leans back and peruses her face. He has hazel eyes. Warm. Kind. She stares up at him.

'Is he…?'

'Don't speak,' he says. 'The back of your throat might be burned. Here, drink this.'

Gently, he lifts her and puts a water bottle to her lips. The feel of the liquid on her tongue and then slipping down her throat – warm as the water is – is heavenly. She can't stop looking at him.

'You'll live,' he says abruptly and gets up off the floor where he has been kneeling next to her.

She flops her head back down. Something is underneath it – a bag of some sort? She feels woozy. Her chest is tight. It feels like it does after she's had an asthma attack. She wiggles her fingers down by her thigh, near the pocket of her shorts. The hazel-eyed man – Harry, is it? – sees her reaching and leans across to hand over her inhaler.

'Here,' he says. 'Take it easy, though. Your system's had a shock.'

It comes back to her in a rush. Running through the trees, the flames grabbing at her, screaming Raffy's name. She jerks upwards but Harry takes her by her shoulders.

'No,' he says. 'We haven't found him.' He looks at her seriously. 'But we will. I will find him. Please believe me.'

Weirdly, she does.

She sits up and drinks more water. She breathes in the steroids from her inhaler. It's such a familiar taste in such an alien situation. She looks around. They're in the clearing where she'd left

190

Eliza. Someone has rigged up makeshift lighting and it burns artificially into the trees. It's drizzling, but both she and Harry are soaking wet. She has no memory of being brought here. She turns, and there's Eliza, hunched on the ground watching her.

'You were knocked out by the smoke,' Harry says. 'Then luckily it rained. That dealt with the fire.'

'He gave you mouth to mouth.' Eliza is so white with shock that her face is almost luminous in the pitted dark of the clearing. 'I thought you were going to die.'

Lou coughs and brings her knees to her chest. 'Great holiday I organised, by the way. Wait and see what I've got planned for Christmas.'

She looks at Eliza for a moment and they laugh.

'Ah. Yeah. Maybe stick to finance,' Eliza says, rubbing a hand over her eyes.

'Sorry,' Lou says to the unsmiling Harry. 'We must be hysterical.'

'It's totally understandable.' He nods and turns to Noah. 'Can you get her back to the resort? I can organise people from here to keep on searching for Raffy.' He looks over at the small group of milling guests and resort staff who have made their way up from the beach. 'But I must deal with the body.' Harry gets to his feet. 'Zikri, you'll come?'

Zikri gives a sombre nod.

Eliza starts to cry. 'What's going on here?'

'What body?' Lou struggles up on to her elbows. 'Is it Adam?'

'I saw it,' Eliza sobs. 'Hanging there. It was awful. Just like...' She stops, her cries muffled as she buries her head in her hands. 'What is this place? What's happening here?'

'I don't know yet,' Harry says, after a brief, bewildered pause.

'What was the explosion?' Noah asks, moving to crouch on the ground next to Eliza.

Lou begins another bout of coughing. 'Is it him?' She manages. 'Please tell me. Is it Adam?'

'Take it easy.' Harry holds out a hand to her. He exchanges a look with Zikri. 'I'm not sure. About any of it. The body is considerably... disfigured. As for the explosion, from the sound of it at least, it was dynamite.'

'Dynamite?'

Harry nods at Noah. 'I think so. A few boxes of it maybe. Could be stashed in that burnt-out hut. From first sight, it seems to have been where the fire originated. But honestly, I don't know.'

'Where are the police?' Lou holds up a hand to stop Harry preventing her and gets up on to her knees. 'Why haven't they come? Because it's bullshit about the weather. I don't believe it. It wouldn't stop them if they knew people were dying here.' She sits back on her heels and wraps her arms around herself. Her voice cracks. 'I mean. We need help. Now.'

'Yeah, but we didn't contact them, did we?' Noah says. 'It just occurred to me. We were supposed to, over at Timba. But we found the boar in the septic tank and then the explosion went off.'

'But *Lars* called them,' Eliza says. 'On Sunday morning. As soon as we knew Adam had gone missing. Lars made the call.' She looks round, asking for confirmation that this is right.

Harry grimaces, exhaling loudly into the sky.

'What? What is it?'

'It's just that... we only have Lars's word for it that he called the police, don't we?'

'What did you say?' Noah asks in a low voice.

'And Lars isn't here any more, is he?' Harry kicks at the ground. 'Makes me think perhaps he didn't bother making too much effort to get the police involved before he split. Zikri, were you with Lars when he called them?'

Zikri wrings his hands. 'No, boss.'

'So unless somebody else did, and just isn't saying,' Harry says, 'I think we'd better work on the basis that the police and coast-guard don't actually know, at this stage, that anyone is missing.'

# 35

## LOU

She can't think about that body swinging from the trees. Charred and burnt and strung up to die. She can't think that it might be Adam. The idea will send her mad.

She has to focus on Raffy.

The body was that of an adult, Harry said.

So it's not Raffy. Raffy is still out there somewhere.

She yells out for him, calling his name. Even though her voice is nearly gone, and her chest feels rough and raw, it's all she can do.

Everything on this island, that she once thought was so perfect, she now realises is her enemy. The sea and its tides, the rainforest, the range of hills, the animals and the tropical plants, the setting of the sun and the pitch-darkness it brings. Soon she will only be able to see what lies in the coverage of her torch beam.

But she can call.

Raffy would know her voice anywhere – even now as it rasps. He will hear her, now that the noise of the storm and the explosion has passed, and the island is lulled once again only by a warm breeze and the night murmurs of cicadas. He will hear her, wherever he is.

She will call all through the night if that's what it takes. She will walk up and down the beach and into the lower ranges of the forest in a wide loop, calling and singing his name. She will do it all night, and all day, holding Monkey in her arms, waiting for her boy to come back to her.

The crabs skitter sideways along the beach again. She cuts a path right through them, keeping her sightline low, at Raffy's height; ignores them scratching and pinching at her toes. She thinks only of her boy somewhere under this darkening blue sky, hoping he's taking comfort from the pinholes of starlight that are beginning to scatter and multiply above.

After a while, she turns off her torch as her eyes adjust to the night. She hears the whispers of the jungle; she can follow the arc of the bats as they hunt. She forgets that she is separate from it all as her feet sink into the sand, crunching on to tiny mollusc shells crusted with salt from the ocean.

As she walks, she focuses on Raffy, on where he could have gone. In her heart, she doesn't believe he has been taken or abducted. Raffy has always been a boy filled with curiosity, but also with great courage.

He would have gone off looking for Adam, that she knows. Once the shock of him disappearing had worn away. Once he saw that the adults weren't succeeding in the hunt, he would have taken matters into his own hands. Again, her stomach clenches. She should have known this when she took that bloody sleeping pill.

Because Raffy has always had a bravery based on what's right. On what he believes to be right. Look at his reaction to the fish bomb, at his outrage at the pain caused to the marine life. He's always been a knight, she thinks. First knight among equals, with the courage and goodness of Lancelot, the innocence of Percival.

Lou stops.

Harry had said that the island explosion was likely caused by dynamite stored in the hut at the epicentre of the fire.

Raffy knew that whoever had planted the fish bomb had used dynamite to make the explosive.

So maybe – if he'd found the hut and the dynamite – maybe he had tried to mete out a little justice?

'Lou?'

From nowhere in the darkness, Harry appears next to her on the beach.

'Jesus, Harry. You scared me half to death.'

194

'Ah. Sorry. I was just worried about you. You should be resting. After earlier. With everything… I don't want you collapsing on me.'

'It's fine. I'm fine. Listen. I'm thinking things through. I think Raffy went off this morning to go and look for Adam. It's the only reason he would have left me this morning. I don't know what he saw or found, but I reckon he must have discovered that hut.' She points a finger at him. 'Where you said the explosion probably originated. That's why Monkey was there. Because he dropped him there. It's the only thing that makes sense.'

Harry nods. 'I've been coming to that conclusion myself. But listen—'

'I think he saw the dynamite and figured it was something to do with the fish bomb. I don't know.' Lou ignores him, raking a hand through her hair. 'Maybe it's all bullshit. But I have to go back up there. I have to keep searching for him. Will you come?'

'Of course. But Lou—'

She holds up a hand. 'I know. But I have to do it. We'll only go to the place where the body is when there's nowhere else to look.'

'It's not that. Will you listen to me?'

She stops.

'I can't be positive, of course. But my instinct is that the body isn't Adam's,' Harry says. 'I think it's Che.'

'The man who worked for you?' Lou asks. 'Why?'

'To hang a person up like that,' Harry frowns. 'It's barbaric. It's a message of power. Of strength. It's more likely to be to do with Che, that's all.'

Lou looks up at the sky and exhales. 'We can't know for sure, though. Can we? Not now.'

'No, we can't,' Harry concedes.

'So, let's go,' Lou says.

'It's dark now, Lou. It will be hard to see anything, let alone a little boy. We might have to wait till it's lighter.'

But Lou is already off, marching up the beach and crossing the forest line.

She keeps on, calling his name, surrounded by the ancient sky and the ancient sea, overlooked by the ancient volcano.

The jungle welcomes her in like an old friend. The darkness is nothing to her. Every step she takes will bring her back to her boy – she can feel it. She's not afraid any more, not of anything. Not even this place, this Fire Mountain.

They walk for a long time.

Tonight the forest seems louder than ever.

An assault on the senses; a requiem of tropical colour and squawks and buzzes and shrills and beeps, drips and echoes, rustles and thuds. After a while, the noises blend until the onslaught softens and becomes a hollow cathedral deep in prayer.

Lou keeps calling, following in Harry's footsteps. As her calls match the night sounds, for a moment she forgets who she is and why she's there. She disappears, becomes merely part of the ecosystem, from its mulch to the overstorey. They both are, she and Harry. And for some strange reason, she feels sure that the forest will do them no harm.

A kilometre beyond the skeletal frame of the burnt-out hut, they duck their heads under a bower of wet banana leaves and enter a dank cavern of vegetation. The darkness is inky, rich with rainwater.

But then a gust of wind parts the canopy and a shaft of moonlight pierces through. It circles a tiny pill bug, curled up tight on the ground.

And there is Raffy.

Lou's knees buckle like a paper fan as she lifts him to her, brings him in close and breathes him in.

Her boy.

She follows close behind as Harry carries him down to the resort. As they go, Raffy stares at her, his face an exhausted moonscape. Monkey's head bobs happily at his shoulder, back in his rightful position with his master.

At the bar Raffy ducks Lou's kisses like a normal kid, and that buoys her. It's only when she draws him on to her lap and they feed him water and then apple juice, sticky and sweet for the shock, that she feels the tremble of his little thighs, the hard, fierce squeeze of his hand on hers.

She swallows her tears, turns over Raffy's burnt palms and applies the cooling gel that Zikri has given her, wrapping light

196

gauze around them to stop mosquitoes landing on his skin. Sara kneels at Raffy's feet, dabbing antiseptic cream on to the cuts along his shins. He has one bad cut on his forehead. It probably needs stitches, Lou thinks, but after giving him paracetamol, all she can do is clean and cover it with yet more gauze, fixing it in place with surgical tape.

He talks to her as he crams French fries into his mouth, licking salt from his fingers, eyes wide on hers with fear of punishment.

'I only wanted to find Daddy.'

'I know you did, baby.'

'Early this morning I couldn't sleep. So I got up and I thought I'd ask Captain Lars for a paddleboard. Because then I could go out round the reef and maybe he'd be there. Asleep past the headland.'

He puts a salty hand on hers.

'Are you mad, Mama?'

She looks at his tufty hair stuck up in a shock, his shorts all covered in mud, and she has to take a breath before she answers.

'No, baby. I'm not angry with you. At all.'

He puts his head on one side. A little crafty now he has returned a conquering adventurer.

'My throat hurts.'

Lou smiles. 'Ice cream?'

Raffy gives an eager nod. 'I followed him. Captain Lars,' he says. 'It was still really dark. And they got in this car? A red one with no roof?'

'Sounds like the Timba jeep,' Harry murmurs from his station at the bar.

The memory of Adam's voice slams into her head like a wrecking ball razing a building to the ground. On the veranda that night. He had driven a jeep, he'd said.

'They?' Lou asks. 'Who was Lars with, Raff?'

'Zoe,' he says with certainty. 'From kids' club. I climbed in this bit at the back. I wouldn't have done it,' he says in a hurry, noticing Lou's eyes widen. 'But Lars was talking to her about going to see the old man. And I thought they meant Daddy.'

'How did they not see you?' Lou asks, amazed.

Appalled, Raffy pauses with a chip halfway to his mouth. 'They were all slobbering over each other. It was disgusting.'

*Nice*, Lou thinks. *How nice.*

Then he forgets about that, grinning widely as Sara brings over a huge bowl of chocolate ice cream. 'Plus it was dark. And there was this other man there too? He had big hair with a line running round it like this?' He traces a finger around his head just above the tips of his ears.

'Che,' Harry says, his shoulders dropping a little.

He looks washed out, Lou thinks, watching him tap on the bar for Zikri to replenish his glass.

'We drove to this place where all the houses were on these long legs,' Raffy continues. 'So I had to hide. And then they had this big fight.'

'Who did?' Harry asks. 'Who was fighting?'

Raffy looks over, his spoon in his mouth. 'Lars and the old man that was on the boat when we first came here. Remember, Mama?' He stops and takes out the spoon, looking down at it sombrely.

'What is it Raff? You didn't like the shouting?'

'No, I didn't. I wanted you. I was scared. And then... the man with the hair. He...' His voice drops to a whisper and Lou has to lean in close. 'He shot a gun in the air.'

'He did what?'

'He shot a gun.'

'At someone? Who did he shoot a gun at?' Angry, vengeful adrenaline rises in Lou, remembering Adam on their veranda, telling her about the gun. Her dismissal of it as drunken rambling. Why hadn't she taken him seriously? Why hadn't they made sure that the police had been called then and there?

Who is Lars Van Graan? Just what is he involved in?

And what has he done to her son?

'Wait. Hang on a minute.' Harry pushes his hands through his hair as if this will help his brain to work. 'Raffy – you're saying all this happened... early this morning?'

The boy nods. 'Yes.'

'But Che went missing yesterday. On Sunday,' Harry points out. 'So where has he been since then? And why did he go off in the first place?' He turns round. 'Zikri? Come on, you must know something about this.'

The barman tightens his lips as he considers the cloth he's using to dry a glass. 'Che and Alif are from different families,' he says eventually.

Harry slams his glass down. 'I'm getting pretty sick of that being the answer to everything around here,' he says. 'Zikri. Come on, we all live together. Don't we?'

The barman doesn't answer.

Lou removes the ice cream from Raffy and brings him round the table and on to her lap. She wipes away the chocolate smears from his mouth and lays his head on her chest, strokes his hair.

'I was really scared. They were all shouting, and a man took a chicken and threw it at someone else and it was so noisy. I just ran, Mama. I ran away, up the road. Nobody even saw. Then once I got into the forest, it was quiet. I hid for a while. I don't know for how long. Under these big leaves. And when no one came after me, I started walking. Trying to find my way back to you.'

'Jesus.'

Lou looks up as Harry pushes himself back from the bar, rigid veins standing out on his arms. He stares at her and holds out a hand as if he wants to touch her or comfort her, but he loses momentum and his arm hangs weightless before dropping by his side.

'What happened then, darling?'

'I walked for ages and then I found this hut. I was really thirsty and I thought it might have water inside. But it was locked.'

Raffy pauses again, as if ashamed.

'Whatever happened, you can tell me,' Lou says. 'I'm not going to get angry, I swear to you. OK? You did what you had to do. It's all OK. I promise.'

After a moment, Raffy sniffs and wipes his nose with the back of his hand.

'I was so thirsty. I found this log and dragged it over to the hut and climbed up and there were these boxes inside. I thought they might have water. I don't know. So I...' He stops, unable to look at her.

'You broke the window to get in?'

He nods.

'It's OK. Really, it is. But what was in the hut, Raffy? What was in the boxes?'

He frowns. 'I thought they were candles at first. I couldn't work it out. And it was dark. It had got really dark. Then I remembered I'd found some matches on the beach clean-up, and I'd put them in my backpack. I thought I could light a candle and find my way out of the forest.

'And then I realised, Mama. I realised what they were.'

Raffy shakes his head.

'They weren't candles. They were *dynamite*. Like they used to kill the fish.' He stares at her. 'So then I knew I could use them to create an SOS so you'd find me. And *then* I realised...' – he looks at her, eyes shining – 'that I could blow it all up so no one could use it to kill the fish ever again.'

Lou is silent for a second or two.

'Oh, Raffy,' she says, kissing him on the head. 'You brave, brave boy.'

'I lit one of the sticks and threw it into the hut. But I don't really remember what happened next. When I woke up, I just knew I'd lost Monkey.' He picks up the toy from the table and brings it to his face. 'And I was somewhere else. I didn't know where I was.' A tear rolls down his cheek. 'So I lay down and waited for you to find me.'

Lou looks down at her son, curled up on her lap.

He gets it, she realises. Unlike the philosophy of his literati grandfather and ambitious father, he understands it's not what you do that matters, it's who you *are*.

Behind the bar, Zikri straightens and peers out beyond the fringe of the atap, where there is the faintest hum of a motorboat and a tiny intermittent flash of blue light.

'Polis.'

As she sees the officers disembark, Lou feels a relief so intense, it almost takes her back to childhood. That sensation of being

200

able to hand the whole mess over to an adult and say: '*There you go. Deal with this, please. I'm going to sleep.*'

But life isn't like that, is it? She is the grown-up. She is the parent. Thankfully, the baby is blissfully unaware of anything bad taking place. She's just enjoying having the undivided attention of Tita twenty-four hours a day.

And Raffy has an unwavering faith that she will make everything better for him. That she is strong enough for them all and she will protect him, no matter what happens.

She can only hope that he's right.

# 36

## ELIZA

She can't stay on the island any longer.

Seeing that body hanging from the tree has ripped everything open. Images shuttle through her head on a rolling news ticker. Fireworks built from memories explode their colours into the dull and starless sky.

All the anger and rage she's had. Where is it now? Where has it gone?

She had left them all in the clearing. She had needed to be alone. To come and stand at the shore and watch the gentle tip and turn of the water.

The sea is so calm now, as if they had only imagined the monsoon. As if they had invented the rain and the thunder, the violence and the noise. But then, real fury needs no fanfare, does it? She knows that it's as quiet and cold as frozen earth.

She hears the sound of voices and stumbles in the other direction, back up the beach to the hut she shares with Noah and the children. There, she drops down on to the bed, her head in her hands.

'What are you doing?' The door bangs open and Noah comes inside. 'I've been looking for you everywhere. Raffy's been found.'

'Oh thank God.' She doesn't look at him, curls her knees underneath her chin. 'How is he? Where was he?'

'He's fine. A bit beaten up but OK. I don't know where he's been. As soon as I knew he was all right, I came looking for you.' He narrows his eyes. 'What's going on? You look spaced out. Are you still feeling odd after fainting like that or is there something else?'

She thinks about all the ways she could answer, and then realises that the time has come.

Because there is something else. And she has to tell him about it.

'The police will be here soon,' she says. 'They'll be here soon and they'll be asking questions. Malaysian police.'

'What's the matter, Eliza?'

'That girl with Adam.' She seeks him out as fading light creeps through slatted shutters. 'Zoe. Were you with her too?'

Noah frowns. 'Zoe? With Adam?'

'Yes. The night Adam went missing. He was with Zoe. The other backpacker from the kids' club.'

Noah's expression flickers.

'You look confused, Noah.' Eliza's tone is sharp.

Without warning, he rounds a fist and slams it into the wall. 'Why is it always me that's wrong? It's always me that's done something bad, isn't it? It could never be you, right? Oh no,' he sneers. 'Don't try and drag me into this, El, yeah? I didn't do anything with any girl.'

'I'm not saying you did, but the police are coming. I'm just telling you. Detectives are coming who know nothing about us. Except they think they do. They think they know about drunken expats who leave their children alone while they get up to . . .' she flutters delicate fingers across the bed ' . . . God knows what.'

'Oh yeah? What about you and Adam? If anyone's got anything to be worried about, maybe it's you?'

Eliza brings her shoulders back, like a gymnast about to take to the floor. 'Adam,' she says thoughtfully. 'Me and Adam. Is there even such a thing?' She glances at the space where Noah smacked the wall. 'Was there ever? Maybe it's time we started facing some facts.'

'What do you mean? What facts? What are you talking about?'

'Come and sit.' She puts a hand down on to the bed.

'I'm fine here.' He folds his arms.

'OK. Well . . .' She feels herself mumbling and tries to focus, to bring all her thoughts into some kind of cohesion. 'All right. I need to start with my mother. That's where this begins.'

'Your mother.' It's a statement.

'Yes. Even though we never had any money. Even though my father was gone. It was enough just being with her. I loved Mum more than anyone.'

'Yes, babe. I know.'

Eliza shrugs. 'But she didn't love me the same way, did she? Those are the facts, Noah.'

He stares at her.

'When we went to South America,' she goes on, 'in Mum's head I was finally independent. I was twenty-one. I had a steady boyfriend. She believed that her duty was done.'

'No...' Noah shakes his head, but she puts up a hand.

'Just let me say it,' she says. 'Now I was gone, she was free to do what she'd wanted to do for years. She couldn't live without the man she loved. So she took her own life.'

'It was a tragedy, babe,' Noah says gently. 'She never got over his death.'

Eliza emits a hollow laugh. 'His death.'

She gets up from the bed and puts her arms either side of his head, above his shoulders, up against the wall.

'Except he wasn't dead,' she whispers. 'He wasn't dead at all.'

She runs a finger down his cheekbone, tears in her eyes, her voice so soft it can barely be heard over the swish of the fan above them, the pull of the tide outside.

'When she died, Mummy left a note where she named my father. A man who was very much alive. A man whose name I recognised. A name that made me realise that I wasn't *actually* a dearly loved child of tragic circumstances. That *actually* I had been abandoned by both of them. That *actually* I hadn't been loved at all.'

Noah slumps down against the wall, his eyes fixed on hers.

Eliza moves away, taking deliberate footsteps in line with her thoughts.

'Who was I now, if I wasn't who I'd thought, for all those years? I didn't know. I ended things with you,' she turns to him, her hands outstretched, 'I stopped contact with everyone. And I wrote to him. My father. I asked him to come to the funeral.

I waited for him in that church. God, it was cold. I can see it now. Blue paint peeled from the ceiling, wallpaper torn from the angels' faces.

'I knew he wouldn't come. And he didn't.

'So then he ceased to exist for me. I cut him out,' she slices a hand across her chest, 'out of my mind and my heart. He only existed in order for me to hate him.

'And it felt good, Noah. It felt really, really good.'

He straightens and clears his throat, dumbfounded. 'Eliza, but who... ?'

'But the trouble is,' she continues, 'hate doesn't fill a void. It's like a bad-luck pond. You, and Sam and Chloe filled it for a little bit, but even they weren't enough after a while.' She opens her mouth for a second in a silent scream. 'Isn't that a disgusting thing to say? I sound like my mother,' she spits and snaps her mouth shut, turning away.

He goes to her and touches her back. Moves her around to face him.

'Eliza,' he says softly, and she bucks against him as if he's trying to capture a wild animal.

Then she stops, breathing hard, her eyes black and fathomless. 'Who is he? Your father?'

She takes his hands in hers and begins to weep a gentle wash of tears. For once it feels good, to feel the surge of his name rise up inside her and make itself known.

'He was my mother's professor. Benjamin Carter.'

'Benjamin... ?'

'Carter. Yes,' she closes her eyes, 'Adam Carter's father.'

# 37

## LOU

When the police arrived, officers had spent a long time talking to Harry and Zikri before spreading along the beach with powerful torches, rigging up artificial lights.

They told them they were awaiting the arrival of their chief inspector who was travelling down from Kuala Lumpur. Until he did, and the light returned the following morning, they seemed reluctant to do much immediately, particularly once they realised that Raffy had been found.

And still there is no sign of Adam, nor a proper identification of the body. They are able to leave the island, now the weather has calmed, and earlier, Lou had seen the Lancashire family complaining loudly, demanding to be taken to the mainland then and there. But everyone has been instructed to stay on Pulau Kalah, at least until tomorrow. A couple of officers remain on guard, sitting sentry in the restaurant. They seem redundant, though, Lou thinks; mainly concerned with tucking in to plates of nasi lemak from the girls in the kitchen.

As Raffy sleeps on a rattan sofa, Lou's chest feels like she's run three marathons through the great smog of London. She sucks deeply from her inhaler at the same time as ordering a whisky from Zikri behind the bar.

'Medicinal,' she rasps, as the liquid sears her throat. 'So.' She looks at Harry, sitting on the bar stool next to hers. 'What's the plan?'

Harry lifts his eyebrows. 'The police will be back tomorrow. They'll find Adam, Lou.'

She meets his eyes with hers. No need to say the obvious – that Adam may have already been found.

'They confirmed that Lars had never contacted them?'

'Yes,' Harry sighs. 'Massive error on my part. I would have done it myself, of course. With the disappearance of Che. But...' he shrugs. 'I assumed they'd be here, guns blazing, with a missing tourist. You get more reward points for finding Westerners.' He blows out his cheeks.

'So we have to assume that Lars is responsible,' Lou says. 'That he was never searching for Adam that first morning after he went missing. That somehow Adam has got mixed up in whatever's been happening over at the kampong. With this dynamite business...' She passes a hand over her eyes. 'You know Eliza saw Zoe with Adam that night – the night he went missing? And Raffy says she was at the kampong on the morning of this fight. Whatever that was about. Are the police going to question her? She seems to be tied up in this too – in whatever Lars was involved in.'

'There are another couple of their guys over at Timba. She won't be going anywhere. She'll be questioned tomorrow.' Harry rubs his brow at the same time as rotating his neck. 'Zoe Tilleman. Very much a Lars template. They buy into the dive lifestyle, the beach vibes,' he shrugs. 'He plays on it. Kids, back-packers, travellers – whatever you want to call them – they come here because they want to run away. Escape their lives, who they really are. They start to pretend they're someone else. A kind of... caricature.'

'It's pathetic,' Lou scoffs.

Harry turns down his mouth. 'Haven't you ever wanted to be different? Come to a foreign country and thought you could start all over again? Be the person you always wanted to be but never thought you could?'

Lou rubs her lips together, remembering her fantasy of Pulau Kalah; of coming to the island and being free and at one with nature. How she imagined being here would resolve all the bad things in their lives so that she could walk away from her relationship with Adam with minimal effort.

'Well, yes,' she admits. 'But I would never hurt anyone.'

Lou slumps on her stool, her hands tight around her whisky glass. She feels like crying.

Zikri tuts and clears his throat. 'What has happened here on Pulau Kalah. Mr Harry, you know. It is a local matter. It is not for others to concern themselves over.'

'Not concern myself with my husband and child going missing?' Lou stares up at him.

'Yes, Ma'am Lou. Of course.' Zikri tops up her glass. 'But we have a saying here in Malaysia: *bagai aur dengan tebing*.

'It means that, to survive, the bamboo and the riverbank must help each other, they must rely on each other. This is how we live here. When this order is disturbed, survival becomes... precarious.'

'Well who's disturbing it?' she asks. 'Lars? That man Che? We still don't know what's happened to him. Just as we don't know with Adam.'

Zikri glances at a table in the corner where the Dutch couple sit drinking wine. He comes in closer. 'Mr Lars grew up here as a boy. He knows the different families, the different loyalties.

'But things change. What an old man like me wants, our grandchildren think too little. It's not enough to eat, to live the way we always have. They want more. People like Lars. Young people like him. They get drunk,' he screws a lid back on to a jar of maraschino cherries, 'not on wine, but by bright lights.'

Harry shifts on his stool. 'The body of a wild pig was put in the septic tank at Timba,' he tells Lou.

'Why?' she frowns. 'To poison the water?'

'It's an old-school message. It's not something the kids would do. Right, Zikri?'

The barman rolls his eyes in the affirmative.

'Some people don't like us. Think we're encroaching on a traditional way of life. So they sent us a little message to warn us. Tell us to get off their patch.'

'*They* put a pig in your septic tank?' Lou clarifies. 'Who's they?'

She and Harry look over at Zikri, but he remains silent. He pushes a cloth back and forth across the bar like a meditation.

'Che worked with me at Timba like a lot of his family. They believed in what we were teaching. They understood about sustainability,' Harry says. 'But...'

'What?'

'I don't know where Che's loyalties really lay,' Harry sighs, finishing his beer.

Zikri gives a weary whistle through his teeth. 'I'm tired now, Mr Harry. I've been here many years. Working for Mr Dirk and now his son.' He looks beyond them, out into the darkness where the ocean turns its tides and the moon hangs low. 'We are a people of the sea,' he says, his eyes faraway. 'That gives us life. Nothing else.' He comes back to the room with a gruff laugh. 'Not even your dollars and ringgits.'

'Someone's split the two communities down the middle: Turtle Cove and Timba,' Harry says, after a pause. 'The bamboo and the riverbank. Someone has been playing them off against each other.

'Both places employ local people, both of them promote eco-tourism. They're good for the local population. But there's all this bad feeling between them. Why?'

'Maybe this is what Adam got involved in?' Lou says. 'When he was suspicious about Lars and the dynamite. Maybe he found out something he shouldn't. Maybe *through* that girl, Zoe?' She puts her hands on the bar. 'And now maybe they're holding him somewhere and they don't want him to be found?'

She gives Raffy a quick look as he moans a little in his sleep on the sofa. 'I should get him to bed,' she says, the trauma of the day coming back to her in a wave of exhaustion.

'The police are here now, miss,' Zikri says. 'All will be well.'

'Come on,' Harry looks over, 'I'll carry him to your new quarters.'

Lou goes to collect Laila from Tita, then hurries back to where Harry waits for her, holding Raffy in his arms. They are no longer in their old hut. She couldn't bear to stay there, surrounded by all of Adam's things. Now, they're closer to the restaurant. Outside, she can hear the two-tone humming of a night chorus of insects and the sporadic rhythm of conversation in the kitchens. She likes to hear people outside. It's comforting, remembering that she's not alone.

Harry lays the boy gently on the bed while Lou settles Laila in her travel cot. He lifts a hand in goodbye and she follows him out to stand underneath the little electric light on the veranda, moths darting between them through the shadows.

'I just want to say thank you,' Lou whispers.

'What for?' Harry asks in a low voice.

'Well, for saving my life? You carried me out of the fire, didn't you? I was unconscious. I probably would have died in the forest. From all the smoke.'

Harry rubs the back of his neck uncomfortably. 'Look, um. Anyone would have done it. Noah was there. He, uh . . .'

'Yes. But *you* did it.' She touches his arm. 'We don't know if Noah would have done it, do we? But we know you did. Because you did. You see?'

Harry looks confused at this logic. 'Ah . . .'

'Yes. So we have *you* to thank.'

'OK. Well . . . you know. Not in the habit of . . . such things. But I'm glad you're in good shape now and that the boy is all right.'

Lou nods, glancing behind her at the pulled-to door. 'He'll be OK, won't he? Surface wounds, that's all, isn't it?'

In the absence of a reply, she sighs.

'I know. Who can say?'

Harry clears his throat and shoves his hands in his pockets. 'It'll be OK. Now the storm's calmed down.'

Lou looks up at him. 'Thanks, Harry. Really. I don't know what we'd have done without you.'

Harry starts down the steps of the hut, then stops. 'The guys here are pretty clued up, you know. They do know what they're doing. I know it's hard to trust people with all the differences, the language and whatnot . . . But give them a chance.'

'Oh, I'm sorry. I'm sure they do. I just mean, well, it's reassuring . . . having you around . . .'

Harry gives her one of his quick smiles and walks off into the night.

By the light of the moon streaming in through the open curtains, she leans on an elbow and gazes down at Raffy. He murmurs in his sleep, his face scrunches and he clenches, then relaxes his fists. She wants to step inside his head and remove all of the awful memories he must have from this weekend. Wipe his brain clean and fill it with ice cream and cheeseburgers and Tottenham goals and riding his bike and swimming.

Next to him, Laila's brow is clear, her hands raised up beside her head as if she's high-fiving the world in her sleep. Give me a child until they're seven, Lou thinks, remembering the Aristotle quote.

Please, she thinks, as she finally allows herself to cry in the dark. Please let Raffy's seven years have been enough to mould him, before this nightmare stole in aged eight and made its terrible mark.

# 38

## Eliza

*Tuesday*

It's so quiet in the bar, they can hear the gentle swell of the surf. Sara comes and places two coffees in front of Eliza and Lou.

'Morning, Sara.' Eliza points behind Lou's shoulder. Someone has written in chalk on the information board that the tenders will be leaving for the mainland after lunch.

'Have you seen that? Seems as though the police might finally be giving permission for people to leave.'

An aroma of garlic and onion comes from the kitchen. It feels weirdly normal, just another day in paradise. Earlier, they had deposited the children in the kids' club themselves. Julie had sworn that not one child would leave there without an adult chained to their side.

Eliza doesn't like it but it's better for the kids to be distracted. And playing up in the treehouse, it's harder for them to see the sombre uniforms of the search teams trawling the beach and the rainforest paths.

Lou has lost weight. She seems elongated in grief, as if the very top and bottom of her are stretching away from her middle, desperate to avoid touching any piece of her heart. Even her face is drawn, creases of misery carved like thick lines either side of her mouth.

'I'm not sure how I can go on.' Deep in her own reverie, Lou ignores Eliza's question.

'What do you mean?'

Lou makes a rough sound, somewhere between a laugh and a cry. 'Oh, well. Letting my husband drown himself, first of all. Or, if not that, getting himself hanged in a local dynamite-trading war that I couldn't even be bothered to listen to him about?' She holds up two shaky fingers. 'Then turning my brain to mush so I didn't even notice when my child left my care. Fucking my head up so much that I thought another child was mine.' Lou picks up her coffee cup but clatters it back down on the table without taking a sip.

'Lou. You have to give yourself a break.' Eliza leans towards her. 'Adam was drunk. He's a grown-up. He should be able to take care of himself. He's not your responsibility.'

Lou shuts her eyes, not listening.

'And Raffy,' Eliza goes on. 'You had to sleep. You were beside yourself. How could you possibly predict that would happen? Come on,' she reaches out a hand, 'it's not your fault. We know whose fault this is, Lou. And it's not yours.'

Lou opens her eyes and Eliza nods at her.

'I think Lars has got a lot to answer for,' she says.

They fall silent, gazing out at the ocean. Eliza brings her knees to her chest in her chair. She can't think of anything more to say. She seems to have run out of words.

'Adam's dead, isn't he?' Lou says after a while. 'I mean. Even if that...' she swallows '... body isn't his. It's Tuesday. The island is small. There are communities that live here. Everyone seems to know each other. If he was alive but injured, he could have found help. Yesterday, all that noise with the explosion, the fire. He would have known where to try and head, wouldn't he? It would have given him something to aim for – if he was lost in the jungle? He could have headed for the direction of the fire.'

'We don't know, Lou,' Eliza says. 'Maybe he was... frightened to go towards it.'

'Adam doesn't get frightened,' Lou says, lifting her eyes from the horizon where she has been studying the sea like a manuscript.

'Yes, but this isn't like catching a spider in the bathroom, is it? Maybe he walked in on something he shouldn't. Saw something he shouldn't have seen. We know someone – most probably

Lars – was storing dynamite for some reason. But there's so much we don't know. Adam doesn't know the police are here. If—'

'If, if, if...' Lou sounds utterly defeated. 'I don't think we're ever going to find out what's happened to Adam.'

Eliza opens her mouth but, still, the comforting words she wants to provide won't come.

'Mrs Carter?' A barrel-shaped man lumbers into the bar. From his weighty gold chain and the radio attached to his belt, Eliza guesses this must be the chief inspector for whom they've been waiting.

He is puffed, his physique clearly better suited to the air-conditioned spires of Johor Bahru across the water than the humid and mosquito-filled foothills of Fire Mountain. He's wearing long socks for some reason, with the kind of sandals Eliza associates with trainspotters. Nevertheless, his benign appearance fails to put her at ease.

As he sits heavily in a chair next to them, patches of perspiration leaking from the armpits of his lemon-yellow shirt, she feels her pulse quicken, a cold sweat break out on her own skin.

Lou sits forward. 'Is there any news?'

'Oh, I am most positive. Ah, Mrs Fisher, we haven't met,' the man says, accepting a glass of ice water from Sara gratefully. He gulps at it and places it carefully on the table. Then he takes out a handkerchief and dabs at his mouth. 'May I introduce myself? Inspector Khan from the Johor Bahru police force.'

Eliza shakes his hand. It's sticky. Afterwards, she resists the temptation to wipe her fingers on her skirt.

'It is most unfortunate what you have experienced on your holidays, here on Pulau Kalah.' Khan gives them a sad smile.

'But what's going on?' Lou cuts in. 'Have you found anything? Have you found Lars Van Graan? Where is Adam, Inspector Khan?'

'We do have some news, yes.'

Lou stares at him but he shakes his head.

'Unfortunately, not directly in relation to your husband although I have no doubt the trackers will find him. But no. In this case, what we *have* found is that the man who was so brutally killed in the explosion was a local worker named Che bin Jalal.'

'Che,' Eliza says. 'The man who worked for Harry at Timba.'

Lou sinks back into her seat. 'Oh, thank God.' She covers her face, crying silently into her hands.

'It is now confirmed, yes,' Khan says. 'It is not Adam Carter.'

Eliza stretches awkwardly to put a hand on Lou's knee, her eyes on Khan. 'Then he could still be alive? Injured in a remote place? Somewhere impossible to find?'

Khan inclines his head but doesn't respond.

After a few minutes, Lou recovers and looks up with a resolute air. 'OK.' She takes in a shaky breath. 'But with the greatest of respect, Inspector Khan, despite this news, I am still at the end of my tether. And so I must now take steps to involve the British Embassy. I don't see any other option.'

Khan opens his palms. 'This is your right, of course.' He inhales, looking skyward. 'I am sure, however, that your husband will be found within hours. My team are experts in these matters.'

Lou leaps up, her fingers tangling through her hair. 'We don't *have* any more hours. He doesn't have any more hours. He's had too many already, lying somewhere injured, dying of thirst. Why can't you understand this? We thought you were coming two days ago. We've wasted all this time already.'

Eliza goes to her as Lou begins to sob, her entire body shaking. Under her fingers, she feels as fragile as one of the bone-white cuttlefish shells that lie empty on the sand, that get tossed in the surf and splinter into a thousand pieces.

'It's OK,' she whispers. 'It's OK.'

Lou buries her head into Eliza's shoulder and she holds her friend's head as she once held her twins, trying to imbue her with love and calm and shelter from everything terrible that's happening around them.

Then she notices that the inspector has himself got to his feet and has moved with surprising agility to the top of the steps that lead down to the beach.

Following his gaze, Eliza feels blood drain from her face as her hands freeze like claws on Lou's hair. Further down the beach is a cluster of people. A mixture of police officers and the khaki-wearing trackers. At the back of the group, her peripheral vision makes out the tall figures of Noah and Harry. Incredibly, to their left, she sees the white-blond hair and tanned figure of Lars.

But it is the middle of the crowd where her eyes get stuck.

As the gathering make their way up the beach, their pace is stilted and slow. They are carrying a stretcher, low to the ground. It's heavy and hampers their progress across the sand.

Eliza's hands lift and hover in the air. Lou raises her tear-stained face, blinking and adjusting after the cocoon of Eliza's embrace. Seeing Eliza's expression, she turns round, fast as a whip. And then she's gone. Racing down the steps and on to the beach. Calling and screaming Adam's name. Desperately begging for this not to be true.

But it is true.

Eliza sinks to the floor, a cry deep inside her, stuck in her ribcage, her hands still holding the now empty shape of Lou's head. She watches as Lou reaches the men and drops to the ground, touching the figure on the stretcher with agonised fingers. She watches as Lou looks up at them all with their bowed heads, as she searches their faces for any sign that this could be a mistake. But they do not respond.

The trackers have done their work. They have found Adam, just as they promised.

But the Adam they have found is not as he was.

This Adam is bloodied and shrivelled, with a caved-in skull and a fatal wound to his stomach.

The Adam the trackers have found is dead.

# 39

## NOAH

'He's actually a good guy,' Harry says, digging his thumbs into his eye sockets as if to rub away the memories of the past few days. 'Inspector Khan, I mean. He's a good man. Honest. Intelligent.'

He pours them both another shot of rum from the bottle he's taken from behind the bar. Zikri is busy down on the beach, loading the departing guests and their baggage into the two resort tenders.

The police have put Adam's body into the cold storage room at the back of the kitchen. Nobody liked to mention health and safety even though Noah had certainly thought about it. But what else could they do? The heat was melting his body beyond any kind of recognition, and they couldn't carry him all the way round to Timba to the air-conditioned bunkhouse there.

'He'd been attacked, hadn't he? Adam, I mean,' Noah says. 'From what I saw of him on the stretcher. That wasn't a drowning.'

Harry doesn't answer, just traces the rim of his glass with his finger.

'Two murders,' Noah says. He watches his hands shake a little as he lifts his drink. The phrase echoes in his head like a shout in a cave. *Two murders, two murders.*

Behind them, the sea washes in and out interminably. The sound of it is beginning to send Noah insane. A creak in a door that needs oiling, a distant car alarm that isn't muffled. He thinks back to a time when – God, when was it – only a day or so ago? When all he had to worry about was getting a report emailed over to his office.

Now, after everything he's heard from Eliza; with Adam dead; how can he care about any of that ever again?

Without warning, he leaps from his stool and strides behind the bar. Grabs the wind chimes that dangle and tinkle in the wind incessantly and rips them from their hook. He dashes them to the ground and grinds his flip-flops into them, splintering the polished wood, silencing them for good.

Harry stares at him.

Breathing heavily, Noah gives an embarrassed smile and shrugs.

'Sorry,' he says. 'It's been driving me mad for days.'

He comes back next to Harry and downs his rum, rolls his neck around until he hears it crack.

Harry drains his glass as Inspector Khan comes into the bar. He shakes Harry's hand and introduces himself to Noah before hoisting himself up on to another bar stool. Harry passes him a glass of rum which he considers for a moment before swiftly knocking it back. He lifts his eyes to the sky.

'Ah. May Allah forgive me.' He smiles at Noah. 'Don't look so worried, Mr Fisher. There are no gods or magic for me.' He pushes the glass towards Harry, who refills it. 'How long have you been married, Mr Fisher?'

'Seventeen years.'

'You are close to your wife, I'm sure.'

'Of course.'

'But you haven't known Mr and Mrs Carter long? They are new friends of yours?'

Noah feels his heart rate quicken. These questions. Does Khan know about the bombshell Eliza dropped on him yesterday? Does he know that Eliza and Adam are half-brother and sister?

'We met them about eight months ago,' he says carefully. 'When we moved to Singapore from London.'

'So nice, I can imagine. To make such good friends, far from your home town. But,' Khan bends his head to one side, 'you are all from the same area, I believe? All from London? Yes,' he smiles at Noah's affirmative nod, 'I was at university myself there. Criminology at the London School of Economics. Yes,

Mr Fisher,' he taps his thigh with a finger, 'Inspector Khan was there too.'

Noah gives an uneasy smile. The policeman seems to be suggesting he's been following them around for years. He tries to keep his breath calm, act normal.

Khan swivels on his bar stool as if to look for something and hops down. 'Would you mind...?'

He indicates a basket on a table behind them and tilts it upwards so Noah can see inside. 'What are these, Mr Fisher?'

'Um. Oh, they're... that's my phone. And...' Noah takes the basket and rifles through the pile '... this is Eliza's. See? We've got the same photo of the twins on the back cover.' He looks up. 'Why have you got them?'

'Oh, come on, Noah,' Harry says wearily. 'This is a murder investigation. What did you think was going to happen? That you'd all be allowed to head off back to Singers as if none of you might be involved?'

'No. But...' Noah gives a laugh. 'Well, I've been with you most of the time, Harry. So what are you suggesting?'

Khan rests his hands on the table. 'When you hiked to Timba with Harry, Mr Fisher, you took your mobile phone with you, did you not?'

'Yes. I did.'

'There's Wi-Fi signal there, isn't there? Turtle Cove has purposely restricted it, here at the resort. To aid rest and relaxation.' Khan gives him a sly smile.

Noah starts to feel cold, even as the sun beats down on the atap roof of the bar. He recognises it as the first sign of adrenaline. Soon he'll have pins and needles in his fingers and toes.

'Yes,' he says. 'What of it?'

'You sent your wife a WhatsApp message, didn't you? Once you arrived at Timba. To let her know you were safe and sound. You forgot, I imagine, that even though you had Wi-Fi at Timba, your message couldn't be read by Mrs Fisher as she had no Internet at the resort.'

Noah studies the policeman, trying to work out what Khan is getting at.

'But, strangely, the message *was* read. On your wife's phone. We have seen the blue ticks.' Khan straightens. 'Maybe it means nothing at all. But you see, don't you? What it tells us?'

Noah's mouth is dry but he forces himself to reply. 'Um, I suppose?'

Khan nods. 'Yes indeed. It tells us that at some point your wife was not at the resort. That she left Turtle Cove. Either that or someone took her phone when they went wandering off. Because she was able to open and read your message, you see? And she'd only be able to do that if she herself had signal. And, as we know...'

'There is no Wi-Fi signal in the Turtle Cove resort,' Noah says slowly. His mind whirs. *How did Eliza pick up that message? When did she leave the resort?*

He can hear her back in the hut, her arms either side of him against the wall. That look in her eyes, almost empty, vacant.

What had Eliza said to him yesterday?

*He only existed in order for me to hate him... And it felt good, Noah. It felt really, really good.*

Oh God, Eliza, he thinks. What have you done?

Khan points at him as if he has won a round in a quiz show before returning to his stool.

'It is a sad thing, is it not? What all of this conundrum will look like to the world, to the press? When we take Mr Carter's body off the island and he is transported back to Singapore. What will people say? Oh, Malaysia is unsafe. Tourists are murdered in Malaysia.

'Do they care so much, Mr Fisher?' Khan stares at Noah in earnest. 'Those people. If they hear that a local man was killed? No, not so much. But for Mr Carter, oh yes.

'Appearance is all. Justice must be seen to be done. The murderer of Adam Carter will surely face the death penalty. Unless of course,' Khan picks an invisible piece of fluff from his shirt, 'this murderer has already suffered a similar fate.'

'What do you mean?' Noah frowns, then his face clears. 'Oh, I see. Che. The body hanging in the tree.'

'Do you know anything about dynamite, Mr Fisher?'

'Not really,' Noah answers, darting a *what's he going on about now?* look at Harry. 'Nothing specific.'

'But you were not as concerned with the fish bomb on your dive trip as Adam Carter, I understand?' Khan nods, leaning on the bar. 'Yes? I think that was true?'

Noah sits back, surprised. 'Oh. Well, maybe not. Who told you that?'

Khan sips from his drink but doesn't answer.

'Yeah, well. Maybe I thought Adam was making too much of a thing about it. They do happen, fish bombs. I just wanted us to have a good trip. Didn't want any drama. I thought he was causing trouble.'

'I see. He was liable to be provoked, was he? Mr Carter?'

'Yes,' Noah agrees readily. This is more comfortable ground. 'He was.'

'He was certainly provoked on the night he went missing, I think. You might have been the one responsible, perhaps?'

Noah briefly shuts his eyes. 'Well, look. Of course you're going to ask about that. I get it. It looks bad. But we were friends. Good friends. We'd had too much to drink. We had a stupid falling-out. I can't even remember what it was about.'

'Was it perhaps that he was angry with you? And you felt it was unjust?'

Noah looks at him. 'You know I'm a lawyer, right? If you're going to start questioning me properly, we should probably get to Johor and think about conducting an interview under proper conditions.'

Khan laughs. 'Mr Fisher, my apologies. No, no. You are not under caution. I'm just trying to work out – just for my own curiosity, you understand – how it was that Mr Carter's body came to be found lying outside a cache of dynamite.'

'What?' Noah stands up, his hands and feet tingling. *A cache?*

'Yes,' Khan beams at him. 'A coincidence, I'm sure you'd agree, after the fish-bomb incident?'

'I don't understand. Adam had found a cache? How? When?'

Khan places his empty glass carefully into the middle of the bar. 'I think you know the answer to that.'

Noah blinks at him from behind his glasses. 'What did you just say?'

'Yes. I think that was at the root of your argument with Adam on the beach...'

'What are you talking about?'

'You overheard Mr Van Graan, didn't you? One of the Turtle Cove staff – she had been babysitting for your group I believe – Tita? She saw you from her hut when you were listening outside his office. Van Graan had been talking to Che bin Jalal about the fish bomb. He was being blackmailed by Che, in fact. Held to ransom because Che wanted the explosives for himself and he was willing to commit murder,' Khan glares at Noah, 'if Lars Van Graan did not accede to his requests.'

Noah sidesteps away from the bar. 'This is completely out of order. The man was talking in Malay. I couldn't understand a single word he said. I definitely couldn't hear what the other person was saying down the end of the phone line. So how I would have managed to fathom all that from what I heard is anyone's guess. And why would I be arguing with Adam about it anyway?' He rubs a hand over his head. *Stay cool.*

'Lars was on the phone, you say?'

'Yes.' Noah crumples a napkin on the bar and throws it on to the sand. 'At least, I assumed that because I couldn't hear a response. I heard him slam something down, like a receiver. But I didn't *see* him.'

Khan looks at the napkin on the ground for a moment.

'All right. Then, maybe your argument with Adam Carter had its roots in something closer to home? A battle of ego? What do men normally fight over?'

Noah stares at him.

'Women, Mr Fisher. Maybe you were jealous that Adam was flirting with your wife?'

Noah laughs angrily. 'Who's telling you all of this? Oh, let me guess. Lars himself. Right. Nice one, Harry. Spot on. Khan is an honest and good man? Bollocks.'

He moves to leave the bar but stops and turns back, his breath caught hot and hard in his throat. 'Next time you want to talk to

222

me, make sure you've got the right paperwork, Inspector. None of what we've just discussed is admissible and you know it.'

He strides off, praying that what he's said is true. He has no idea about the intricacies of Malaysian criminal law, but he had to fight back, he had to say *something*. He marches down the steps to the beach, his heart tight in his chest. Ahead of him, the sea is like glass but, for the first time, it doesn't seem beautiful.

For the first time, looking at it, he feels afraid.

# 40

## Eliza

'But I don't understand it.' She stares at Noah as he throws their clothes into the two weekend bags they'd brought with them. In the next-door bedroom, Sam and Chloe are plugged into their iPads.

'How are they allowed to look at our mobile phones? They're private.'

'They just are,' Noah says. 'It's the law in Malaysia. It's irrelevant, though, isn't it?' He looks up at her, a pair of swimming shorts in his hands. 'The issue is – the only way that message could have been opened on your phone was if you hit Wi-Fi signal by leaving the resort. Which means you've lied to me. Because you never told me you left Turtle Cove.'

Eliza pauses for a second, then shakes her head. 'That's not the point. When they took all our details – which we gave them *freely*, by the way – they said they needed my passcode. And I asked them then: I said, why do you need it? And they told me it was just for security purposes. The guy gave me his name but I can't remember it. Fucking *hell*. It's so sneaky.'

'Did you hear what I said? I'm saying you have lied to me.'

'What? No. I haven't. When have I lied to you?'

'Adam has been murdered, El.' Noah pulls the zip across on the bag and snaps the clasp together. He looks around the hut, moving to another pile of clothes in the corner, bundling them into his arms and shoving them into the other bag. He's filled with nervous energy. She can feel it fizzing from him; an almost chemical reaction. 'Of course they're going to be asking questions.

It wasn't so long ago that you were telling me this yourself. They need to know where everyone was on the island when Adam was killed. It's obvious.'

'Don't start getting angry,' Eliza warns, the threat of tears in her voice. 'I can't cope if you start having a go at me. I don't know about that message, all right? I didn't know you'd sent it.' She shuts her eyes for a second, trying to think. 'When would it have come through?' she whispers, and then her head snaps up. 'OK. So... It must have been when I went after Lou.'

But he's not paying attention, he hasn't heard what she said. She goes over and grabs his hands, forces him to stop his manic packing.

'Listen to me. I'm not denying it, Noah. I *did* leave the resort. I'll go and tell them this right now. I went after Lou to try and look for her. When she announced at breakfast that she was going to go and look for Adam herself? Remember? It was then. Before she came back soaking wet after the rain started, right before the explosion? You can ask Tita. I told her I was going, because I went to her hut to find Lou and the baby, and Tita was the one that said she'd gone. Why would I do that if I was planning on murdering Adam?' She stops and takes a breath. She can hear that she sounds vaguely hysterical. 'I went out into the rainforest, up the path where you went with Harry. But then I freaked out. I didn't like it on my own. I didn't know where I was going and I was worried about getting lost. But...' her eyes dart around the room, thinking, '... I must have hit the Wi-Fi zone at some point without even realising it. That must be why, Noah.

'God, this is what it's going to be like, isn't it? They're going to twist everything. Make us look guilty.'

She finally grabs Noah's attention, and his gaze clears as he registers what she says. 'You followed us to look for Lou? And you told Tita? You're sure you did? She'll back you up on that?'

'Yes.' Eliza wraps her arms around her torso. 'I mean, I think she will. We definitely had that conversation.'

'OK. OK.' Noah drops the clothes he holds in his hands and exhales. 'That woman is bloody everywhere, isn't she? In this case, it's good, though. Because I agree with you about twisting

225

stuff,' he says darkly. 'They're making up some rubbish about me overhearing Lars talking about dynamite with the dead guy Che. Not that it's a crime to overhear stuff, obviously. It's what they're implying. I don't like it, El. We don't have representation here. No way of knowing what's going on. Even Harry – who I thought I could trust – even he seems in the pocket of this Inspector Khan.

'What am I going to say to the firm, the partnership? The press are going to get hold of this. It's a fucking nightmare.'

Eliza puts a hand on his chest. 'We *have* to get home. Everything will be OK once we're home. We can work it all out then. Surely they can't hold us here indefinitely without charging us? Or giving us some cause? They've let other guests go. Why not us?

'The more I hear, it's obvious, isn't it? Adam basically got involved with something to do with the locals, this bloke Che whoever he was.' She swallows. 'The man who was hanged. It's to do with that. Nothing to do with us. So why don't they let us go?'

Noah lifts her hand away. 'Maybe they know something. About your background.'

Her *background*. For a moment, she can't think what he's talking about. Then, like plummeting into cold water, she remembers. She's told Noah about Adam.

Her brother.

She gives an empty little laugh. 'How could they possibly know about that? The only people that know about it are dead, or they're me. Or you,' she says archly then flushes, regretting saying anything.

He laughs harshly. 'Only just, babe. By the skin of my teeth.'

'Noah, there was no need for you to know—'

'I'm sorry, but what the actual fuck?' He reels round, snatching off his glasses, the tendons in his neck tense as guy ropes.

'I couldn't deal with it. I didn't want to talk about it. I wanted to forget it. Put it all behind me.'

'You *left* me...' he says. 'You didn't let me go to her funeral. And you knew then, didn't you?'

He waits.

'We are *married*, Eliza.'

'What's it got to do with that? With us?'

'Well, as it turns out, quite a lot as it goes. From where I'm standing today.' He laughs again and then stops and the silence is brutal. 'This is too much. I can't work it out, split the fucking atoms.' He shuts his eyes briefly and takes a breath. Puts his glasses back on. 'Why are we here, Eliza?'

'What do you mean?'

'Why are we friends with the Carters?'

She turns away. Can't look at him as she talks.

'Eliza...'

'OK,' she rips her head from side to side, 'OK. I'll tell you. Just give me...' She waits a beat. 'Look. Right before we left for Asia, a mother at the twins' old school told me that a good friend of hers lived in Singapore and I *must* have heard of him.

'Adam Carter was his name, the author and son of the famous Benjamin. They were a lovely family, she said. I should look them up when we arrived. Singapore was so minuscule, it would be impossible to avoid them anyway.'

She pauses for a minute, her voice small like a child's.

'Would you have believed me, if I'd told you the truth? It was like my mind completely fractured. I tried to talk to you, but it was impossible. Then I tried to get us out of the move. I did. Remember? And then...'

'Then, what?' Noah asks.

'I began to feel curious, I suppose. As the move date got closer, I read his books, researched him online, studied family photos on his Facebook page. Then I found myself putting the twins into the same school in Singapore as Raffy.' She turns round defensively. 'It is one of the best, anyway.'

He shrugs as if he couldn't care less.

'And it really didn't take long to meet them, did it? And I genuinely did like Lou.'

'What about Adam?' Noah asks with emphasis. 'What did you think about him?'

Eliza blows out a bewildered half-laugh. 'I was a bit dazzled by him, I think. Intrigued. Bloody amazed that I shared DNA with this bolshy, charismatic, irritating man. He was so different from me. But... he was also my *brother*.'

She wipes tears from her eyes with rough fingers.

'Yeah, all right then,' Noah concedes. 'But I still don't get it. Why didn't you tell Adam? How could you be friends with them like this, and not say anything?'

She moves to the bags on the bed and starts rearranging the bundle of clothes Noah has shoved inside. 'It wasn't the right time.'

'It's just… *weird*. Coming away like this for the weekend?'

'I was getting to know him. Seeing if we could have a proper relationship. And… also, I mean. How do you bring it up? Right?' She stares back at him. 'What's the etiquette for something like that?'

'Well, I guess… But what did you want? From him?'

'I don't know. Nothing. I didn't want anything. I didn't tell him because I didn't know if I was ready or not.'

'Ready for what?' Noah starts to sound impatient. 'What were you waiting for?'

'Stop it…'

'Just like me.' He folds his arms, staring at her. 'When were you ever going to tell me? Huh?'

'Listen to you. Look at you,' she points at him. 'Look how aggressive you are. Why would I come to you when you're like this? I don't like it. And I tried, I really did. In London. But you were – you *are* – obsessed with work. It's all you ever think about. It's all you see. Not me,' she stabs a finger into her chest.

'I do it for our family. For all of us.'

'Oh, come *on*. You do it for yourself. Why can't you admit it? You're so determined to make something of yourself. Be the boy come good. Show your mum. Show your family. Prove you're better than them.'

She breaks off, seeing the hurt wash over his face.

Noah exhales and drops his arms like all his fight is gone. He comes to where she stands by the bed and sits, hanging his head, delicately bringing his fingertips together across his knees. He has such elegant fingers, Eliza thinks. He's so strong, but so fine, all at the same time.

'Isn't that what we all do, El?' Noah says, looking up at her. 'Isn't everyone trying to prove things to their families? Trying to make something of their lives? Trying to be better than the person they've always been told that they were?'

There's a thump and a giggle from the room next door and they look at the wall, towards the sound.

Eliza sinks down, kneeling in front of him. 'I never had a proper family,' she says. 'The people who are supposed to love you unconditionally... they left me. My father,' her mouth twists on the word. 'And then my mother.'

'When you came back to me,' Noah says, 'I thought I was enough. I really believed you'd decided I could give you the family you'd always wanted.'

'You did. You have.'

He shakes his head. 'It's not true, though, is it? I've always worried. Doubted it. Maybe,' he takes a deep breath. 'Without making excuses, maybe that's what I stick my head in the sand about. The drinking...' He shrugs and looks at her with a sad smile.

'You are enough,' she tells him. 'Look at me. You are.'

'Then why are we here, Eliza?'

All the thoughts she's had over the last few days flutter through her head. It's October, she remembers. She misses the seasons, here in Asia. Misses the sight of autumn leaves picked up by the wind, swirling through dust on the ground.

She stands and straightens the wrinkles in her skirt. She turns to the mirror and lifts her hair into a ponytail and ties it up. Puts on a dash of lipstick and some mascara. Analyses her reflection.

'You asked me what I would have said to Adam. If I'd told him the truth about him being my brother.'

'Yes?'

'It wasn't fair,' she says.

'What wasn't fair?'

She goes to the door and throws it open, lets a cone of bright yellow sunshine spill into the hut.

'That was what I wanted from Adam,' she says. 'That was what I wanted to say.

'I wanted to tell him that it wasn't fair.'

# 41

## LOU

She opens the door to the cold room and, right away, has to take a step back. She can't help it: she's gagging with her hand over her mouth. Surely, whatever that smell is, it cannot be Adam?

She looks back over her shoulder to check Raffy hasn't snuck up behind her. Over in the restaurant, Sara and Julie are sitting with him watching *Incredibles 2* on a laptop. After she'd told him that his father was dead, she had wondered if she would be able to get through this. Whether she would have the strength to wake up every morning and see his little face, so serious but so stoic at the same time.

She would rather he screamed and cried and kicked out at them all. But he has taken the news like a soldier. Like a knight. And onward he battles, letting the news settle inside him like a feather. She doesn't think she will ever be able to match his bravery. And watching him fight to hide his tears and his grief is almost too much to bear.

She has to see Adam. They've told her she shouldn't. That he isn't the Adam she knew. But she has to see him one last time.

She has to say goodbye.

She puts on the mask they've given her as well as pulling her T-shirt up over her nose and mouth. She makes a silent apology to Adam that she can't accept him as he is. The smell is like nothing she's experienced, though. She lifts up the sheet that covers him and realises they were right.

He is gone. Not only in the way his handsome face has been shredded into tatters, sunken into pockets of flesh and liquid and shadows. But even if his shell were untouched, she knows he's not there any more. That spark he had, that *life*, the essence of him that made him so Adam: convivial, infuriating, charming, sometimes cruel. Never, ever boring.

All of that has evaporated.

She hovers her hands over his body, and she cries. He was a terrible husband. But he was also the best. Ignored by his father, emotionally leeched on by his mother, he had come into her life, strutting like a peacock with a heart riddled sore by those bullets. She had loved him. She had hated him too. But, God, she had loved him.

And now, he is gone.

'The valiant never taste of death but once.'

Lou rests her hands on the table where Adam lies and bows her head. 'Julius Caesar,' she says. 'Very apt for Adam.'

'Come outside, Mrs Carter,' Inspector Khan says from the doorway. 'Come out, into the light. Let us see the small hero, Raphael.' Lou gently replaces the sheet and leaves the cold room. She looks over to see that Raffy has fallen asleep on Julie's lap. She's turned off the computer and seems content, patting his back and gazing out to sea.

Lou gives them a short wave and joins Khan at a nearby table.

'I didn't know Mr Carter. But he strikes me as the man who didn't fear death.'

'You're right.' Lou acknowledges the fact with a smile. 'Adam lived his life very much as if death was something to be completely ignored. Not because he was afraid. Quite the opposite, actually. He was very aware of it. Particularly after his father died. But, perversely, that made him almost... *dare* it to come and get him. And so it did,' she says.

Zikri brings over two coffees. Lou thanks him and sighs, turning the cup around in its saucer. When he has gone, she leans forward.

'What happened to him, Inspector Khan? What happened to Adam?'

Khan nods. 'We think your husband was caught, entirely by accident, in the middle of a local dispute. The man, Che – who was killed in the explosion – we think he saw Adam paddling in the kayak near a dynamite cache hidden in a cave on Ferringhi beach. It's a small beach, not used by tourists at all. It's completely covered in rocks, not a place to relax.

'Our theory is that Adam came on to the beach for some reason. Maybe to look for drinking water before returning to Turtle Cove? Anyway, Che discovered him or… he found Che,' Khan opens his palms. 'Adam had been seen the night before in the kampong. There had been a fight about Che stealing dynamite from another local family. He'd been using it as leverage to get cut in on a deal he perceived he'd been denied. When he saw Adam, Che thought he was snooping, spying on him. That he'd report the dynamite cache to the police. Let us hypothesise there was a tussle.'

'And he killed him?' Lou stares at Khan. 'Just like that?'

'Well…' Khan takes a sip from his coffee and looks out to sea for a moment. 'His family say not. They say Che returned to the kampong immediately after the fight. He was in a clear panic. He told them Adam had fallen and hit his head—'

'Of course they'd say that,' Lou interrupts.

'Yes,' Khan admits. 'But when he was found, Mr Carter also had a wound to his stomach. The family knew nothing of this. Che mentioned only the fall. We won't know until after the autopsy what it was that proved fatal – that or the head injury. But it remains a possibility that Adam was killed after the fight with Che. By somebody else.'

Lou puts her head in her hands. 'By whom? How will we find that out for sure? And what about the fight that Raffy saw on Monday morning in the kampong? He says someone let off a gun. And Adam told me he'd seen Lars with a gun. What's been going on here, on Pulau Kalah? All of it is so…' She tails away, unable to find the words.

'Well,' Khan says. 'And really, Mrs Carter, you must understand that none of this really involves Adam. He was just in the wrong place at the wrong time. Che had found the cache a while ago on his walks to work at the turtle sanctuary every morning. He realised it was being used to supply others in his community.

It made him angry. Envious. So he had been stealing little bits of the dynamite store and hiding it in a hut not far from here—'

'The place that Raffy discovered?'

'Precisely. Yes. Che was using what he'd stolen as a means of extortion over Mr Van Graan. Unfortunately,' Khan says with a grim shake of his head, 'Lars Van Graan has been getting himself involved in matters he should not be meddling in. Selling dynamite to others in the community to help them fish.'

Lou sits up in her chair and then slumps down again. 'Adam thought that was the case. But we didn't believe him. We laughed at him. I told him he was jealous of Lars.' She gives a little laugh. 'Always the way with Adam,' she says. 'At first, you feel pissed off with him for getting into trouble. And then you feel guilty for giving him a hard time about it.'

Khan gives a sympathetic shake of his head.

Lou rubs a hand over her face, exhausted by all this news. 'So where has Lars been?'

'Ah. He has also been in what you call the flat spin.' Khan finishes his coffee and pushes the cup and saucer away. 'After the fish bomb during your husband's dive, Lars realised he had to contain Che and his psychological games. Che was threatening to disrupt further dives. It would harm Lars's business. Everyone's business, in fact. They couldn't have tourists frightened to come and dive the reef for fear of being blown up.

'He agreed to cut Che in on the amounts he was selling to the local community. Really, Mrs Carter, we are not talking large quantities here. Van Graan is clever. He knows it is more a case of I have and you have not than any desire to destroy, that gives him power over these people. Anyway,' Khan shrugs, 'the man with whom the arrangement had originally been made – Alif—'

Lou frowns. 'The old man? The boatman?'

'He is not so old. Maybe fifty,' Khan smiles. 'Yes, Alif. He felt betrayed by this agreement with Che bin Jalal. He sees him – rightly or wrongly – as part of a new order. The turtle sanctuary. He disagrees with it wholeheartedly. He has been sending them messages for a while now, indicating his displeasure...'

'The pig in the tank...'

'Indeed. As part of the agreement with Van Graan, Che had told him where he had been storing the explosives he was skimming from the cache—'

'In that hut,' Lou says.

'Yes. Ah, I digress.' Khan shakes his head. 'Anyway, when Che came back to the kampong frightened he had killed Adam, he called Lars. But Lars's first search with Zikri, if you remember – it was early on the Sunday. Only around ten a.m.' Khan lifts his eyes to the sky briefly and then places a warm hand on top of Lou's.

'What is it?' she whispers.

'I am sad to tell you that Che did not return to the kampong with his sorry tale until after midday on the Sunday.' Khan looks at her with mournful eyes. 'So, when Lars took his first search for Adam, he went authentically. He knew nothing then about Che or any fight with Adam. He only knew that Adam had gone out into the ocean, late at night, after too much to drink.'

'What?' Lou scoots back her chair, not believing what she's hearing. 'What do you mean? You're saying Adam might still have been alive when Lars first went looking for him?'

'It is possible, yes. We will know more from the autopsy and the official time of death. But my theory is that Adam was asleep somewhere at that point. And when he woke, he had the raging thirst. And it was this that led him to Ferringhi beach.'

'How do you know Lars didn't find him? How do you know it wasn't Lars that killed him and took him to the beach?'

'Because Zikri and Lars's stories match. And they also correlate with the timing of the witnesses in the kampong,' Khan says softly.

'Oh my God. I don't know what to believe any more.' Lou stands up and goes to the low wall of the restaurant, stares out at the sea.

'On the second search, the one Lars made with Alif,' Khan continues, 'they found Adam.'

Lou spins round, her hands at her heart.

'He was lying on the beach at Ferringhi. Alive, but unconscious. Lars didn't know what to do. If he called the police, they would find the dynamite. He didn't have time to shift it, there was too much. Alif and he couldn't move Adam on their own. He needed to buy time.

'And then the monsoon alarm was raised. They were as stuck as all of you. There was nothing that could be done. Everyone had to wait.'

Lou glances over at Raffy. He is still asleep as her heart pounds so loudly she can't believe it doesn't wake him.

Khan tracks her gaze.

'The following morning – on the Monday – is when young Raphael went in Lars's footsteps to the kampong. Lars had already told Che to lie low. Now Harry was looking for him. Things were becoming unmanageable. Alif was out of control. He blamed Che for the danger he'd put them all in by the attack on an *ang moh*. If Adam survived, he would make trouble by reporting them all to the authorities. If he was dead, their businesses would be ruined. Their livelihoods destroyed. On top of that, they were facing a criminal charge. So the orders were given,' Khan says. 'Che had put them in this situation and so he must be dealt with.'

'This is a small island,' Khan says. 'Horizons are not large. Van Graan exploited their needs. But he, too, is simple. Distracted by his own desires.' Khan tuts. 'Stupid of him to bring the girl to the kampong. He is a man that thinks with his...' Khan waves a hand over his trouser area and then clears his throat, embarrassed.

He shifts position on his chair.

'So, perhaps, he was not on the ball when young Raphael followed them. And then, when this smallest hero finds the explosives,' Khan's eyes shine, 'the game is afoot!'

Lou stares at him.

Khan nods. 'If Raphael survives, Van Graan knows he has to disappear before your boy is found and tells all. He calls Zikri and instructs him to look after things. Then he leaves for the south of the island where he will wait for the weather to clear. His plan is to sail a local boat – a sampan – to a nearby holm and stay hidden there until the police have gone.'

'But you found him?' Lou asks.

His mouth turns down. 'I wish I could take this honour. But it was in fact the loyal barman Zikri as well as your dependable marine biologist, Harry, who snagged him for us, Mrs Carter. Persons who know the land, the sea. Who care about its future. Men like Zikri, they are the older guard.' Khan minutely adjusts the gold watch he wears on his wrist. 'My sense is they have lost patience with the Van Graan family and their hold on the island.'

'Yes.' He taps the table with his hand. 'Government rules and regulations concerning fishing quotas and conservation are not for us to decide. Similarly, we must let the law mete out justice, do you agree?'

'Well, yes,' Lou says. 'Of course.'

'Ah,' Khan sighs. 'But so many of us prefer to take these matters into our own hands. And so, Che paid the price for his disloyalty.'

Lou frowns. She puts her index fingers to her temples. She is getting a tension headache. 'But we still don't really know what happened to Adam.'

Khan pats her hand. 'We will.'

She looks over again at the sleeping Raffy, at his little back rising and falling with his breath.

'When can we go home, Inspector?' she asks. 'I want to get Raffy back. And Laila. They need to be at home with their things. I need to ...' She pauses. 'I don't know. Being stuck here on the island. It's like a wound that still bleeds, the longer we stay here. We need to heal, Inspector. I need to heal. I can't go on like this, I really can't.'

'I absolutely agree,' Khan replies. 'And I will not keep you here any longer than is necessary. But, you understand. Singapore is a different country to Malaysia. We are friends with our Singaporean brothers. But everything must be as settled as possible before people start crossing any borders.'

'The other guests, though?' Lou points out. 'They've been allowed to leave.'

'That's true. But we don't have much more to establish. And those other people ...' Khan waves at the sea. 'We can rule them out, Mrs Carter. I think you understand.'

She closes her eyes wearily.

'Ah, I can see Mrs Fisher over there on the beach,' Khan says loudly, making her jump. 'Let me see if I can find out some other things. Don't worry, Mrs Carter. We won't keep you much longer.'

He walks off and Lou watches as he hurries along the shoreline. She shivers in the warm breeze, following the shadows of passing clouds as they dance across the sand.

She leans back in her chair and closes her eyes, going over everything Khan has said. And thinking back to something she didn't mention. That she hasn't said to anyone.

When they brought Adam's body up the beach and she'd run to see him, she'd been distraught, crying, sobbing, unable to take it in. But, as she'd walked back up with him, she'd been almost calm. She'd known from the time he went missing that this reality was always possible. Now it had happened, she had to focus on Raffy and helping him get through it.

So when she got back to the bar, she was breathing normally, her eyes were clear. And so she was fully aware, and she had seen the expression on Eliza's face as they brought Adam's body past.

Eliza looked stricken.

Lou knows that Adam wasn't cheating on her with Eliza. But there was something there, she's sure of it. Some kind of connection between them. Every which way she analyses it, she believes it to be true.

She just wishes she knew what it was.

Because thinking back on how Eliza had looked when she had seen Adam's body, she just can't tell.

Had Eliza been heartbroken? Or terrified?

# 42

## NOAH

From their hut, he hauls their bags up to the dive shack. He chucks them into the trailer the staff use to wheel the luggage down to the tenders when guests depart.

It's a blatant act of defiance as Khan hasn't said they can leave. But he has to do something. He is being hamstrung and it's killing him.

The twins have run up alongside him on the beach and he now deposits them at a table in the restaurant and orders two Oreo milkshakes from Sara. He tries to make his mind go blank as he sits there, watching chocolate moustaches emerge on their upper lips as they drink and chatter to each other.

'Cheers.' Sam clinks his glass against Chloe's. 'I'm going to have five of these. Let's pretend they're beers like Daddy drinks.'

'Get really drunk,' Chloe says.

Noah turns his head.

'Lars won't even talk to me.'

An American voice cuts in above the children's. It's the girl, Zoe, standing just outside, whining to Julie.

'All he says is I gotta leave A-SAP. That he'll wire me the money he owes. Won't even help with the flight. After everything I did for him. Seriously. My luck. Fucking men.'

'Get really drunk like Daddy, like this,' Sam bashes his head down onto the table.

'Hey, watch your language, girl,' Noah bellows at Zoe. 'There are kids here, yeah?'

She glances over, rolling her eyes. Julie pulls at the sleeve of Zoe's T-shirt, giving Noah an apologetic look. Zoe peels herself off the wall of the restaurant and slinks away.

'I'm going outside, kids,' Noah says. 'I need some air.'

He is trembling.

Behind him, in the dark, cool storage room, is Adam's decomposing body. Adam is dead.

Adam is Eliza's half-brother.

His kids think he's a drunk.

And even though it kills him to admit it, he still can't shake the feeling that Eliza has somehow been involved in Adam's death.

He doesn't know how. He can't ask her and he doesn't think he ever will. If he's honest, he's too scared to hear the answer.

But he knows her.

He knows her every which way and round about. He has always been proud of his ability to read Eliza, to see past her beauty, past her exterior. To see the real her.

He knows that Khan has questioned her. That she told him about leaving the resort to look for Lou, and that Tita has confirmed that she did ask her the way. That explains the Wi-Fi activation on the phone and the fact that his message to her downloaded as it did.

It's not that, though.

It's the fact that she kept the secret of Adam from him for so long. How could she do it? He has been totally betrayed. Eliza has deceived Adam. But she has also deceived him. He – Noah – who loves her more than anyone in the world.

That look on her face.

*He only existed in order for me to hate him... And it felt good, Noah. It felt really, really good.*

He stumbles out and away from the restaurant, down to the end of the beach where high tide has foamed around the cluster of rocks, their surface sleek as sealskin. He takes off his flip-flops and stands in the surf, letting the water swirl round his ankles, looking out at the horizon and the endless blue of sea and sky.

He has to change. Things have to change.

He shuts his eyes against the surrounding paradise. He's had too much and he's sick on it. It means nothing. They don't belong there, Eliza and him. He wants to rip a hole in that perfect cobalt sky and step out of it into the grime and shit of London town. Talk to someone in a language he understands. Not all of this ma'am and boss shit. Yes sir, no sir, three bags full of your finest explosives, sir.

*Fuck.*

How has he not realised how damaged Eliza is? How angry she is – even now – at the death of her mother? How did he miss her discovering something this cataclysmic – that she had a *brother*?

What are they doing here in Asia? Why have they come? Just to make money and then what? Come to these perfect, pristine beaches and get pissed? Scream and fight and smash everything they have to pieces?

'It is beautiful out here, is it not?'

Inspector Khan stands behind him, his trousers rolled up to his knees.

'Over there, you can see Pulau Tioman.' He points. 'See? In the distance?'

Noah squints in the same direction and can just about make it out. He doesn't really care, though. He sighs and shoves his hands in his pockets, looking down at his bare feet in the water.

'You love your wife very much, Mr Carter,' Khan says.

Noah's jaw tenses involuntarily. 'Of course I do.'

'She is also very beautiful.'

He can't help it, his whole body jerks with anger towards the detective. 'It's not that, man. Yes, of course she is. She's stunning. But it's her mind I love. The whole of her. She's vulnerable and scared. She's been treated so badly in her life. By her mum. Her dad. I just want to be there for her. Be her family. Her *real* family.'

'She has no family?'

'She has us.' Noah smacks his chest with his palm. 'Me and the twins. That's all we need. No one else.'

Khan twists his mouth. 'Sometimes friends become like family. Friends become so close, they *feel* like family.'

Involuntarily, Noah starts to laugh. And once he starts, he can't stop. He laughs so hard, he has to bend over and put his hands on his knees to catch his breath.

'Feel. Like. Family,' he gasps. 'Shit. You couldn't make it up.'

Khan watches him with interest, a smile playing on his lips. 'Ah,' he says after a moment, 'my wife. She always tells me I have no humour. I must refer her to this episode.'

'Man,' Noah straightens and wipes two fingers over his mouth. The laughter drains from him as quickly as it had come. He clears his throat, hooks his thumbs into his belt loops.

He's said too much.

'We'll look after Lou,' he says.

'Sometimes, Mr Fisher,' Khan says, 'the version that's presented to the world isn't necessarily true. It may not be a lie,' he clarifies. 'But it is not totally accurate, all the same.

'Much like this very place. This painted lady. We admire her, revel in her beauty, but underneath it all, there's a darkness to her. As we've discovered.'

Noah doesn't respond. He's thinking of Eliza. How beautiful she is and how it veils all of her sadness. He feels an insect bite his leg and, at once, he's had enough of this conversation. He has never wanted to leave a place more than he does Turtle Cove right now. Abruptly, he turns his back and goes over to where he dropped his flip-flops.

He strides up the beach, gripping his sandals in clenched fists. It's an effort to walk barefoot in dry sand and, when he gets to the restaurant, he's puffed and breathing hard. He glances up, into the interior that's dark against the dazzle and glitter of the beach. There is Eliza, sitting waiting for him with their children.

She holds up a hand to him, and he takes it.

His wife. For better or worse.

# 43

## LOU

The baby gazes at her intently, her dark eyelashes curling up to soft eyebrows. Her cowlick still stands to attention in the middle of her head. She seems to have grown in the last few days. Her cheeks bloom, full of health and milk, and sea-blown sleep in arms that rock her.

In the long periods when Lou was away searching for Adam and then Raffy, Tita has somehow managed to get Laila to take her feeds from a bottle. God only knows how she did it and Lou doesn't even want to think about the screaming and hollering that Laila will have sounded while Lou was gone. But somehow, she knows that Tita won't have come at the task in the same way as Lou would have done.

The same way as the *old* Lou would have done.

She realises, as Laila grabs her finger, that part of her anxiety with this child is that she has always been trying to control her. For four months, she has wanted her daughter to fit in with her routine. To sleep when Lou tells her it's time. To eat on a schedule that Lou has devised. It's true that, if Laila is on a timetable that fits in with her day, life will be easier when she goes back to work. But now...

Now everything has changed.

Will she even be going back to work?

Why did she want to go back to work in the first place? It's not like they need the money. She realises now it was to try and carve back her identity. That person she had lost in the last few years. Work had given her that.

But now...

It still seems so impossible, sitting on a sunlounger gazing at the ocean, with her daughter placid in her arms, that her life looks nothing like it did only four days earlier. She spins with the thought of it, every time she remembers that Adam is dead. Will there ever be a day, she wonders, when that sentence – those words – doesn't cause her to feel as if she's collapsing from a great height, deep into a valley of a life that is utterly unimaginable?

She thinks of life before this holiday. She had wanted to be apart from Adam. She had made the decision before they had come here, to Pulau Kalah. But she had never dreamed that the children would be without their father forever. That he would leave such a gaping hole in their lives.

She looks up the beach towards the restaurant and sees the Fisher family sitting together on plastic chairs on the sand. They look oddly formal. As if they're posing for a studio photograph. She hasn't really spoken to any of them since Adam's body was found. She senses their awkwardness, their unease, that they don't know what to say to her. That they seem almost embarrassed by the glaring fact of their family, still intact and entire. Whereas she is so visibly alone. A widow. A single mother of two.

She wonders, though, why Eliza is avoiding her. Why she hasn't come to comfort her, to grieve for Adam with her? What is it that stops her? What is it that makes her turn her back on her friend in her hour of need?

They must be desperate to leave the island, she thinks, adjusting the muslin swaddle around Laila.

But still, Khan won't let them go.

Lou turns to the other end of the beach where the inspector has been in the dive shack with Lars for over an hour. He also spoke to Eliza for a long time on the beach earlier. Surely he can't be suspicious of her? She's thought about it. Realistically, there *is* a small window of time when Eliza claimed to be looking for Lou, when she could in fact have left the resort to kill Adam.

But why?

Even if they were having an affair, it doesn't make sense.

If there was a connection – and the more Lou analyses it, the more she begins to doubt herself – it certainly wasn't romantic. It feels as though the link between them came more powerfully from Eliza. That she was the one with the deeper interest, the more intense fascination.

Lou has always been sensitive. Her emotional antennae pick up vibrations from people all the time. And the feelings she has about Eliza and Adam aren't anything to do with sex or attraction. Weirdly, the instinct she has is actually quite the opposite: that Eliza was always – and very covertly – *angry* with Adam.

But why? What had he done?

Killing a person seems such a sort of, well... Lou has to admit this to herself, such a *brave* thing to do. She could never do it herself. Even in self-defence. Murder has always felt like such a wilful destruction of your own being. The ultimate ending of another's life, yes. But, more than that... it's the ruination of any part of your character that you might justifiably argue was moral and right. It's such a frightening idea, that Lou would never be able to go through with it in a million years.

But what about Eliza?

She has her suspicions about Noah, too. He is devoted to Eliza in a blind, all-consuming way that means she can imagine he would do anything for her. He has always been cagey about the night that he and Adam fought on the beach. She has seen how strong he is even though his height belies the heft of his frame. Adam was so drunk that even Lou had managed to hit him off guard. Is it totally impossible to imagine that in the early hours of Sunday morning – threatened by Adam and riven with jealousy – Noah had found him sleeping drunkenly in the kayak and angrily pulled him out into the water? Just a couple of tugs and one hard push, over a few baby waves, and Adam would have been out into the ocean, with Noah left free to turn round, walk back up the beach and climb into bed with Eliza.

Lou stares out at the blue, breathing in the salt on the air. She watches the clouds puff past slowly, the breeze lazy and warm until the next time the monsoon picks up its skirts and makes the wind run.

These theories are beyond ridiculous.

The obvious explanation is the most simple one. The theory that Khan has laid out. Adam's death was just a terrible case of being in the wrong place at the wrong time. A blow to the head, a tumble over the rocks, his poor delicate brain cleaved open on the sand.

But she can't forget about the stomach wound. It just won't leave her thoughts... She worries it and she worries it like a scab that will never heal. Nothing seems to bring her peace and she genuinely fears that the constant picking of these thoughts is going to be the end of her.

A shadow falls over her and the now sleeping Laila, where they sit under the umbrella of a palm tree.

'Hi Lou.' Harry is there on the sand. 'How are you?'

Lou looks up at him, shading her eyes. 'Hi Harry. I looked for you earlier.' She gives a sad little laugh. 'Because I have to thank you again. For finding Lars.'

He takes a seat on the sand next to her and rests his arms on his knees, looking out at the sea. 'What Lars did,' he says, 'it hurt us all. You don't need to thank anyone. I'm just...' He inhales. 'I'm just so sorry that any of this happened.'

'How did you find him?'

'Pulau Kalah isn't big,' Harry says, scratching his nose. 'There are only so many places a person can go.' He gives her a quick glance. 'It's why, I'm afraid, I knew things weren't good for Adam. When he didn't turn up straight away. It meant that either he'd drowned and we'd never find him until the sea gave him up. Or someone didn't want him to be found.' He sighs. 'The camp in the south is inaccessible but it's not impossible to locate.'

'Zikri helped you.'

'Yeah. He'd had enough too by then, I think.'

They sit for a few minutes in silence.

'She looks like Adam,' Lou says after a while, gazing down at Laila. 'Blue eyes. Messy hair.' She smiles as the baby mewls in her sleep. 'Big dreams.'

'Khan will let you leave soon,' Harry says, putting his chin on his hands. 'Will you be OK getting back to Singapore?'

'I'll be OK.' She looks over at him. 'Will you be OK? You've lost… staff. It's been a hard few days.'

'Did you hear that Zoe's leaving?' he asks. 'She's transiting through Singapore next week, so I heard.'

Lou bites the inside of her cheek, feeling the anger rise in her again. Mainly towards Lars, but even towards young, naive Zoe. All of those people on this island that had injured and killed. Hurt her boy, her son. Taken his father from him. Caused so much damage, even down to the bloody fish in the sea, floating to the bottom, their innards blown out by the dynamite Che had used.

She doesn't know when this rage will leave her be. When she will ever feel calm again.

She looks up to find Harry's eyes on her.

'Do you remember when you were a kid?' he asks.

'Yes,' Lou answers, not sure where this is going.

He nods. 'And you used to sit in a car and wind down the window and put your arm all the way outside? Make your hand flat? Used to pretend you were an aeroplane with the rush of the wind hitting the back of the hand and the hairs on your arm, the speed of the car? Remember?'

Lou shuts her eyes and all she can hear is the rolling of the tide, whooshing over a million tiny broken glass fragments of white sand, moving in and moving out, watching her hand spread wide out of a car window, dandelion heads fluffed, seeds spinning through the air, holding her baby close.

In a moment, the feeling is gone, and the peace recedes like the waves.

But it was there.

'Yes,' she says, opening her eyes. 'There was nothing like it.'

# 44

## ELIZA

They bring out Adam's body on a stretcher, covered in a dark sheet.

It looks like a funeral cortège. Six policemen holding Adam aloft on their shoulders just as they would with a coffin.

Next to her, she feels the warmth of Noah's body. How *alive* he is; his blood red and vibrant, pumped by his strong, working heart through his veins.

As the stretcher passes, she catches Lou gazing at her distantly. Their eyes meet and she tries to convey with her expression how sorry she is. Because she is. She had never wanted Adam to die.

The staff have lined up, dressed in full uniform. Just as they had when the Carters and the Fishers first arrived on the island. This time, though, there are no glasses of rum and coconut. Their hands are empty, their eyes downcast.

They manage to get Adam into the police boat without incident. Inspector Khan follows the procession down to the shore, and salutes the officers. They return the gesture as the engine turns over and the prow of the boat gently cleaves the shallows before heading out into open water.

It's dignified. Adam would have liked it, Eliza thinks, as tears burn her eyes.

Khan stays there, watching the white-blue foam of the boat's wake until the vessel is just a dot on the horizon. Then he turns and he, too, catches Eliza's eye. But his is not a distant look. It is very close, the scrutiny of a laser. Impossible to either duck or hide.

Beside her, she feels Noah stiffen and realises that he feels the weight of Khan's gaze too. 'The tenders are ready,' he murmurs into her ear, putting a reassuring arm around her shoulders.

And they are. The staff are piling the remaining luggage into the boats from the trailer. Lou remains standing on the beach, facing the direction that the police boat took. She has one arm around Raffy and Laila is snug in the papoose. They are going home.

'Let's go,' Noah says. 'Let's get into one of the boats.'

But Khan is already approaching. He's smiling at her, loping easily up the beach. As he reaches them, Eliza takes a breath. She can't help it. Khan frightens her. He seems to know everything about her, as if she is a book that he has opened up and is reading with relish.

He stops in front of them and opens his mouth to speak. *This is it*, she thinks. *This is where he is going to arrest me.*

Earlier on the beach, he had come to her and they had stood on the shoreline together, gazing out on the horizon. He had asked her about her movements over the weekend, from that Saturday night onwards, and she had tried to explain. She had trembled a little but, she thinks, that could easily be attributed to nervous exhaustion.

She had very nearly walked away from him, having made no mistake at all. Right until the very end of their conversation when she had told the inspector how sorry she was that Adam had died, and she had meant it.

'Yes,' he had agreed. 'But he did not suffer a great while, by all accounts. He was unconscious and it did not take long for death to find him.'

She had breathed in deeply, filling her lungs with the cleansing salt and brine on the air, even as she knew that what he said was not the case at all.

'But, no, Ma'am Fisher?' Khan had murmured softly. 'It did not happen as I say?

'It is interesting, is it not,' he had continued, his gaze fixed on the watery line where the sea meets the sky, 'that Lars Van Graan returned to Adam Carter's body on Monday, before he left the resort? Really,' he sniffed, 'there was no reason for it. Unless he hadn't been entirely sure that Adam was dead and needed to finish the job. *Or* because he needed to plant some evidence. Something incontrovertible that would prove it was Che who had committed the deed. So that there would never be any doubt and the matter would be closed. Life on Pulau Kalah could resume. Paradise would not be lost.'

She hadn't looked at him at all. She had only nodded.

'Imagine, though, what he must have thought. When he arrived and a new injury had mysteriously appeared since he had last set foot on Ferringhi beach. A wound in Mr Carter's stomach. Fresh blood. Still warm.'

She had said nothing. Whatever Khan had seen in her face, what could he prove? Nothing.

He had talked for a while, but in the end, there had been no more to say, and they had walked up the beach to the bar together.

Now, Khan holds out a hand to Noah. After a second's hesitation, Noah shakes it. Khan slaps his other hand on their interlocked fingers.

'Mr Fisher,' he booms. 'On behalf of my countrymen, I must – and can only – apologise.'

Noah flicks Eliza a look. What does Khan mean?

'Malaysia is truly a beautiful country,' the inspector continues. 'We have many, many things to delight and bewitch our guests. Beaches, and diving. Further north we have our famous tea plantations. The metropolis of Kuala Lumpur. The colonial relics and street art of Georgetown in Penang.' He whistles at the thought of it all. 'I am truly sorry that the Fisher family have had such an upsetting experience in our wonderful home.'

Eliza stares, thinking he must have gone quite mad.

Still, she smiles and nods. 'Oh no, Inspector,' she says. 'In fact we would love to come back. Once we have helped Lou with…' she looks over at the boat where Lou sits, her back rigid and unyielding '… everything that she needs.'

'Actually,' Khan says sharply, 'that is something I do wish to request, if I may.' He takes Eliza by the elbow and steers her a little distance away. There he whispers to her beyond anyone's hearing.

'Mrs Fisher, I have this one thing to ask of you. It is, I hope, not too much. Indeed, I think it will be helpful for you as well, in the long run.'

'What is it?'

'Please, Mrs Fisher. Do not help Mrs Carter. Rather, do the reverse. Or, at least, let the reverse be the help you provide. Leave her be. Take yourself away from Singapore and go home. Go back to your home in London. Make a life for you and your family there. Leave Mrs Carter to grieve for her husband without you. You can see why I ask this. Can't you?'

She looks at him, a foot shorter than she. He takes her in owlishly, his eyes bug and wide. She notes his heavy gold chain, his lemon-yellow shirt, stained with sweat; his bushy grey hair swept over to one side. He watches her calmly as if he sees the pain inside of her, knows how her heart breaks for her mother, swinging softly in the morning sun.

'You will do as I ask.' He nods and pats her arm. 'You will remember our conversation on the beach, I think. You will remember that long after you have returned to your rightful home.'

Khan turns on his heel and ambles back to the dive shack.

Within half an hour, she and Noah and the twins are cresting the waves on their way to the mainland. They took the other tender, separate from Lou and her children.

The boats moor simultaneously at the jetty at Mersing.

Eliza and Noah take their bags and get the twins settled into their seats in the roasting-hot interior of their car that has been sitting without shade for five days. As Noah drives them out of the car park, Eliza turns to see Lou sitting in the driver's seat of the Carters' car. A police detective is next to her. Before Lou puts the car into gear, she stares for a long while out of the windscreen, at the smears of dust across the glass.

Four hours later and Noah pulls into the driveway of their house in Bukit Timah. Inside, their helper, Tess, takes their bags and sorts out their laundry. The twins jump straight into the swimming pool in the garden and Eliza and Noah have a gin and tonic on the deck overlooking them.

They sit in silence, as the sun drops heavy, and their part of the planet rotates into night-time.

As it does, Eliza knows that Khan is right, and that she will soon be gone from this place.

And that she will never see Lou again.

# 45

## ADAM

*Monday: one day earlier*

A laser burns into him as it crawls up his legs. It rises in tiny increments over a few centimetres of skin at a time. It is a poker, white-tipped with fire. It is the never-ending passage of a slow and steady scorpion. The pain will kill him with its laborious tenacity. It is the—

But actually, it's only the glare of the sun that has sought him out feet-first where he lies otherwise in the relative cool of a shadow of a large rock.

Above him, he can just make out the purple apex of Fire Mountain, beyond the shelf of the cliff that he lies beneath. He doesn't know how long he's been lying there. Time has become meaningless. There has been warm rain and burning sun, and periods when he's slept. Once he opened his eyes and the world was covered in stars. The next time he awoke, they were gone and the night was rich and thick as velvet. Once, an animal snuffled at his feet, and up his torso, its snout prickly and damp across his cheeks.

He doesn't know whether it's been hours or days since he answered what he'd thought was a wave hello and set all of this mess in motion.

He can't move. His legs don't work. A while ago, in this new form of time, he brought delicate fingers to the back of his head and felt a tiny crevasse, a couple of millimetres he estimates, of soft tissue. His skull, cracked open like an egg.

Around him, there is the strong smell of iron. His body feels light, as if filled with air, and not with the blood he needs to pump his heart. He is leaking over the sand. His life is draining out of him like a dripping tap. Only his legs are solid and heavy. But he cannot move them. He assesses he has been paralysed. A catastrophic knock to the head. A twist of his spine.

He is beached. Like a fish or a whale. If he could, he would say some things at the indignity of him lying spread on the ground like a speared fish left to dry out in the sun. And his speech would start with *for fuck's sake*.

Are his injuries enough for him to die, though? His breath is shallow. But that's the dehydration, he thinks. And that won't kill him anytime soon. He will die here at some point. But, if he's not going to be found, then let death come quickly.

Not like this.

After the attack from that idiot guy who thought he wanted to steal the dynamite, the idea of dying had seemed almost exciting. Soon, he would find out the answer to the question that every human being wanted to know. He had thought for a long time about it, imagining where he might go. Would it be like sleep? Deep and dark, and filled with the weird stitching together of images that happens in dreams? Or would it just be a void, a chasm of nothing?

Since then, though, he has been thinking about the most random stuff. Tottenham Hotspur, for some reason. For his football team that he will never see play again. Never find out if they can ever finally win in Europe. He tries to find it inside himself to laugh that – even at death's door – their loss against Liverpool in the Champions League final still pisses him off. But he is finding it harder to breathe and his laugh sounds more like a sigh.

He thinks about how he hasn't finished his book. Will his publisher complete it posthumously? he wonders. That is a more pleasant thought. His epitaph. And his funeral. How well attended it will be.

Then he thinks of Lou and his children. Of the cruel proximity of them all – just around the headland. How worried they'll be. Searching for him. Looking for the kayak.

The kayak is gone. Who knows where it is? Floating off to the other side of the world, perhaps.

What will they think? That he drowned? That he capsized drunkenly into the sea and drifted to the bottom of the ocean in a booze-filled haze? How he wishes he had drowned, rather than eking out the last few hours of his life in a state of chronic dehydration, feeling his body grow slowly redundant, hallucinating his way into his final demise. How much better to sink into cool water and let the waves fill his lungs, wash away the blood, let the fish nibble on his skin until his bones are picked clean.

The sound of footsteps cuts into his thoughts. He can't move his head to see where they're coming from, or who it is. His failing heart gives a last-chance boom in the hope that this means rescue.

The steps halt with the sound of a skid of rubber sole on rock. He waits for the shout of his name. The relief his rescuer will feel once they come over the bluff and find him there on the sand.

The burn of the sun on his legs is blocked by a shadow. He strains to see who stands over him, but their face is haloed by the sun.

He tries to move his fingers. Sounds gurgle in his throat.

The pain of movement is mixed with exhilaration when he sees his saviour is Eliza.

Beautiful Eliza.

His angel.

But then she begins to speak and the blood that oozes out of him turns cold.

Then he feels rage.

Because he realises he is going to die and very soon.

He wants to tell her that she's wrong. That *life* isn't fair, sweetheart. Yes, Benjamin was a dick, but he was a dick to them *all*.

But his voice has gone. He has already spoken his last words.

He sees something like a blade but he is dazzled. Maybe this is heaven. A sensation of pure light that hides all the badness, all the wickedness down on earth. In fact, it's so much better this way. Not to have to witness it.

Then he does see. Images. Flashes of his life. His childhood bedroom. His mother's trembling hands. The dog he had as a boy. His father at a bar, bending to kiss a woman who wasn't his wife. His son Raffy running along the beach, grinning at the beautiful simplicity of his life.

Thunder rolls above him, climbing over the top of Fire Mountain and falling down its ravines. He smiles as it reaches him, as the power of the rain reaches him, drenching him as if he is, finally, sinking underwater. Down in the quiet of the deep, with a hundred miles of ocean pressing down on him.

He feels a sharpness placed into his hand, the top of the blade, the sharp invasion of its tip as he pushes against it. Blood bubbles in his mouth as his stomach gapes and the waters lap and close over his head. He lets go then, at the warmth that fills him up, at the peace that takes his hand as he goes.

Down and down he goes, down into the deep of the void.

# 46

## ELIZA

*One year later*

Eliza drops the twins at school and makes the short walk from its gates to the coffee shop on the high street. There, she orders a black Americano and a chocolate croissant.

She's put on weight since they've moved back to Richmond. She doesn't care. She likes it. It's changed the shape of her face. Erased the haunted, hungry look she always used to have when she was thin and living on gin in Singapore.

She opens up her laptop and logs on to the Wi-Fi. Arriving back to the UK in the middle of a global pandemic hasn't been ideal but at least it's meant she can work from home. When they'd announced their return, her old job had immediately contacted her and reinstated her full-time. Now the twins are finally back at school, she can concentrate on kick-starting a career she's let slide.

Noah has settled into his role as partner of a new law firm and they are once again living in their sunny house in the side streets between Richmond and Twickenham, enjoying the change in the seasons as autumn gets ready for winter, and the twins get excited about the prospect of a proper – albeit socially distanced – Bonfire Night the following week.

After she's worked through her inbox and looked at a Zoom presentation for the next day, Eliza logs off the company website and checks the news. She's reading about the upcoming US elections when a Google alert pings on to her screen.

The name causes ice to run through her veins.

Carter.

She had never removed all the alerts she'd set up when she'd first found out about Adam's existence. When, for the few weeks before they'd moved to Singapore, she'd been so obsessed with him that she could spend whole days randomly trawling websites and old articles, piecing together scraps of information about his life.

But this alert doesn't concern Adam.

It's about Lou.

Eliza peers at the screen.

There's a photograph of her with the turtle guy from the island – Harry Wells. The notice says they're getting married after tragedy struck Louise Carter when her husband was killed in a horrific kayaking accident in Malaysia a year ago.

It's a good-news story, so necessary in these Covid times. Something heart-warming to read over your cornflakes. Louise is marrying the man who devoted most of his life to save the green turtle from extinction. They have now set up an educational NGO together on the Malaysian island of Tioman. They moved there with her two young children before lockdown, and have spent the time swimming, fishing, and generally enjoying being in paradise.

Eliza gently closes her laptop screen.

She tries to remember what she is learning in her online therapy sessions. That she is loved, and valued by her own family. That this family is hers alone, and it is profound and filled with hope. That she does not need to destroy others to bring meaning into her life.

She has tried to forget, since they left Singapore. She has tried to forget that weekend. All of the panic, the emotional carnage. The trauma that had resurfaced.

Inspector Khan had known.

She didn't know how he did. But he had spoken with her on the beach, just before they had left the island. He had read *The Kingfisher*, he said. When he had studied in London as a young man. And he knew, from the background checks the police did on them all, that Eliza's mother had been a student

257

at King's College, where Benjamin Carter was a professor of English literature.

When Khan had told her this, she had never been surer, than that he somehow knew everything. He had said two things that she didn't understand at the time. Both of them strange, neither of them really making sense until now.

She had been terrified of Khan. Afraid that he could read her mind. She had barely listened, barely spoken, not wanting to give herself away. She had convinced herself it wasn't real anyway. It wasn't really to do with her. It had just been a terrible mistake. She hadn't wanted it to happen. There was no intention, no design.

She isn't that person. She never has been. Never will be again.

And yet, the Fates had conspired.

They had come together like fire on the mountain, and she had seen them. She had heard them.

She had tried to follow Lou through the jungle but she'd never caught up with her. She'd wandered aimlessly, thirsty and sad. It was so easy to lose your way in those tangles of vines, and ferns and roots the size of tree trunks. She'd ended up down an unmarked path, arriving on to a small rocky beach.

And there he was.

Not yet dead, but certainly dying. Very close to death. His lips were white with dehydration. Blood crusted around his nostrils. When he saw her, he managed one spasm, a jerk of muscle as if to reach out a hand. She knew she could have helped him. She could have brought water from the spring in the cave to him and rubbed it on to his gums and his parched lips. She could have taken out her phone and seen from his WhatsApp message that Noah wasn't far away. He'd arrived in Timba safely, so he and Harry could have come around the coast by boat. They could have saved Adam, perhaps.

But she didn't do those things.

Instead, she talked. She told Adam about the pain she'd felt. How unfair it all was, what had happened to her. All the hurt she'd rolled up in a bundle, tied up tight with string and carried on her back without really even knowing how heavy it was, until she'd found out about him.

And even then, she'd hoped that maybe his love could save her. That *he* could be the family she'd never had. But it hadn't worked out like that. He just wanted to fuck her. Just like her father had done with her mother.

She talked, and she talked and talked.

She saw his eyes change. She saw them move from relief to injury, and then to fear. But he said nothing. No apology. He gave her no comfort. He lay with glassy eyes, skin so raw from sunburn that it had blistered. And still it wasn't enough. She wanted something from him, for everything she'd suffered.

She found the piece of broken coral on the beach. Its edge as sharp as a blade. She held it out to him, but he was weak.

It would be days, she told him. Days before he died of thirst.

She put the coral spear in his hands, his palms on its end, its pointed spike pricking through his T-shirt.

He pushed it into his stomach as if it were the most wonderful feeling he'd ever had, rapture spread across his face as he travelled out and upwards and into the void.

'When is a murder committed?' Khan had asked her. 'Is it when the life is taken? Or is it earlier, when it is conceived? When a killer knows that the path is there to be taken. Even if only in his mind. Or, indeed, *her* mind,' he had smiled.

Eliza gets up from her table in the coffee shop. She decides to walk down to the river, to watch the winter water flowing downstream under the grey skies of London. She makes her way to the promenade that runs underneath Richmond Bridge and sits on a bench. It's quiet at this time of year. It's cold.

She thinks about Khan and what he had said. Now she understands it. He had said that, often, what we see is what is really true. Many times, we are beguiled by the beauty of a jewel, but the fact of our captivation doesn't make the stone any less precious. She hadn't wanted to think about what he meant. She had buried it along with all her memories of that weekend. Her shame and her guilt.

He was right when he had told her to leave. Lou has recovered and maybe she wouldn't have done if Eliza had been there as a constant reminder of what had been taken.

Khan had meant that our perceptions are only that: they are only thoughts and ideas that flit through the air like our dreams. Somewhere in all of this, she could believe that Benjamin Carter had really loved her mother. He had also loved his wife and son. And maybe he had also loved the daughter he never knew. He was *The Kingfisher*, after all. Territorial. Selfish. But still capable of love. She could choose to believe this. She could choose that gift.

She watches as a mallard duck takes flight over the water. Is it enough to be sorry? To live with the regret? Does she need to give Lou and Raffy her eye for Adam's? Can a wrong ever fully be righted when the hurt is this hard?

Above her, thunder rumbles. She decides to walk across the bridge, over the river, to take the long path home. As she begins, the rain washes in from the sky, soaking her to her skin.

Still, she keeps on walking.

# ACKNOWLEDGEMENTS

I began writing *The Cove* during lockdown in Singapore, at the beginning of the global pandemic in 2020. I finished the final edits having moved back to London after living for a decade in Southeast Asia. So, this book is, in many ways, my farewell letter to a part of the world that I will always love. It's where my daughters spent their formative years and where we have a million happy memories.

And now it's here, brought to life by the wonderful team at Raven.

Katie Brown, who edited it ferociously without me really knowing – such is her positivity and happy spirit! Thanks so much, Katie – it has genuinely been excellent working with you.

Thank you to Lilidh Kendrick for her brilliant edits. And to the eagle eyes of Kate Quarry, Sarah-Jane Forder, Amy Tan, and also Catherine Best.

To Amy Donegan and Maud Davies for their amazing energy and cheerleading skills. To David Mann for the most beautiful and striking cover.

To Marcy Posner, who makes me get up so early – at the crack of dawn, no less – to talk to her in her beautiful house in Palm Springs. But it's always worth it because her advice and support is bloody amazing. Thank you for backing *The Cove*. I thought you'd like it and thank God you did.

And where would I be without Ariella Feiner? Pretty much nowhere, frankly. Thank you for remaining calm in the face of total chaos, of still smiling after hours of endless Zoom calls and for generally being the best agent ever.

The island of Pulau Kalah is a fictional island, but it was inspired by a wonderful resort where, as a family, we holidayed many times. Everyone returned safe and sound: tanned, relaxed and happy – not a murder in sight! But to all the people I've met and known (and quizzed for research purposes!) on Pulau Sibu in beautiful Malaysia, thank you.

Thank you to Will Jelf for providing the seed of an idea for this book many years ago. Seed ideas can take a long time to germinate!

Thank you to Jeroen Van de Waal for his invaluable advice and help on diving, his knowledge of the Malaysian archipelago and the truly dreadful effects of dynamite fishing. For more information, please have a look at www.orcanation.org.

Thanks to Michelle Yong and her kind donation to the Breadline Group for a name in *The Cove* (thankfully not Mr Cuddles).

Thank you to my early readers – Matthew Kasper and Brenda Foong. To Tom and his font suggestions. And to the ever-supportive Singapore Writers' Group, who I hope will continue to flourish and thrive and create amazing work. Thanks also to Dre Johnson for the odd – and generally very odd – query.

As always, thank you to Mum and Dad for their advice, their time, and their love. It's good to be home.

This book is really about family. About connections, and love and loyalty. I am very fortunate to have some friends who feel as close as family, so massive love – as well as raising a *very rare* goblet of wine – to them.

Finally, to Connie and Indy. Thank you for being so brave, so loving, so funny, and for being such good company here, there, and everywhere.

# A NOTE ON THE AUTHOR

ALICE CLARK-PLATTS is a former human rights lawyer who worked at the UN International Criminal Tribunal in connection with the Rwandan genocide and on cases involving Winnie Mandela and Snoop Dogg. She is the author of *The Flower Girls*, and the police procedurals *Bitter Fruits* and *The Taken*, the latter of which was shortlisted for the Best Police Procedural in the Dead Good Reader Awards 2017.

# A NOTE ON THE TYPE

The text of this book is set in Linotype Sabon, a typeface named after the typefounder Jacques Sabon. It was designed by Jan Tschichold and jointly developed by Linotype, Monotype and Stempel in response to a need for a typeface to be available in identical form for mechanical hot-metal composition and hand composition using foundry type.

Tschichold based his design for Sabon roman on a font engraved by Garamond, and Sabon italic on a font by Granjon. It was first used in 1966 and has proved an enduring modern classic.